PALE H

PRAISE FOR THE PROJECT EDEN THRILLERS

"Sick didn't just hook me. It hit me with a devastating uppercut on every primal level—as a parent, a father, and a human being."—**Blake Crouch**, best selling author of Run

"...a gem of an outbreak story that unfolds like a thriller movie and never lets up, all the way to the last page. Absolutely my favorite kind of story!"—**John Maberry**, *New York Times* bestselling author

"...not only grabs you by the throat, but by the heart and gut as well, and by the time you finish you feel as if you've just taken a runaway train through dangerous territory. Buy these books now. You won't regret it."—**Robert Browne**, best selling author of Trial Junkies

"You think Battles was badass before? He just cranked it up to 500 joules. CLEAR!"—**PopCultureNerd.com**

"Brett Battles at his best, a thriller that also chills, with a secret at its core that's almost too scary to be contained within the covers of a book."—**Tim Hallinan**, author of the Edgar-nominated The Queen of Patpong

ALSO BY BRETT BATTLES

The Jonathan Quinn Thrillers

THE CLEANER
THE DECEIVED
SHADOW OF BETRAYAL (US)/THE UNWANTED (UK)
THE SILENCED
BECOMING QUINN
THE DESTROYED

The Logan Harper Thrillers

LITTLE GIRL GONE
EVERY PRECIOUS THING

The Project Eden Thrillers

SICK
EXIT 9
PALE HORSE

Standalones

THE PULL OF GRAVITY
NO RETURN

For Younger Readers

The Trouble Family Chronicles

HERE COMES MR. TROUBLE

PALE HORSE

Brett Battles

A PROJECT EDEN THRILLER

Book 3

What Came Before

TIME IS RUNNING out for the human race. First it was the test, a contained release of the KV-27a virus by its creators at Project Eden. It proved so successful that the world gave it a name, the Sage Flu, and collectively breathed a sigh of relief when it seemed to burn itself out.

It left its scars, though, on Army Captain Daniel Ash and his children, Josie and Brandon. His wife was one of the Sage Flu's first victims, and he was later accused of being the man responsible for its release. Ash had nothing to do with the spread of the disease, but he did plan on doing something to keep it from happening again.

Aligning himself with a group that worked out of a secret facility in Montana, calling itself the Resistance, Ash, along with several others, went in search of the Project's headquarters, a place known as Bluebird, in hopes of stopping Project Eden's true plan—the removal of over ninety-nine percent of mankind so that humanity could have a restart.

He found Bluebird on Yanok Island above the Arctic Circle, where he ran into former Project member Olivia Silva. She, too, had been looking for Bluebird, but while it seemed their goals were the same, she was not entirely forthcoming.

Back in Montana, at the Resistance's headquarters known as the Ranch, a Project Eden attack squad was spotted heading their way. Having no choice, Resistance leader Matt Hamilton sealed up the underground bunker where members were hiding. Two people were not able to make it inside on time. One was Daniel Ash's son, Brandon.

At Bluebird, Ash, Olivia, and the people they'd brought along took over the Project Eden control room. Ash was relieved when they were able to stop the virus's release, but the feeling was short-lived as Olivia revealed her true plan and input the go code.

As her finger hovered over the keyboard, Ash aimed his gun at her, and…

And I looked, and behold a pale horse;
and his name that sat on him was Death,
and Hell followed with him.

—Revelations 6:8

IMPLEMENTATION DAY

THURSDAY, DECEMBER 22nd

World Population
7,176,323,921

Change Over Previous Day
+ 280,229

1

DANIEL ASH LOCKED eyes with Olivia Silva, his gun held out in front of him.

For a moment it was as if time itself had frozen solid.

Then the corner of her lip curled up in the slightest of smiles.

Oh, God. No!

Even as he thought this, he squeezed the trigger, but her finger was already plunging toward the ENTER key.

2

MARTINA GABLE'S PLAN had been to sleep as late as possible. She'd arrived home the previous evening, after spending the first few days of her winter break getting in some extra workouts at Cal State University Northridge's athletic facility. Like most freshmen, she had wanted to come home right away, but she knew if she put in a little more time at the gym, it would go a long way toward scoring points with Coach Poole and the other members of the softball team's staff. As good as she had been at the game in high school, she was just one of a hundred or so equally talented players at the university vying for a spot on the squad.

It had been a good move. Only two other freshman girls and one sophomore had hung around, and the coaches seemed both annoyed that more hadn't stayed and pleased that Martina and the other three were there.

Instead of trying to one-up the other girls, Martina had gotten them to work together, helping each other like teammates would. It wasn't any kind of strategy on her part; she was just good at that kind of thing. But it was clear from the comments she received from the coaches before she left that her leadership skills had not gone unnoticed.

Finally, once the staff had left for the break, she drove the two and a half hours back to her hometown.

Sleeping in her own bed for the first time in months, she was sure she wouldn't open her eyes until noon, but by eight o'clock she was wide awake. With a groan, she pushed the covers back, swung her legs off the bed, and pulled on the running clothes she'd laid out the night before.

Five minutes later, she was out the door, and heading east toward town. When she'd left for college that August, it had been blazing hot. That was to be expected, of course. Ridgecrest was located at the northern edge of the Mojave Desert, so blazing hot in summer was the norm.

Winter was a different thing altogether. Most days wouldn't rise above fifty degrees and many were considerably colder. On this particular morning, three days before Christmas, the temperature was hovering just above freezing. If it had been cloudy, there would have been a good chance for some snow, but the sky, as it was most days, was clear.

As soon as she reached that blissful state she always felt when she ran, the cold became a distant memory and her mind turned to other things, like the gifts she still had to buy for her parents and a couple of her high school friends she was getting together with that evening. And, of course, Ben.

On she went, past the track homes, the churches, then down through the old business district on Balsam Street. Would it be tacky to get her dad a gift card to Home Depot or someplace like that? Probably, but it would be so much easier, and he'd undoubtedly be happier in the end.

You can't do that, she told herself. *Just talk to Mom. She'll know what he wants.*

A car horn honked, the driver waving and smiling as the vehicle passed by. It was Mrs. Henson, one of the secretaries at Burroughs High School.

Martina waved back, then returned to her thoughts of Christmas and her parents and her almost boyfriend. There had been several days that previous spring when she was sure she'd never see another summer, let alone Christmas, but she'd been one of the lucky ones who'd survived after contracting the Sage Flu during the outbreak. That was a nightmare she never wanted to live through again, yet if it hadn't been for the quarantine, she and Ben would have never met.

The truth was, though she didn't know it, she could never live through a hell like that again. At least not in the way she did before. Her exposure to the virus had given her immunity. So if the Sage Flu bared its fangs again, she would not fall victim.

Of course, the same couldn't be said about nearly everyone else she knew.

MONTANA
9:35 AM MOUNTAIN STANDARD TIME

LIZZIE DEXEL WAS not a typical recluse. She had lived, if not quite thrived, for many years right in the middle of Denver, Colorado. It hadn't been easy, and she had been prone to the occasional panic attack, but she had made it work. She'd even had a couple friends. Well, one work friend, anyway. When she left for the day from the accounting office where she was employed, she would go straight home, make some dinner, and watch Animal Planet until it was time to go to sleep. She had no pets. She liked cats, but was allergic, and dogs took too much work. So she contented herself with watching them on TV.

When her brother Owen died, things had changed. He'd been even worse with crowds than Lizzie. The one time he had visited her in Denver, he had barely left her apartment, and when he did, his eyes watched every face he passed. He was much happier in his isolated home in Montana, where he was able to feed his paranoid belief of a coming war.

That's where his body had been found. He'd been chopping wood behind his house and had apparently suffered a heart attack. If Lizzie hadn't become worried because he wasn't answering her calls, it could have been months before anyone found him. As it was, his body lay on the ground for nearly two weeks before the sheriff drove out and checked, giving the bugs and the animals plenty of time to take what they wanted. Needless to say, it was a closed casket funeral.

Being the only one Owen kept in contact with, Liz had inherited his house. At first she thought she'd sell it, but after spending a week there going through his things, she found she liked the solitude. She thought if she did a little redecorating, and lost the survivalist theme, his place would actually be nice.

Back in Denver, she had worked out a deal with her firm to work remotely from Montana.

It didn't take much to convince her bosses that it was a good idea. She did great work, but was a bit of an oddball in their view, kind of a loner who had a paranoid streak in her. She, of course, would have said the description fit her brother, not her, but she never really had been good at seeing the truth about herself.

At the end of summer, she moved permanently to Montana, and settled into her new life. The only times she saw anyone in the months that followed were on the two occasions she'd gone to town for supplies. No one ever visited her house, and she believed no one ever would.

It was probably for the best that she didn't realize how soon that belief would be shattered.

OUTSIDE MUMBAI, INDIA
9:12 PM INDIAN STANDARD TIME

THE ROAD SANJAY and Kusum had been traveling on was really no more than two rutted tire tracks running through a stretch of wilderness outside their home city of Mumbai.

Sanjay had been forced to drop their speed to a crawl, so that the front tire wouldn't get caught in a hole and fling them both to the ground. Kusum's arms were tight around his waist, but he knew she was only trying to hold on, not showing him any kind of affection.

Despite his protests, she'd been right when she accused him of kidnapping her. But what choice did he have? When he'd found his cousin Ayush dying in a makeshift hospital

19

room, then learned the truth about the "miracle malaria spray" they had both been hired to help douse the city with, he'd had no other option. The spray had nothing to do with saving lives. In fact, quite the opposite. They and others hired by Pishon Chem would be covering Mumbai with the same deadly virus from which Ayush had been dying. Sanjay had stolen some vaccine, talked Kusum into joining him for lunch, then kept driving the motorcycle he'd rented until they were well out of the city.

He'd done it to save her. He *had* to save her. She was all he ever thought about, all he cared about—especially now that Ayush was surely dead. If that meant kidnapping her, then so be it.

When he'd stabbed the needle into her arm, and injected her with the life-saving vaccine, she had all but flown into a rage, thinking he had drugged her. He'd tried to explain what he had seen and learned, but naturally she didn't believe him.

"I promise if I'm wrong, I will take you back and turn myself over to the police," he told her. Finally, she had reluctantly agreed to stay with him.

As they came around a turn, Sanjay immediately jammed on the brakes. The back of the bike fishtailed right, then left, before stopping at an angle to the road.

Kusum immediately released his waist. "What's wrong?"

"There." He nodded at the road ahead.

A pool of water, perhaps twenty meters across, covered the road. He didn't think it was very deep, but knew it would be better to cross it in daylight to be safe.

"We'll stay here."

She looked around. "Stay where?"

"Here."

"In the jungle?"

"It's not that much of a jungle. We'll be fine."

"Are you crazy?"

"It's just for one night."

"I'm not sleeping here."

"Fine. You can stay awake."

He gunned the engine, circled the bike around to the way

they'd come, then turned into the wilderness and drove them back amongst the trees and bushes until he found a wide spot that would work for their camp. Killing the engine, he flipped down the kickstand, but Kusum didn't move.

"Please," he said. "Get off."

"I will not."

"Well, I'm getting off, and when I do, you'll fall."

She huffed in frustration then climbed off the seat, making sure her foot kicked him as she did. Once he was off the bike, he stretched, and retrieved the bag he'd strapped to the handlebars that contained the food they picked up earlier.

He sat down in the small clearing and opened the bag. "Have something to eat."

"I am not hungry," she said.

"You need to eat. It's important."

"I told you, I am not hungry."

"All right."

He pulled out the container of *vada pav*, quickly ate two pieces, then took the bag with the remainder back to the motorcycle and hung it over the handlebars so insects would be less likely to find it.

"When you get hungry, it's here."

He stretched out on the undergrowth and glanced at Kusum. "If you're not going to eat, you should at least try to sleep."

"I told you, I am not sleeping here."

"Kusum, please. I am not your enemy. What I have done is only because I care about you."

She glared at him, her eyes full of fire. "If you cared about me, you would have taken me home already."

In a few days, you will see how much I care, he thought, but he said nothing, hoping he was wrong.

Hours later, he stirred, his eyes opening for just a moment. Kusum was on the ground a foot away from him. Tentatively he reached out and put a hand on her shoulder. At first she tried to pull away, but then she stopped. A moment later, she scooted back against him, and he could feel her body shake as she cried.

3

THE RANCH WAS on fire.

The dormitory, by far the smaller of the two buildings of the Resistance's headquarters, was already well on its way to total destruction. Even if a hundred firefighters had been on site, there would have been nothing they could do.

The Lodge was a different story. Though it too was being consumed by flames, there would have still been the possibility of saving some of the structure, given its massive size. But the nearest fire crew was over seventy miles away, and they had received no emergency call.

Nor would they.

Just before ten a.m., three helicopters and several ground vehicles had been spotted rushing toward the Ranch. There was no question who had sent them, or what their purpose was. They were a Project Eden attack squad, coming to eliminate everyone there.

"Full cover," Matt Hamilton, the head of the Resistance, had ordered.

Giant impenetrable doors had been sealed, locking everyone into the large underground bunker deep below the Lodge, and the self-destruction of the two surface buildings was triggered. The burned wreckage would block the two main entrances into the Bunker, and, Matt hoped, keep the killers above from finding a way in.

"Don't worry," Rachel Hamilton said. "Jon will keep him safe." She was Matt's sister and closest advisor, so it wasn't surprising she knew exactly what he was thinking.

"I know," he said, though he wasn't as sure as she was.

"He'll get Brandon out."

This time Matt simply nodded.

Though most of the people who had been at the Ranch when the helicopters were spotted were safe in the underground facility, Jon Hayes and Brandon Ash had been caught outside, unable to get back before Matt was forced to seal up the Bunker. While Jon had received the training all Resistance members were given, Brandon was just a kid. To make matters worse, Matt himself had promised the boy's father he'd watch over him.

He just hoped Jon and Brandon had done what he ordered, and were already in the woods, trying to get as far from the Ranch as possible.

"Intruders on ground," someone announced.

Matt looked at the monitors displaying feeds from cameras hidden around the compound. He zeroed in on a view of the open space near the Lodge, where one of the helicopters had just set down and a half dozen heavily armed men in fatigues, helmets, and body armor were jumping out. As they rushed toward the burning building, the second helicopter landed and more men joined the others.

"Dear God," someone said.

Matt could sense fear filling the room.

"Hold it together," he ordered. "They can't get in. You all know that."

There were a few nods, and a couple of grunts of agreement, but the anxiety level remained high.

On the screen, the attack squad circled the Lodge, while a smaller detachment raced over to the dormitory. When it was clear no one could be alive in the burning buildings, they regrouped, then split again, and headed in teams of three into the woods.

It's okay, Matt thought. *Jon and Brandon are far away. They won't be seen.*

"Matt?" Christina Kim called out from the communication terminal she was manning.

"In a minute," Matt said.

"No. Now."

He turned. "What is it?"

Her eyes never left the monitor in front of her as she motioned for him to hurry over. She said into her microphone, "Your signal's weak, but you're getting through."

Matt walked quickly to her desk. "Who is it?"

"Pax," she said as she handed him a second headset.

Matt donned it and pressed the earpiece tight to his head. Pax was his right-hand man, and was currently above the Arctic Circle in search of Bluebird, Project Eden's control center. "It's Matt. Are you there?"

"Good to hear your voice, Matt," Pax said.

There was a lot of interference.

Matt put his hand over his mic and said, "Can you do anything about the signal?"

Christina shook her head. "I'll keep trying, but that's the best I've been able to do so far."

He took his hand off the mic. "Any luck?"

"Bust here," Pax said. "The science facility on Amund Ringnes Island is legit."

The assumption had been that Bluebird was posing as a scientific research outpost on one of the far north islands. The Resistance had narrowed it down to the most likely ones, and sent the team—headed by Brandon's father, Daniel Ash—to see if they could pinpoint its exact location, and do whatever they could to stop Project Eden from initiating its plan. The team had then divided in half so they could check the final two possibilities at the same time. Pax led one group to Amund Ringnes Island, while Ash led the other to Yanok Island.

So if Bluebird wasn't on Amund Ringnes…

"I haven't been able to reach Captain Ash," Pax said. "Has he reported in to you?"

Though Matt knew the answer, he glanced at Christina. She shook her head. "No," he said. "We haven't heard from him since before they left for Yanok."

"I was afraid of that. I've also been unable to reach Gagnon to arrange pickup." Gagnon was flying the seaplane that shuttled the men to the islands. "I guess it doesn't matter at the moment. Even if I did reach him, I doubt he'd be able to get here for a day or two."

"Did something happen?"

"A storm happened. It seems to be a pretty big one. We've taken shelter in an unmanned research outpost, and won't be going anywhere until it calms down a bit."

"I understand."

There was a pause. "Matt, Bluebird's got to be on Yanok. I'm sure Ash has already figured that out, so I'm surprised you haven't heard from him."

"Could be caught in the storm, too."

"Could be, but he wouldn't let that stop him until he knew for sure. We're running out of time. Implementation Day could be tomorrow, for all we know."

Implementation Day, when Project Eden would activate the release of the Sage Flu virus on the world.

Matt glanced over at the others watching the assault team search the area around the Lodge. "Actually, Pax, I'm pretty sure it's not going to be tomorrow."

"KEEP MOVING!" HAYES yelled.

Brandon jerked back around. He hadn't even realized he'd slowed down, but he hadn't been able to help glancing over his shoulder to search for the helicopters thumping in the distance. He couldn't spot them, though, with the thick forest cover barely allowing him a glimpse of the sky. He picked up his pace, and soon caught up to the man who was trying to save his life.

"The emergency stash is only about five minutes from the top of the ridge," Hayes said. "We can rest when we get there."

"I'm fine," Brandon told him, not wanting to show any weakness.

Hayes gave him a smile. "Glad to hear it."

When they reached the top, the trees parted enough for them to see two columns of smoke rising into the air from back toward the Ranch. Brandon knew that at the bottom of the larger column would be what was left of the Lodge, and below it, underground, the Bunker where his sister Josie and the others were hiding. He hoped she was all right, and that the security measures Mr. Hamilton had taken would be enough to protect her and everyone else.

A part of him wanted to rush back, and do what he could to help them. What that would be, he had no idea, but running away just seemed wrong.

As they started down the other side of the ridge, he said, "Do you think they can get into the Bunker?"

"No," Hayes said, and started walking again.

Brandon grabbed his arm. "You can't know for sure."

The man turned toward him. "Matt knows what he's doing. The people from the helicopters won't be able to get to them. You and I, we need to concentrate on our own survival right now. Playing guessing games about what's going on back there isn't going to help us. Okay?"

Brandon frowned, but said, "Okay."

A few minutes later, Hayes stopped.

"Is this it?" Brandon asked, looking around. There was nothing there but more trees.

Hayes approached a broken branch sticking out of the ground. No, not a branch, Brandon realized—an old rusted stake.

Hayes aligned himself with it, then marched off a couple dozen paces to the west. The place where he stopped was just a small open space, maybe ten feet in diameter at most, and looked pretty much like everywhere else.

"Give me a hand," Hayes said. He dropped to his knees and began pushing away the ground cover.

Brandon joined him. He almost asked what they were looking for, but as soon as he started moving the dirt and dead vegetation, he saw a flat metal surface. It took them less than a minute to completely clear it.

"Come over to this side," Hayes said.

Brandon repositioned himself, and together they put their hands underneath the four-foot-square plate and lifted. The metal was heavy, but they were able to get it up and to the side. In the space beneath was what looked like a sewer lid, only it had no holes in the top, and instead of being metal, it was plastic. Embedded in the surface were two handles about six inches apart.

Hayes put a hand in each, and turned the whole thing like the lid of a jar. It took two complete rotations before it came free. Underneath was a round shaft stuffed with items in airtight packages.

Hayes set the lid to the side, then began pulling the packages out and handing them to Brandon. By the time they finished emptying the cylinder, the area around the hole was littered with bags. Hayes started going through them one by one, separating them into two groups.

When he finished, he pointed at the bags to his right and said, "Those go back in. Can you take care of that?"

"Of course," Brandon said.

While he put the unwanted bags back in the storage cylinder, Hayes opened the others. The first contained a standard hiking backpack, while in the second was a smaller bag, not too dissimilar from the book backpack Brandon had used for school. Hayes began filling each with contents removed from the other bags—food, bottles of water, clothing, two sleeping bags, and a few things Brandon couldn't identify.

"Shall I put the top back on?" Brandon asked when he was finished.

Hayes shook his head. "We need to put all the empty bags in first."

Brandon collected the bags and stuffed them down the hole.

Once that was done, Hayes said, "You'll take the small pack."

The bag looked full, and had one of the sleeping bags strapped to the bottom.

"Don't worry, I didn't make it too heavy."

"I'm not worried," Brandon said.

"All right. One more check around to make sure we haven't forgotten anything, then—"

A low, rhythmic noise echoed softly down the hill. Both Hayes and Brandon cocked their heads.

"One of the helicopters," Brandon said.

Hayes looked around, his gaze settling on the half-full storage cylinder.

"Get in!"

"What?"

"Get in! Now. We don't have time to talk about it."

"You said they might have a thermal scanner. Won't they be able to see us?"

"Not through the lid and the ground."

Brandon looked at the hole, then at Hayes. "But...we both can't fit."

"I'll get rid of them, and come back for you."

"No!"

"If you don't get in, you'll get us both killed."

The whirling of the helicopter rotors was growing louder.

"Now!" Hayes shouted.

Brandon jerked back in surprise, then climbed into the hole.

"Here," Hayes said, shoving the small backpack in with him. "I'm going to leave the screw top off, and just pull the plate over."

"But...but..."

"It's going to be all right," Hayes said, grabbing the metal plate and tipping it back over.

As it was closing down on him, Brandon said, "How long will I have to—"

"It's going to be fine."

The plate fell the rest of the way to the ground, plunging Brandon into darkness. He could hear scrapes on the other side as Hayes covered the plate with the loose ground they'd scraped off. For several seconds all was quiet.

Then the helicopter roared overhead.

4

THE MOMENT THE bullet left his gun, Daniel Ash started running toward the front of the room. His aim had been true. The slug slammed into Olivia Silva, spinning her off the chair.

But had it been in time?

He paid no attention to the huddled group of men on the floor, or their dead colleague who lay nearby. His focus was completely on Olivia, and the computer she had been using.

She was now on the ground, clutching her blood-soaked shoulder. Through clenched teeth, she said, "Very good, Captain Ash. I'm impressed." She sneered. "But not as impressed as I could have been."

Ash looked at the computer. On the screen, in deceptively small letters, was the simple phrase:

ACTIVATION COMPLETE

Dammit!

He blinked, but the words remained the same. His bullet may have hit its mark, but it had not stopped Olivia from transmitting the go code that would commence the release of the virus on the world.

Project Eden's restart of humanity had begun.

He looked down at her. "You've got to stop it!"

"Stop it? Even…if I could, why would I?"

He whirled around and glared at the group of men, the leaders of Project Eden. "Deactivate it!"

No one moved.

He rushed forward, pointing his gun from one man to the next. "Turn it off. Stop it. Now!"

"We can't," one of the men said.

Ash turned to him and put the muzzle of the pistol against the guy's forehead. "Turn it off!"

"Can't be done. Once activated, it can't be stopped."

"Bullshit! You've got to have some sort of override."

"Ash!"

He looked up. Chloe was standing in the doorway at the back of the room.

"We've only got a few more minutes!" she yelled. "We've got to go!"

Before punching in the go code for the virus, Olivia had begun the self-destruct sequence for the Project Eden facility known as Bluebird. From that moment, they'd had fifteen minutes to exit the building. Half that time was already gone.

"Olivia activated the virus!" he told her.

Chloe's eyes widened in horror.

Ash looked back at the men on the floor. "Override it!"

"There is no override," another man said defiantly. He was the one who'd been sitting at the computer when Ash, Olivia, and the others had barged in and taken over, the man who was supposed to have activated the release. "What's done is done. Welcome to the new world, Captain Ash."

"Ash, we've got to go!" Chloe said.

Ash ran back to the computer, hoping there was something—*anything*—that might indicate the men were wrong. But there was nothing on the screen other than:

ACTIVATION COMPLETE

Sitting beside the keyboard was the open envelope Olivia had taken from the man who'd been at the computer. Next to it was the piece of paper that had been inside. Ash snatched it up. There were only five characters on it:

EXIT 9

The activation code, he realized. He started to throw it down, then stopped himself. *What if...?*

"Ash! Come on!" Chloe called.

He typed in E-X-I-T-9, and hit ENTER. Nothing happened.

He tried the code backwards, 9-T-I-X-E, knowing it was a long shot at best. Nothing again.

"Ash!"

He glanced toward Chloe. She was frantically waving at him to join her.

"Give me a second!" he yelled, then input EXIT 9 again.

ACTIVATION COMPLETE

He tried once more.

ACTIVATION COMPLETE

Someone tugged at his arm.

"Ash," Chloe said from beside him. "We're out of time. We need to leave now!"

"We've got to stop this!"

"We *can't* stop it! We tried, but we can't. Do you want to die here, too? Because that's what's going to happen if we don't move *now*."

He balled his hands into fists as he stared down at the computer, more frustrated than he'd ever been in his life.

This time, when Chloe grabbed his arm and pulled, he didn't fight her.

"Sorry to ruin your...day, Captain Ash," Olivia called after him.

He twisted out of Chloe's grasp and stepped toward Olivia.

"What are you doing?" Chloe asked.

"She started this," he said. "She's coming with us. She needs to answer for what she's done."

Before he could grab Olivia, Chloe yanked him to a stop. "Are you kidding me? She's going to *die* here when the building goes up. That's about the best solution we can get. Come on!"

He stared down at Olivia.

She smiled at him again. "Goodbye, Captain."

Snatching his gun off the desk where he'd left it, he pointed it at her head.

"Go on. Do it," she said. "You know you want to."

Damn right he did. No one would ever come close to matching the number of dead that would undoubtedly lie at Olivia's feet. Billions, if the Resistance's projections were correct.

Her smile broadened. "You can't, can you? You're too good for that. You'd never shoot an unarmed—"

He pulled the trigger, blowing the top of her head off, ensuring she'd never speak another word.

"Satisfied?" Chloe asked. "Can we go now?"

There was no satisfaction in killing Olivia. His inability to stop what she'd already unleashed made her death a footnote to what he knew would be happening next.

Without responding, he headed for the door, Chloe running right beside him. When they entered the corridor, they found two members of Olivia's strike team waiting there.

"Where is she?" one of them asked.

"She didn't make it," Chloe said as she tried to push past them.

The man grabbed her arm. "What do you mean, she didn't make it?"

Ash shoved him away. "She means Olivia's dead."

The other man raised his rifle, aiming it at Ash. "You killed her, didn't you?"

Before Ash could respond, two shots rang out, and both men dropped to the ground.

Chloe, her gun held near her waist, said, "I don't know about you, but I'm getting the hell out of here."

They raced down the corridor, retracing their path back to the emergency tunnel. Somewhere behind them, Ash could hear others running in their direction, the Project Eden members who'd been held captive in their own command center now trying to escape the coming destruction.

"This way," Chloe said, turning down a smaller hallway that Ash almost missed.

At the end, they could see another one of Olivia's people standing in the open entrance to the tunnel, waiting.

"Close it behind us!" Ash yelled as they approached.

"Where are the others?" the man asked.

"Not coming," Chloe said.

"What happened?"

As they neared the door, Ash could hear the Project Eden members turning into the hallway. "Just close it!" he ordered. He rushed through the opening right behind Chloe.

The man hesitated a moment, then followed him and shut the door.

Ash went over to the monitor mounted on the rock wall that controlled the entrance, and touched the screen, engaging the lock. The others would be able to release it from the inside, but it would at least slow them down a bit. As far as Ash was concerned, none of them deserved the chance at escape. They had all played their parts in the plan to kill most of humanity, so they could all go to hell.

"Give me that," Chloe said to Olivia's man as she ripped the flashlight he was holding out of his hand. "Come on!"

The three of them headed quickly down the tunnel, the flashlight's beam bouncing across the ground ahead of them.

"How much time?" Ash asked.

Chloe glanced at her watch. "A minute if we're lucky."

They weren't.

They made it halfway to the opening of the cave when they heard a low rumble behind them.

"Faster!" Ash yelled.

The sound grew louder and louder as the ground began to shake, and dust and pieces of rock started to fall from the top of the tunnel. Ten steps on, a large chunk dropped from the ceiling and grazed the side of the other man's head, knocking him to the ground. Ash yanked him back to his feet. The man was bloodied and dazed.

"I got you," Ash said, putting an arm around him.

The man stumbled forward, gained his footing again, and began running on his own.

More rocks assaulted them as the rumble became a roar.

Ahead, the tunnel curved slightly to the right. As soon as Chloe reached the bend, she yelled something back at them. Ash couldn't hear her above the noise, but when he reached the point where she'd been, he saw what she was trying to tell him.

The opening of the cave, just fifty feet away. Ash thought he could see some movement beyond it, but it was hard to tell, because the perpetual dark of the Arctic winter was only slightly lighter than the pitch black of the cave.

A loud *boom* suddenly engulfed the tunnel, shaking the ground so hard all three of them were thrown off their feet. A large section of the ceiling crashed down between Ash and Chloe.

Ash grabbed the other man and pulled him back to his feet, then half carried him over the fallen rock. Once they cleared it, Chloe braced the man on the other side. They headed off again just as part of the ceiling behind them collapsed, and bits of rock pelted them in the back.

Nearing the opening, Ash could hear the wail of the wind, and realized the movement he'd seen moments earlier was snow, but not just normal snow. Blizzard snow.

The storm that had been threatening earlier had arrived.

They stopped at the entrance just long enough to pull on the hoods of their jackets, then made their way on the narrow pathway that led across the cliff face back to the relative safety of the island.

"Where are the others?" Chloe asked.

The rest of Olivia's team had left Bluebird not long before them, but the path was empty.

"Back to base," Olivia's man said. "Supposed to meet there."

"Do you know the way?" Ash asked.

"Yeah. I think so."

Think so? Ash thought. He and Chloe had only come this way the one time, and while both were excellent with directions, navigating through a full-on blizzard would magnify even the slightest of mistakes.

They were three-quarters of the way toward the top when the ground shook again. Chloe grabbed on to the cliffside. Ash started to do the same, but Olivia's man began waving his arms around, attempting to regain his balance as he tipped backward toward the edge. Below were rocks, the icy sea, and certain death.

Ash whipped out a hand, snatched the man's sleeve, and tried to pull him back. For a second, he thought they would both go over the side, but then Chloe grabbed the man's other arm and stabilized them.

Ash took two deep breaths, and glanced toward the cave.

The entrance was gone.

Once the shaking subsided, they continued along the path. When they reached the top, they huddled together, the snow whipping across their faces. Even with the flashlight, their visibility was only a dozen feet at most.

"Which way?" Ash asked.

The guy looked around for longer than Ash would have liked, then pointed. "That way. Until we reach the ridge."

Chloe looked at Ash, the silent question in her eyes, "What if he's wrong?"

He grimaced and stared at her for a moment. "Okay, we keep our pace steady, and hold on to each other at all times. Chloe, you lead."

"Goody," she said.

They headed through the storm.

5

CHRISTOPHE DE COSTER paid the cab driver and climbed out onto the sidewalk. It had taken him a bit longer to get to Gare Montparnasse than he'd hoped, but, as was his nature, he'd built a buffer into his schedule, and still arrived at the station in plenty of time to greet Marcus Lunt when his train pulled in.

Lunt was one of the primary owners of the advertising company Christophe worked for, but he had long ago moved into semi-retirement in Bordeaux. Every month, he would make the trip to the capital, spend the next day at the office being briefed on current projects, and head back home. And every month, Christophe would be at the station waiting for him when he arrived, and accompany Lunt to the man's Paris apartment, where Christophe would give his boss a pre-briefing. This ensured that when Lunt showed up the next morning, he would look more involved than he really was in the everyday workings of the company.

Christophe's efforts had helped him steadily move up the chain of command, and, if everything went as hoped, by this time next year, he fully expected to be named the new president.

As he walked toward the station entrance, he noted that construction on one of the buildings across the street was still ongoing. Now, in addition to the scaffolding and piles of building materials that seemed to have been there for months, there was a large metal box on the street right out front—a shipping container, if he wasn't mistaken.

He'd all but dismissed it when the most curious thing happened. The top of the box seemed to split lengthwise, then each section started to rise, creating an opening. Casually, he glanced at the building, thinking the construction people must be working late—an unusual thing, to say the least—but he could see no one around.

Odd, but then again, if a construction worker walked through his office and saw how advertising operated, that person might find things strange, too.

Nearing the station entrance, he thought he could hear a hum coming out of the shipping container.

Ah, he thought. *A portable workshop. What a great idea.*

He passed through the doorway and joined the crowd inside. As he headed for the platform, his thoughts turned to the items he would be discussing with Lunt, and how he would change a few things once he was in charge.

Unfortunately for Christophe, that day would never come.

BALTIMORE, MARYLAND
12:15 PM EASTERN STANDARD TIME

IT HAD BEEN two weeks since Mary Jackson had first called City Hall to file a complaint. The person who had answered listened for a moment, then transferred her to the Department of Public Works. The man she talked to there had seemed pleasant and helpful, and had told her he'd make sure someone came out to check.

But after four days, no one had shown up. Mary knew this because she could see from her living room window the big metal box in the empty lot next to the convenience store. Sure, her neighborhood wasn't the most beautiful in the world, but she'd lived there for over forty years. No way was she going to let it get any worse. And to her, someone dumping a corrugated eyesore right in her view was definitely pushing things in the wrong direction.

So she called again, this time talking to a bored woman who couldn't even get her name right, and again the following day, getting someone completely new who acted like it wasn't the responsibility of his department.

For the next week, she did nothing but stew and watch the box. If she'd been younger, maybe she would have walked over to see if there was a phone number on it anywhere. But at her age, she rarely even set foot on her porch anymore.

She had made up her mind that she would give it one more day then call again, only this time she'd bypass Public Works and go directly to the mayor's office. But her plan changed when the top of the box opened, and it started to hum.

She reached for the phone.

"Office of Public Works. May I help you?"

She recognized the voice as belonging to the man she'd talked to the first time she called, the one who'd seemed so helpful.

"Yes, this is Mrs. Jackson. You've got to do something."

"I'm sorry, ma'am?"

"About the box. I talked to you two weeks ago about it."

"The box?" He paused. "Oh. Oh! The metal box across the street from you."

"You said you'd send somebody out, but they never came. And now the thing has opened up and is making a weird noise."

"Opened up?"

"Yes. Opened up. Did you not just hear me?"

"Are you sure?"

Her lips squeezed together. She was not in the mood to be doubted. "Never mind. I'll call the mayor. I'm sure *he'll* do something about it."

"Ma'am, I'm sorry no one has come out yet. There was obviously a mix-up somewhere."

Yeah. With you, she almost said but held her tongue.

"As soon as I hang up, I'll make a call and have someone come out right away."

"Well, okay. But if I don't see them in the next hour, I'm going to call the mayor."

"I completely understand. Now, could you give me the address again?"

Once she had given him the information and hung up, she sat in her chair and kept an eye on the box. Even through her closed windows she could easily hear the noise. Apparently, she wasn't the only one who noticed the strange sound. Not long after she'd sat back down, a couple of teenagers wandered over to the box.

She watched as one of them boosted the smaller of the two up so he could get a look inside. Something very strange happened then. As the small kid leaned over the opening, the collar of his jacket started to flap like it was caught in the wind. He was only there for a second before he wiped his hand across his face, and jumped off his friend's hands to the ground. He dropped to his knees and covered his eyes.

Mary leaned forward, muttering to herself, "I told them there was something wrong with that. I told them!"

The taller kid hunched over his friend. After several seconds, the smaller one rubbed his eyes and stood up. His friend asked him a question, and the short one shrugged and smiled. The tall one punched him in the arm, and soon they were both laughing. But as they walked away, the short one glanced back at the box, giving it a wary look.

He seems okay, Mary thought. But she still didn't like it.

Twenty minutes later, a Public Works truck turned onto the street, slowed, and pulled into the lot where the box was.

How about that? I guess I should threaten to call the mayor every time.

The man who got out looked at the box with disinterest, walked around it, stopped back where he'd begun, and stared at it again. Finally he pulled out a phone and made a call. As he talked, he gestured toward the box several times, so Mary assumed he was talking to his boss. Finally, with a visible sigh, he put the phone back in his pocket, and pulled a ladder off his truck.

Setting it next to the box, he climbed up high enough so he could look inside. Unlike the kid earlier, he didn't lean all the way over the edge. Still, his hair fluttered from the moving air coming from inside. At one point, he touched his cheek and rubbed it for a moment. When he moved his fingers away, he looked at them as if there was something on them.

When he climbed back down, the disinterest he showed earlier was no longer on his face. He whipped out his phone, his conversation considerably more animated than it had been the last time.

Within ten minutes, two more Public Works trucks and a city-owned sedan arrived. Five minutes after that, the fire department was on the scene.

Mary smiled. They should have listened to her earlier. At least now she'd get the damn thing out of there.

Unfortunately, she was mistaken. The only thing that would be moving was Mary, when she was taken to an evacuation center halfway across town, where, in a few short days, she would take her last breath.

OCEANSIDE, CALIFORNIA
9:16 AM PACIFIC STANDARD TIME

BECKER WAS GETTING impatient. He'd been sitting in his car for over an hour now, parked at the side of the road. What he shouldn't have done was down the entire cup of Starbucks coffee as fast as he had. Now he had to piss. Bad.

He looked at his watch. Maybe something was wrong. His eyes moved back to the shipping container on the back of the parked truck just down the street. If things had gone according to plan, the Implementation Delivery Module—or IDM—should have opened by now. Was there some sort of delay? Had the directors decided to reschedule?

If that were the case, somebody would have called him by now, right?

He picked up his phone. He had a good signal, but there were no missed calls.

Then what the hell is taking so long?

He bounced his legs up and down, attempting to ease some of the pressure on his bladder.

"Come on, come on, come on," he whispered.

Then, as if magically obeying his command, the top of the IDM began to rise.

With a sense of relief, he smiled. It was really happening. The new world they'd been working toward was about to arrive.

He shifted his gaze past the truck, to the buildings about two miles away—Marine Corps base Camp Pendleton, directly downwind from the module.

He picked up his phone and hit the preset number. "It's me," he said. "It just opened."

6

THE DECADES IT had taken Project Eden to move from an idea for a better world to the actual Implementation Day had been wisely spent in preparation. With a goal as large as theirs, it was vitally important that *every* detail was well thought out.

One of the priorities on the list was the creation of storage facilities to ensure that those chosen to restart humanity would have the supplies they needed to guarantee their survival through the transition. The depots were spread across the world, and were designed to serve the dual purpose of storing the supplies, and acting as a shelter for Project members during the unfortunate but necessary step of killing off over ninety-nine percent of mankind.

It wasn't that the members needed the facility to avoid contracting the KV-27a virus—all had been vaccinated—but after the release of the disease, there would likely be a period of chaos until the pandemic burned itself out. It was believed this would not last for more than a month, meaning those taking refuge in the depots would barely make a dent in the storage supply.

Depot NB219 was located just north of Las Cruces, New Mexico. By all appearances, it was just another farm along the Rio Grande. If the local population had been given a tour of the facility, they would have been shocked to find out how much of the place was actually underground.

Due to its remote location, on Implementation Day NB219 was one of the least populated facilities, with only forty-three Project members using the living quarters. One of those present was the Project's primary fixer, a man named Perez. His status as the Project Eden directors' golden boy made him not only the highest-ranking member at the depot, but the second highest of all members not currently at Bluebird. So while he didn't immediately insist on taking over for NB219's facility director, he did make sure he was involved in every decision.

When the hour of implementation approached, he joined Director Kane and his assistant Claudia Lindgren in the main conference room to monitor the events.

There were some tense moments when the hour came and went without any reports that activation had occurred. Then, nearly five minutes late, a message appeared on the television screen:

ACTIVATION COMPLETE

Soon after that, news started to trickle in from spotters scattered around the globe that the IDMs were going live.

Kane smiled broadly. "I think we should break out the champagne."

Claudia rose from her chair and pulled a bottle of Dom Perignon out of the small refrigerator along the wall. She grabbed three glasses from a nearby cabinet, and returned to the table.

As she popped the cork and started to pour, Perez said, "None for me."

Kane's smile slipped a little. "Are you sure? It's a special occasion."

"I'm sure."

The director looked like he didn't know what to do.

"I'll have one with you," Claudia said. She held a glass out to the director.

With a weak smile in Perez's direction, Kane raised it in

the air. "To the new beginning."

"The new beginning," Claudia repeated.

They both took a drink.

Perez's refusal to join them had not been any kind of anti-alcohol stand, nor was it based on the fact it was still morning. As someone who had routinely killed people for the Project, he clearly understood the sacrifice the rest of the world was about to make. To him, celebrating that was beyond inappropriate. But he said nothing.

As it approached ten thirty, he watched the monitor for the expected follow-up message from Bluebird. When it didn't come on time, he thought perhaps it would be delayed the same amount of time as the activation message.

But five minutes passed with nothing. Then six. Then seven.

"Are we still online?" he asked.

Kane, red-cheeked from the two glasses of champagne he'd already downed, leaned toward the monitor. "I, uh, think so. Yes, I believe we are. Is something wrong?"

If Kane couldn't figure it out, Perez wasn't going to tell him. "I need someone to open the vault."

"What?" Kane said, confused.

"The vault. I need someone to open it." Perez narrowed his eyes, staring at the director. "Not you."

"Now, hold on. There's no reason for you to take that tone with me. I'm in charge here."

"You *were* in charge. Things have just changed."

"What are you talking about?"

Claudia glanced at her watch, then looked at the monitor, the blood draining from her face.

Immediately she put her glass down and stood up. "I'll take you."

Kane gaped at her. "Claudia, what do you think you're doing?"

Instead of answering, she led Perez out the door.

The conference room was located on the third basement level, while the vault was on level four, the bottom level.

As they rode the elevator down, Claudia said, "It could

be just a communication glitch."

Perez said nothing.

The amount of redundancies the Project had built into their communications system meant the chances of that being the case were extremely low. The second message, the one confirming everything was happening as planned, should have arrived no more than thirty minutes after activation. That was a step built into the Project's plan years ago. The fact it hadn't happened meant something was wrong, most likely at Bluebird itself.

But, as it had done for many possibilities, the Project had prepared for just such a circumstance.

Once out of the elevator, they made their way to the vault where Claudia punched in the code, opening the outer door. Inside was the real vault door. This took not only another code but a retinal and hand scan of an authorized individual. Claudia wasted no time releasing the locks, and within seconds they were standing inside.

One wall was covered with small, numbered doors that looked no different than a wall of safety deposit boxes in a bank. The only difference was that the ones in the Project's vaults were opened with codes instead of keys. Each box contained instructions or information that would be used in different scenarios. Perez went immediately to box A002.

"Code," he said.

"Two-slash-thirty-eight-slash-seven."

He input the characters and the door popped open.

Inside was a single sheet of paper. He read it carefully then handed it to her. "I'm officially taking over this facility."

"Yes, sir," she said, her eyes scanning the page.

"Retrieve the communication codes for the other depots, and have your people start making contact. I want a video conference in one hour with the top four ranking members."

Something had gone wrong at Bluebird after the activation code was sent. Which meant, until someone from the Project directorate showed up, Perez and the others he would soon contact had to take charge.

7

BRANDON FOCUSED ALL his energy on trying to hear anything from the other side of the metal plate that covered his hiding spot. But there was no helicopter, no feet, no anything. Just his own heartbeat thudding in his ears.

Every few minutes he would use the flashlight that had been in the backpack to check his watch. Hayes had been gone over half an hour. Brandon was sure he should have been back by now. He'd only heard the helicopter for a few minutes right after he was buried in the hole, so he thought it had probably flown off somewhere.

How long do I wait?

An image flashed in his mind. Hayes somewhere in the forest injured and needing help. Brandon was the only one around, the only one who could do anything.

Ten more minutes, then go look for him.

He sat on the pile of empty plastic bags, his head cocked to the side so that his ear rested against the metal.

Still silence from above.

When he checked his watch again, he saw that he was already two minutes past his deadline.

All right. All right, I'm going.

But for a moment he didn't move, wondering if he was making the right decision.

"Go," he whispered to himself.

He placed his palms against the metal plate and pushed. It moved half an inch, and came back down. He'd forgotten how heavy it was, plus now it had an added layer of dirt on top of it.

Could he even move it? Would he be stuck in the tube until someone found him? *Would* anyone find him?

The thought of never getting out of the hole was more than enough to motivate him to try again. This time, instead of just pushing up, he pushed up and to the side, hoping that would be easier, and was able to move it several inches before he had to set it back down again.

He gave himself half a minute, then tried once more. After three attempts, he'd moved the plate enough that a wedge of light appeared at one end. All he had to do was get it halfway across the hole and he was sure he'd be able to squeeze out.

He raised his hands to push again, but froze. A soft crunch, not far away, like someone stepping on fallen pine needles.

Hayes? Or someone else?

Brandon held his position. Another crunch, this one farther away, then several more. They sounded too light to be footsteps. What then? Something falling from the trees?

When several minutes passed with no more noise, he pushed on the plate again. The pause had given him the energy he needed, and he was able to move the cover an inch beyond the midpoint.

He rested for a moment, then raised himself so his head cleared the opening.

There was a loud rustle to his left. He whipped around just in time to see several deer hop away. The noise hadn't been Hayes, nor one of the others.

He worked himself all the way out, then leaned over the tube and extracted the backpack. As he stood up, he looked at the metal plate and considered pushing it back over the hole. But the energy it had taken to move it off had already drained him. Shoving it around again would only make him weaker, and he knew he was going to need all the strength he had left.

47

It would just have to stay the way it was.

He turned slowly in a full circle, unsure which way he should go in search of Hayes. His eyes settled on the ridge they had come over about an hour before. While it wasn't completely treeless, the forest was thinner there.

Leaving his backpack by the open tube, he jogged up the hill. As he reached the top, he could hear the distant *thump-thump-thump* of one of the helicopters, and spotted it hovering above the Ranch. He searched the rest of the sky for the other helicopters, but only the one was visible.

He turned his back to the Ranch, and looked down into the valley where he'd been hiding. A carpet of trees stretched out for as far as he could see. To the left the land tapered downward, flattening out to a horizon that looked a thousand miles away. To the right were the mountains that jutted up toward the heavens like a wall marking the end of the world.

Left?

Right?

Straight ahead?

Back to the Ranch?

No. Hayes wouldn't have gone back. That would have been heading directly toward those attacking the Resistance.

As Brandon turned back to the valley, a helicopter suddenly rose out of the trees about half a mile away. Without even thinking, he dropped to the ground, his eyes never leaving the aircraft.

It hovered in the sky for a moment, then turned and began heading in his direction.

Scrambling backward on his belly, he moved behind the nearest tree, then closed his eyes and hugged the ground.

Please don't let them see me. Please don't.

The thump of the helicopter increased until it roared right over his head. A part of him was sure someone inside was looking down at him, and within seconds the aircraft would descend enough so that the soldiers could drop down on ropes and snatch him from where he lay. But after a moment, the pounding of the rotors began to recede as the helicopter passed over the ridge and headed toward the Ranch.

Brandon wasted no time jumping to his feet. He sprinted down the hill to the thicker cover of the forest near the tube, retrieved his backpack, and headed in the direction of the spot where the helicopter had risen from the trees.

As he drew closer, he slowed his pace and tried to minimize the sound of his steps in case some men had been left behind. What he really wanted to do was call out Mr. Hayes's name, but that obviously wasn't an option.

Just ahead, he could see the clearing where the helicopter had landed. In the spring and summer it was probably green with vegetation, but now it was just dirt and rocks and scrub, waiting for the winter snows that, according to those at the Ranch, should have arrived already.

Staying among the trees, he circled around the meadow, looking for movement. It seemed, though, that the helicopter had taken everyone with it.

Just keep going. Get away from here, a voice in his head said.

He turned, planning to do just that, when something odd caught his attention. It was just inside the trees, about a quarter of the way farther around the clearing, a blue shape that looked out of place.

It kind of looked like a tarp or—

No.

Keeping the thought from completely forming, he skirted the edge of the clearing and raced toward the object. But the closer he got, the slower his stride became, as the realization of what it was started to sink in.

The blue was flanked on both sides by offshoots of black.

No, he thought again, taking another step closer.

A blue jacket. Black sleeves.

Another step.

A jacket that had a hole in the middle no wider than one of Brandon's fingers. A jacket that was still being worn.

Oh, please, no. Please.

"Mr. Hayes?"

He dropped his pack on the ground, knelt down, and put

a hand on the man's shoulder.

"Mr. Hayes? Are you all right?" It was a stupid question. Of course he wasn't all right. He was lying there unconscious.

Brandon moved his hands under the man's chest, and carefully turned him onto his back.

For a moment, all he could do was stare, then he twisted to the side and vomited.

Hayes's eyes were open wide, but there was no life in them. There was a gaping wound in his chest right above where his heart was.

The hole in the back of the jacket, Brandon thought. A bullet hole.

His stomach turned, and he wanted to retch again, but he forced whatever was left inside to stay down.

What am I going to do now?

He stared blankly at the ground just beyond Hayes's body.

The Ranch?

One look at Mr. Hayes was reason enough not to go that way.

Think. Think! What would Dad do?

Before the Sage Flu, his father had been just like most dads. He played with Brandon, pushed him to do his homework, taught him how to field a grounder. But after the outbreak, after Brandon and Josie's mother had died and they'd finally been reunited with him, he had started teaching his kids other skills, survival skills they would need if things turned bad. Brandon could tell directions from the stars, knew how to shoot a gun, and even, despite his age, how to drive a car. But he was still a kid. Even he knew that.

As he closed his eyes, his father's voice echoed in his head. "Never let events overwhelm you." It was a lesson he'd preached many times. "Relax. Be logical. And survive."

Brandon repeated the last part silently to himself.

When he felt he was in control once more, he opened his eyes. Hayes was still there, still staring at the sky, his chest ripped open, but the sight no longer repelled Brandon. It was as if he was watching a movie, and Hayes was only an actor on the screen. So he did what he'd seen in films many times—he closed Hayes's eyes.

Dipping his head, he said, "Lord, please take care of Mr. Hayes. He was trying to help me, and probably saved my life. Thank him for me, okay? Amen."

It wasn't the best prayer ever, but it would have to do.

He gritted his teeth, knowing what he had to do next wasn't going to be pleasant. Hesitating only a second, he started searching through Hayes's pockets for anything he might need. He found seventy dollars in the man's wallet first, and in the pockets a folding knife, a book of matches, and eighty-five cents in coins. He'd been hoping to find Mr. Hayes's cell phone, but he didn't seem to have it on him.

He stood up and took a look around the area. So where was Mr. Hayes's backpack? Had the people from the helicopter taken it with them?

No, Brandon realized. Mr. Hayes probably hid it somewhere so he could move faster.

Brandon thought about going in search of it, but who knew how long that might take, or if he'd find it at all? He couldn't chance on the helicopters flying back over and finding him. He'd just have to get by with what he already had.

Keep moving, his father's voice said.

"But where?" Brandon whispered.

Not the Ranch, and not toward the mountains.

The only real choice was to follow the gentle slope down toward the wide horizon. Somewhere out there, there had to be a town, someone he could go to for help. At the very least, there would be a highway.

The decision made, he looked down at Hayes again. "I'm sorry you had to die. I wish I could have helped you." He almost said goodbye, but that seemed too much.

Donning his pack, he turned east and started walking.

8

SIMS WAS SITTING in the command helicopter, looking at satellite images of the Montana facility that was burning about one hundred yards from where his aircraft was parked.

He knew from the moment they'd flown in that the fires had been set intentionally, so the people who had been occupying the building—the same people who had been a thorn in the side of the Project for so long—had either left the area completely or were hiding somewhere nearby. Given the surprise nature of his team's arrival, he found it hard to believe they'd had time to leave. The satellite image revealed there was only one way in and out of the property via the ground, and the portion of his team that had come in on the road had met no one going the other way.

There was, of course, a landing strip not far from the main building. They could have flown out, but he and the others in the helicopters would have seen them for sure.

So where were they?

He studied the photo, looking for any indications of camouflaged buildings or something that might be an entrance to an underground facility. There was the large building and the smaller building, both burning now, and an exercise area that his team had already thoroughly searched. The only other structure was about half a mile away, an old barn that had housed horses. When his men checked it out, they had found no secret doorways or places where people could hide. The only thing they discovered was that someone had opened the doors, and let all the horses out. That had been a surprise. When they were flying in, one of the other helicopters had done a heat sensor sweep of the barn and determined that there'd been several horses inside. A quick check with the pilot confirmed that the door had been closed at the time.

So there was at least one person around.

Sims had ordered one of his helicopters to go in search of whoever it was, hoping if they found someone, that person might be able to point them to where his friends were.

"Dammit," he said, tossing the photo down.

He knew they had to be here somewhere. He just *knew* it.

Outside, he heard a helicopter descending, so he pushed himself up and walked over to the open doorway. The men he'd sent in search of the person who'd opened the barn were back.

As soon as the other helicopter landed, the door flew open and the team jumped out one by one, but they had no prisoner with them. Sims stepped out of his aircraft and strode toward Donaldson, the other team leader.

"I take it you didn't find anyone," he said. The mission had been on radio silence since before they flew in.

"Actually, we did."

Sims looked around. "I don't see anyone."

"He's dead."

A pause. "He was dead when you found him?"

"No. He was armed. We tried to stop him, but when he shot at us we had no choice but to return fire."

"I clearly remember telling you to bring anyone you find back alive."

"I understand that, sir, but I wasn't going to let my team get shot."

"No one said you couldn't shoot him, but you didn't have to *kill* him."

"He moved."

"What?"

"He was running away. I tried to hit him in the shoulder, but he moved to the side so it went through his chest."

"*You* did it?"

"Yes, sir."

Sims looked away, reining in his anger. Donaldson was one of his top soldiers. If he said the man moved into the bullet, then Sims had to believe him. Dammit. It was still a lost opportunity.

"Was he alone?" he asked.

"We spent some time looking around, but found no signs of anyone else." Donaldson paused. "There is something that might be helpful, though."

"What?"

Donaldson reached into his pocket and pulled out a cell phone. "This was on him. According to the call log, he used it a minute or two before we all arrived here."

THE FIRE AT the dormitory was almost out. Matt studied the camera feed, and was satisfied that the auxiliary Bunker entrance in the building's basement was now fully inaccessible. And though the Lodge was still burning above them, the fire had passed the point where it could be extinguished in time to find the main Bunker entrance there.

Now all they had to do was wait until the Project Eden assault team left, then inessential personnel could use the emergency tunnel to get away.

Matt would, of course, stay. If Project Eden had indeed triggered Implementation Day, then he needed to be here in the control room where he could do what he could to put a dent, however small, into its plans.

But had they triggered it or not? Given the attack squad aboveground, it seemed pretty damn likely, but he couldn't afford to make a mistake. The options still open to them would work only once—if that. If he set off the warnings and Implementation had not begun, the Resistance would be like the boy who cried wolf when it really did happen.

One time. One shot. They had to get it right.

For the last hour, Christina and several other communication officers had been trying to contact Resistance members on the outside who were near one of the shipping containers that had already been identified as suspect. They had reached a few people, and sent them to check out the boxes, but no one had reported back yet.

"Matt," his sister called from across the room. "Your phone."

"What?"

"Your cell phone. It's ringing."

He walked over to where he'd left it on one of the tables. The name on the display read J. HAYES. Why was Jon calling? Protocol in this situation was that all communication should be severed. Had something happened to Brandon?

He punched the ACCEPT button. "Jon?"

There was a pause. "No."

Matt froze. "Who is this?"

"You can call me Sims. I assume you're...Matt?"

"Who are you?"

"I just wanted to let you know that you and your friends can only hide for so long, and we'll still be here when you come out."

The assault team. They must have found Jon and Brandon.

Matt paled. "What did you do to them?"

Another pause. "I think we've talked enough. Call me back when you're ready to discuss surrender."

The line went dead.

"What is it?" Rachel asked.

"That was someone from the assault team. He was using Jon's cell phone."

"Jon's?" Her confusion lasted only a second before it morphed into fear. "What about Brandon?"

"He didn't say anything about either of them, but we probably should assume—"

"No, no. No assumptions," she said. She grabbed his arm. "We need to send someone out there to get them back."

"You know we can't do that. If we do, we'll expose our

55

location and get *everyone* killed."

"Brandon's just a boy. You promised Ash you'd watch him!"

"What's going on?" The voice came from across the room.

They both turned to find Josie Ash standing in the doorway.

"I heard you say Brandon's name. Did you find him? Did something happen?" she asked.

"We don't know anything at this point," Matt told her, but it was hard to sound convincing.

Josie stared at him, her eyes wide. "You said he'd be okay. You said Mr. Hayes would take care of him."

"Get her out of here," he whispered to Rachel.

Rachel stepped over to Josie.

"Come on," she said. "Let's go talk."

The two had barely left the room when Christina looked up from her monitor. "Matt. Dale Porter just called in. He drove by one of the containers in San Francisco. It's open, and it's humming."

The entire room went silent.

So this was it.

The end of the world.

Matt said, "I want a second confirmation from somewhere else. Preferably out of the country. As soon as we have that, don't wait for me to say anything. Initiate WC."

WC was not some tricky code. Its meaning was simple and clear.

Worst Case.

It would be another three hours before a second confirmation—this one from Copenhagen, Denmark—came in.

SIMS HUNG UP the cell phone and smiled. The man on the other end of the line had said, "What did you do to *them*?"

He looked over at Donaldson. "You've got yourself a second chance. There's at least one more person out there.

Find whoever it is and bring them back."

"Yes, sir." Donaldson turned and headed quickly back to his squad.

Sims stepped over to the doorway of his helicopter. "So?" he asked.

Inside was an impressive array of communications gear. Included among the equipment was a device that could track cell phone calls and pinpoint the location of both the originator and the receiver.

The technician manning the console was named DeFassio. He kept his attention focused on one of the monitors for a few seconds longer, then looked over.

"You were correct, sir. They're right here."

9

AT TIMES THE snow whirling around them became so thick it seemed as if they were walking through a never-ending wall of white.

Several times Ash was sure they were lost, but then they'd reach a landmark Olivia's man, Kessler, had pointed them toward, and head to the next.

"Which way now?" Ash yelled above the wind.

They had just reached the latest landmark, a small hill with an outcropping of rocks that was quickly becoming covered with snow.

"There's a little gully up ahead. Should be in that direction about a hundred yards." Kessler motioned ahead and slightly to the right. "The camp will be right on the other side."

"You need to rest or can we keep going?"

"Keep going," Kessler said.

They almost missed the gully, their path having veered a little too much to the right, but Chloe spotted their mistake, and guided them back on track.

As soon as they reached the far end, Kessler pointed to the left. "There. See it?"

A canvas drop that had been anchored to the side of the hill was now flapping in the wind, exposing everything that had been underneath it to the storm.

"I thought you said the others were going to be here," Chloe said.

Kessler looked confused. "They're supposed to be. That was the plan."

"Then where the hell are they?"

He shook his head. "I don't know. Maybe..."

"Maybe what?" Ash asked.

"They might have made for the boat."

"Boat? The island's iced in."

"Icebreaker," Kessler said. "About a mile offshore."

"You hiked in?"

Kessler nodded.

"So you think they went back there?" Chloe asked.

"It's the only other place they could have gone."

"What happens when they reach the boat? Will they wait for you?" Ash asked.

Kessler was silent for a second. "They might think I'm dead."

Since the three of them had been in the tunnel when the explosions started, Ash was willing to bet that's exactly what the others thought. They probably decided the sooner they got off the island, the better.

Chloe leaned close to Ash. "We've got to get there before they leave."

"I know," he said. The plane they had arrived on had crashed upon landing, so it was very likely that the only way they'd be able to get off the island was on that ship. He turned to Kessler. "Do you know where the icebreaker is?"

Another tired nod. "Southeast. Straight out."

"Then unless you want to die here, we need to keep moving."

Kessler nodded wearily. "Don't worry about me."

"Good."

"Hold on a second." Kessler staggered over to the remains of the camp. "There should be a GPS tracker here if it hasn't blown away. We'll need that."

After a minute of rooting around, he came up with the device. He turned it on and studied the screen.

"Okay, that way," he said, pointing into the storm.

"No," Ash said. He nodded to his left. "This way first. We have a stop to make."

RED CHECKED ON the pilot again. Gagnon was still out, his temperature warm, but not too hot. The fever had to be from an infection caused by one of the wounds the pilot had received when their plane crashed on the ice just off Yanok Island. In addition to the cut on Gagnon's head, the man had at least two broken ribs and a deep gouge on his leg. Red had done what he could, keeping the pilot's ribs wrapped, changing the bandages as often as necessary, but his biggest concern was that Gagnon had suffered internal damage. If that was the case, there was absolutely nothing Red could do.

What the man needed was a doctor, but Red was beginning to think they were both going to die right there in the makeshift shelter the Resistance advance scouts had used when they'd first discovered Bluebird's location.

It had been over eight hours since Ash and Chloe left them there. That in itself might not have been cause for concern, but just over two hours earlier, the ground had shaken violently several times. Not earthquakes, Red thought. Explosions. He only hoped that if Ash was the one who set them off, he'd been able to do it in time to stop the monsters from Project Eden.

Gagnon groaned, turning his head first one way, then the other.

Red grabbed the pot of warm water he'd heated earlier, poured some onto a piece of cloth, and pressed it lightly against Gagnon's lips. Squeezing, he let some of the water drip into the man's mouth. This seemed to calm him.

Outside the wind howled past the shelter. Red glanced over at the doorway, making sure nothing had blown away, and nearly jumped when the cover moved to the side and someone stepped in.

Ash. Chloe entered right after him, then a man Red didn't recognize.

"I wasn't sure if you guys made it," Red said as he hopped to his feet.

"We weren't sure ourselves there for a little while," Ash said.

"Did you find it?"

"Bluebird? Yeah, we found it." There was hesitation in Ash's voice.

"I felt explosions. Tell me you were able to—"

"It didn't go as planned."

"You mean—"

"They set it off."

Red closed his eyes and rolled his head back. "Holy shit."

"We can worry about it later," Ash said. "Right now we need to get out of here."

"In the storm?"

"If we don't, the only way we have of getting off this island will be gone."

"What about Gagnon?"

Ash looked past him at the pilot. "We'll have to take turns carrying him."

"That might kill him."

"Staying here *will* kill him. At least this way we'll all have a chance."

IT TOOK THEM forty minutes to reach the small bay where they'd come ashore after the plane crashed. It was the only path Ash knew that had easy access to the frozen ocean. Kessler said that his people had come up another way, but he wasn't completely sure where it was, so this was better than wasting time hunting around.

Chloe took charge of the GPS tracker once they were on the ice, while Ash and Red traded off carrying Gagnon every ten minutes. Unfortunately, the only way to effectively to do this and not lose time was to put the pilot over their shoulder in a fireman hold. Not exactly the ideal position for someone with broken ribs.

61

PALE HORSE

The frozen surface of the ocean, as they'd learned when they landed the plane, was not smooth and level. To make it worse, the new snow hid many of the contours and ridges, resulting in each of them falling or nearly doing so more than once. Luckily it never happened with whoever was carrying Gagnon, but it did slow their progress, making the one mile seem like ten.

An hour and twenty minutes passed before Chloe yelled out, "We should almost be there! Maybe another hundred yards."

Without saying anything, they all picked up their pace.

"I think I see something," she said a few minutes later.

As if to answer her, there was a sudden loud crack.

"No!" Kessler yelled, then raced ahead.

"Come on!" Ash said to the others. "They're leaving!" With Gagnon over his shoulder, Ash could only get up to a slow jog, but he urged the others to keep going. "Get their attention!"

He didn't see the ship until he almost reached it, its black metal hull suddenly rising up from the ice.

It was moving. Very slowly, but definitely moving.

"Hey!" Kessler yelled from several feet away.

The others joined in, but there was no reaction.

"Red! Come here!" Ash called out.

Red rushed over.

"Take him," Ash said, handing over Gagnon.

Free of the pilot, Ash backtracked several yards until he could see the dim outline of the deck. His gaze moved back and forth, searching for signs of movement.

There!

It was the shape of a man moving quickly toward a door that led inside. He probably wouldn't hear Ash yelling, so Ash pulled his gun from his jacket, aimed at a spot near the door, and pulled the trigger.

The shape jerked to a stop.

Ash couldn't be sure, but it looked like the man turned toward the side, so Ash jumped up and down and waved his arms. The others, seeing what he was doing, started to mimick him and scream at the top of their lungs.

At first, nothing happened. Then the cracking of the ice began to recede as the ship came to a halt.

10

THE VIDEO CONFERENCE call Perez wanted set up within the hour took four to organize. There were several factors involved in the delay. Number one—and the most time consuming—was determining who the other four highest-ranking Project members were, and where they were located.

The only one on the list higher than Perez was Dr. Henry Lassiter. Dr. Lassiter's purview was the health of Project members. Working under him was a team of physicians—general practitioners, surgeons, and specialists—who responded to all medical issues not related to the KV-27a virus. In effect, he was a hospital administrator whose employees were scattered all over the globe. The doctor himself was at NB772 in the south of France near the Spanish border.

The other three on the list in descending order were: Erik Halversen, Regional Director of Technologies for the Northern Hemisphere, located at NB405 outside Hamburg, Germany; Patricia Nakamura, Regional Director of Supplies for North America, located at NB89 near Seattle, Washington; and Dominick Tolliver, Regional Director of Supplies for East Asia, located at NB294 in the outskirts of Osaka, Japan.

"Are we ready?" Perez asked Claudia.

"Just waiting for Nakamura to come online." There was a pause, then she nodded. "All right. She's live. I can connect you all now."

"Do it."

Perez was pleased with how Claudia had jumped right in and helped without any hesitation. She'd proved herself very useful over the last few hours, something he couldn't say about Kane. The facility director just didn't seem to understand he was no longer in charge. Finally, Perez had had him taken to one of the holding cells. That solved the problem, at least in the short term.

Claudia tapped away at her keyboard. "All right. Here we go."

She hit one more key, and the large screen on the conference room wall came to life. The image was divided into four equal sections: Dr. Lassiter in the upper left, Halversen upper right, Nakamura lower left, and Tolliver lower right.

"Can you all hear me?" Perez asked.

They each responded yes.

"Then we should begin. First, when was the last time any of you was in contact with Bluebird?"

"Hold on a moment," Nakamura said, her eyes narrowing slightly. "There's something I think we need to clear up first. What exactly is *your* position with the Project?"

The question was not a surprise. The four on the screen were all managers with fancy titles. Perez was a wild card, the type of Project operative probably none of them had come in contact with before. But while they might have been confused by his inclusion, the Project directorate had known his worth, and had purposely ranked him as high as they did in case something like this happened. He was someone who could make sure things stayed on track and didn't get tripped up by narrow-minded middle managers.

"I'm Special Operations," he said.

"And that is what, exactly?" This time the question came from Tolliver.

"Use your imagination."

Silence.

"We think there might be a mistake with the information

we received," Nakamura said. She raised a piece of paper a few inches off her desk. "According to this, you're number two?"

"Yes. And?"

A small laugh escaped her lips. "*And* I guess we don't understand how that's possible. You're not even a director."

"You mean *regional* director. You're right. That's not a title I hold. I don't have a specific title, nor do I operate in a specific region. I work everywhere."

"Then I guess I have to go back to the earlier question. Doing what?"

He stared into the camera. "We're wasting time. We have a situation which needs to be dealt with, and you want to get into a pissing match over why the *directorate* saw fit to give me my rank?"

"It's just that—"

"Ms. Nakamura," Lassiter said, "Mr. Perez is correct. We need to address more pressing matters. If the directorate thinks so highly of him, then they must have a reason. It is not our position to challenge it."

Nakamura looked momentarily confused.

Her reaction pretty much confirmed what Perez had already thought, that she'd had an earlier conversation with Lassiter, and someone, perhaps the doctor himself, had come up with a strategy to figure out who Perez was. Chances were, conversations had occurred between all four of his new colleagues.

Time wasters. *Space* wasters. The Project was in the first few hours of implementation, and here they were—the supposed leaders if Bluebird remained out of contact—not able to pull their heads out of their own asses.

These people were even more of a problem than he thought they would be.

"Thank you, Dr. Lassiter," he said. "Perhaps we can get back to my question. Unless you'd like to be the one to keep things moving along."

"No," the doctor said after a second's hesitation. "You're doing fine. Please continue."

"All right. So, last time anyone heard from Bluebird?"

Like Perez, the last message they had all received was the one saying that activation had been completed. In the twenty-four hours prior to that, there had only been routine communications with no signs of trouble.

"I don't know if any of you have checked the weather or not," Tolliver said, "but it appears that a large storm has moved in over Bluebird. It's possible that could be affecting communications."

"Actually, not possible at all," Halversen said. "The systems that have been put in place work no matter what the weather."

"Well, *something* happened," Nakamura said.

"Yes," Perez agreed. "And there's no way we can know at this point what that is, so speculating about it is useless." Nakamura started to open her mouth, but Perez went on. "We've all read the document from box A002. The instructions are clear. In the event of a loss of communication from Bluebird, this committee is to be formed with the purpose of focusing on the continuation of the Project's goals. What we need to do now is make sure everything is proceeding as planned, and make any adjustments that might be necessary. After that, we can turn to the next steps."

"Hopefully the directorate will be back online by then," Nakamura said.

The others nodded in agreement.

"Of course," Perez said. "We all hope that."

Claudia slipped a piece of paper in front of him. He glanced down at it.

A man named Sims says he needs to talk to you right away.

Perez knew Sims. He was part of Special Operations, too, and commanded one of the Project's tactical strike teams.

"Mr. Perez?" Lassiter said. "Something the matter?"

"No. Sorry." Until he knew what Sims wanted, best to keep this to himself. "Now, about monitoring activation."

"I have an idea about that," the doctor said. "I'm willing

to bet that your background makes you best suited to assess where we are. You could be in charge of that task, and report back to us. What do you think?"

Report back to us? Perez thought. *All right. That's it.*

These people had no business being anywhere near the decisions that would have to be made. He was going to have to take full control himself. It would be best, though, if they didn't see it coming.

He almost smiled. "Of course. I would be happy to do that. Why don't we reconvene in four hours and I can fill you in then?"

Once they'd all agreed, the call was ended, and Claudia put Sims through to the phone on the table.

"Sims? Perez. What's going on?"

"Actually, I was going to ask you the same thing. I've been trying to get through to Bluebird, but no joy. Have you talked to anyone there?"

"No one has. The activation signal went out, but after that, nothing."

A pause. "I was afraid of that. Anyone trying to find out what's going on?"

"Apparently there's a big storm up there, so nothing we can do at the moment. Our focus is on making sure everything else goes as planned."

"Well, that's kind of why I'm calling you."

"Okay. What is it?"

"Who's in charge of security now? That's really who I should be talking to. Called you because the depot I contacted gave me your number, and said you were organizing some kind of leadership meeting."

"You called the right place. I'm the one you're looking for."

"I was hoping you'd say that. My team and I were sent on a special mission today, with instructions to call in a report thirty minutes ago. Like I said, I've been trying."

"What's the mission?"

Sims briefed him about the raid on the Resistance's headquarters.

"So the buildings are destroyed, but you haven't found them yet?"

"Oh, we've found them. We just haven't been able to get to them. They're in an underground shelter. Once we locate the door, we'll have them."

Perez was a practical man. It's what made him so good at his job. While an attack on Resistance headquarters was interesting, he instantly knew it was a needless act of revenge. Whoever was in that shelter would die of the coming plague anyway. Using Sims's team to kill them before that happened was risking the squad members' lives unnecessarily to satisfy the ego of one of the directors, no doubt. A director who was quite possibly dead.

"Sims, I've got some new instructions for you."

11

BRANDON LEANED AGAINST the tree, panting. Once more he could hear the helicopter heading in his direction. He slid around so the trunk was between him and the aircraft, hoping it would mask him from any heat-seeking scanner they might have.

He'd been doing the same thing for what seemed like hours now, running when the helicopter was far away, then using the trees as a barrier when it came near. So far it had worked.

When he'd left Hayes's body, he'd been hoping he wouldn't see any of the helicopters again, but the empty skies hadn't lasted long, and soon the one he was now hiding from had begun its slow methodical search over the forest.

This time it was flying just above the trees on a line that would take it over his position. Once it reached the point directly above him, the only things between it and his heat-radiating body would be a less-than-solid layer of branches. Would they be enough to hide him?

He thought about running to the side out of the helicopter's path, but he worried that he'd already waited too long, and would be seen the moment he took his first step.

Go? Stay?

Stay, he decided.

The treetops began swaying from the wind generated by

the helicopter's approach. Another few seconds and it would be right above him. He squeezed his eyes shut as if doing so would make him invisible, and pressed as tightly as he could against the tree.

Fifty feet away now, the rotors so loud he could no longer hear anything else.

He angled his feet so that he could shimmy around the trunk as the helicopter passed above, and hoped that would be enough to keep him from being discovered.

Twenty feet. His mind screamed at him to move around the tree now.

Wait. Wait.

He held his position.

Suddenly the sound of the engine changed as the helicopter stopped in midair.

He shoved his eyelids even tighter together, sure that he'd been seen, and those soldiers he'd been worried about earlier were descending to the ground.

The helicopter hung in the air above him. Why? What were they doing?

Reluctantly, he opened his right eye, then his left. Very slowly, he tilted his head up. Through a small gap in the tree cover, he could see a portion of the helicopter's tail section. Knowing he was taking a big chance, he leaned a few inches further around until he could see the main cabin.

No ropes. No men hanging below. The door was shut.

Run!

He didn't move, not because he thought the urge was wrong, but because his feet suddenly felt as if they were a thousand pounds each.

Without warning, the engine noise increased again, this time even louder than before. He looked up just in time to see the helicopter turn. It wasn't moving toward him now; it was moving away.

Run!

This time his feet obeyed.

Dodging trees and jumping over dead branches, he raced as fast as he could through the woods in the opposite direction of the helicopter. Every few minutes he'd look over his shoulder, expecting to catch a glimpse of the aircraft following him from above, but not once did he see it.

Run!

Since the helicopter had returned, he'd never been able to go for more than fifteen minutes without it flying somewhere close by, but now he'd been racing through the woods for twenty minutes and there was still no sign of the aircraft's return.

Run!

The gentle downward slope of the ground was a good indication he was heading in the same eastward direction as earlier, but he would feel better if he could get a glimpse of the mountains to be sure.

He glanced over his shoulder again, but could only see the trees. As he turned back around, he caught a split-second glimpse of the dead branch sticking up from the ground just before his shin slammed into it.

Down he went, his backpack crashing into him as he hit the ground, and spilling out several items from inside.

He lay there for a moment, not moving. Once his breath slowed, he pulled the backpack off, and sat up. Head throbbing, he touched the spot where his skull met his neck. His hair felt moist and sticky. He pulled his hand back and saw that his fingers were covered with blood.

He stayed where he was and gritted his teeth through the pain until it dulled enough so that he could check the rest of his body. Cuts and a few bruises, but he was pretty sure he hadn't broken anything.

He slowly repacked the backpack and pulled it on, then rubbed his hand over the back of his head again. There didn't seem to be any new blood, so hopefully the wound wasn't that bad.

He took a moment to figure out the direction the slope was going, and set off again, walking this time. The pain he felt, particularly in the shin that had smacked the branch, lessened somewhat as he walked, but didn't completely go away.

Twenty minutes later he reached a wide spot amongst the trees, not meadow really, barely even a clearing, but it was enough for him to get a look at most of the sky.

There was not a helicopter in sight. Maybe he *was* free.

With a sigh of relief, he checked his straps and continued on.

12

A COLD WIND blew across the waves, occasionally spraying salt water on the decks and windows of the vacation homes that lined the beach. Most of the places were closed up for the winter, while a few were occupied by people who called the area their permanent home.

One, however, was being used by a man and a woman, recent arrivals who had yet to venture into town. Those few locals who knew they were there assumed that they'd come to spend the Christmas holiday along the shore.

But while Tamara Costello and Bobby Lion had basically lived together since the previous spring, they were not a couple. They were friends and colleagues.

And survivors.

When the Sage Flu outbreak had occurred in California, Tamara was a promising reporter for the Prime Cable News network, and Bobby was her equally talented cameraman. They'd been assigned to cover the outbreak, and in the process had started to unearth the truth about what was really going on. If it hadn't been for Matt Hamilton and his people in the Resistance—an organization she had no idea even existed at the time—she and Bobby would have been long dead.

Instead, while everyone who'd known them thought they *were* dead, they'd actually gone into hiding and changed their identities. After the full realization of what they were up against finally sunk in, they had agreed to do whatever they could to help the Resistance stop Project Eden. This meant using their professional talents to make a series of anonymous videos warning everyone about what was happening.

But though they tried to get various news organizations interested, no one took their reports seriously. The only way they were able to get them seen was to post them on the Internet. That had only been incrementally more successful, as hackers from Project Eden would diligently remove them before more than a handful of people saw them.

Still, Tamara and Bobby kept plugging away, hoping that at some point, their videos would become more than just white noise that disappeared without anyone noticing.

Then, less than four days before, Matt had called and told them to prepare the Worst Case video, as it might be needed very soon. This was not a video meant to expose Project Eden like the others were. It was a guide to survival and an explanation of events, and was to only be distributed if the Project's plan went live.

Scared out of their minds, Tamara and Bobby had put the finishing touches on the video, and relocated to their backup safe house on the outer banks.

"If it looks like things are going to shit and you can't reach me," Matt had told them, "upload it. Don't wait for me to give you the go-ahead."

They had spent every moment since arriving in North Carolina watching for that moment. There were three TVs in the house, each tuned to a different news channel, and left on twenty-four hours a day. Plus Tamara and Bobby each had a laptop so they could check the web while keeping an eye on the news. Missing something because they were sleeping wasn't an issue. Neither of them was sleeping much these days, and for the most part, one or the other was always awake.

So far, though, there had been nothing on the news, except a few follow-up reports on a minor Sage Flu outbreak at a St. Louis-area hospital. That event had actually taken place before Matt called them, and very possibly was the reason he'd put them on alert. Though there had been several deaths, the outbreak seemed to have been contained and was dying out.

"Beer?" Bobby asked as he pushed up from the couch.

"Sure," she said, not taking her eyes off the screen.

They were watching PCN, their former network, though that seemed like a lifetime ago. With only a couple days left before Christmas, and all the politicians having gone home, most of PCN's stories were feel-good fluffy pieces—the best gifts for a busy dad, a gingerbread-house competition, and reports from retailers encouraged by the increased spending habits this season.

"Here," Bobby said, handing her a bottle.

"Thanks."

That was the way their conversations went these days. One or two words between hours of silence as they stared at the TV in a constant state of anticipation.

On the screen, one of the PCN talking heads was describing the president's plans for the holidays. Camp David this year with family and a few friends. A turkey and a ham, and candied yams from a recipe passed down through the first lady's family. As he started to list the desserts, the cell phone sitting on the coffee table rang for the first time since Tamara and Bobby had arrived in North Carolina.

They both jumped, and stared at the phone for a moment before Tamara snatched it up.

She pressed ACCEPT. "Yes?"

"This is one call I'd hoped I wouldn't have to make," Matt said.

She let out a groan, and unconsciously moved her free hand over her mouth.

"Go with WC," he told her.

"Are you sure?" she whispered.

"I wish I wasn't."

"When will it happen?"

"It's already begun. Put it up. Keep it up. Get the word out. Let's try to save as many people as we can."

76

The line went dead.

CHANNEL SIX NEWS
5:12 PM EASTERN STANDARD TIME

"…THE ACCIDENT WAS reportedly caused by a roll of carpet. Where that carpet came from, police are unsure. The good news is, there were only minor injuries."

The image of the polished-looking, fortysomething male anchor was replaced by his polished-looking, twentysomething female counterpart.

"Fire department and police officials have received reports of several metal containers spread around the tri-city area that are emitting what some people are calling a hum. A police spokesman says that officers have been dispatched to investigate these reports, but at this point there's been no further information. Victoria Lawrence is on the scene with one of these boxes right now. Victoria?"

The studio shot cut to Victoria Lawrence standing in the parking lot of the Whittington Mall. About fifty feet behind her was a dark red shipping container, the top of which was open. This was the first such report to make it on the air.

"Cheryl, you can see one of the containers in question behind me." As she said this, she turned for a quick look at the box, then faced the camera again. "This is only one of a half dozen sightings that have been called in to our station. The police have yet to arrive at this location."

"Any indication of what might be inside?" the male anchor said.

"No, Paul. We haven't been able to get a look yet. Mall security has asked everyone to stay away, but you might be able to hear the noise it's making. It sounds a bit like the propeller of a small plane. As you can also see, several curious onlookers have gathered to see it for themselves." She turned to a crowd of about a dozen people standing near her, and held a microphone up to the nearest women. "Hi, Victoria

Lawrence, Channel Six News. What's your name?"

"Michelle."

"Any thoughts on what might be going on here, Michelle?"

"No idea."

"I know!" a man yelled behind her.

Victoria moved the microphone toward him. "Can I have your name?"

"Charlie Simmons. And if you ask me, I think it's some sort of PR stunt. Probably some kind of movie promotion. You know, that kind of thing."

Victoria interviewed a few more people, each offering their take on what might be happening. Finally, she turned back to the camera, her smile clearly indicating this was the kind of story you just had fun with because it would end up being nothing. "Paul? Cheryl? What do you think?"

"I'm with the guy who called it a marketing trick," Paul said.

"I was thinking the same thing," Cheryl agreed.

"Well, whatever the case, when we find out, we'll bring the answer to you," Paul said to the camera, sure that the story would probably be forgotten by morning. "Coming up after the break, a bear makes a surprise visit to a Walmart parking lot."

IM CONVERSATION TRANSCRIPT
BETWEEN DOUG MINOR, FREELANCE WRITER, AND
JOSE RAMOS, EDITOR FOR THE BEYOND BLOG
NETWORK
2:21 PM PACIFIC STANDARD TIME

DOUG MINOR: Jose, you there?

JOSE RAMOS: What's up?

DM: Want to show you something. This aired just a few minutes ago on a station back east: <link

redacted>

JR: Hold on.

<time break—1 minute 23 seconds>

JR: They're probably right. Some kind of publicity stunt.

DM: I'm not so sure about that. Did a quick check around. There's some noise online from other places about similar boxes.

JR: A big campaign, then. So what?

DM: Look at this: <link redacted>

DM: And this: <link redacted>

DM: Two other shipping containers. Found in last couple days. First in Australia, and the second in Cleveland. Both exploded.

JR: Okay, a bit creepy. But has anyone proved that they're connected?

<time break—14 seconds>

JR: Doug?

DM: Holy shit! Turn to PCN.

PCN NETWORK BROADCAST
5:26 PM EASTERN STANDARD TIME

"…AT THE MOMENT."

The speaker was Fredrick Price, PCN's number one evening anchor. The image being broadcast was shaky and slightly out of focus, and was centered on a long, dark rectangular box sitting at one end of a large lot. There were no people in the shot, but there was movement, low and steady across the ground.

"What you're seeing is a law enforcement reconnaissance robot being used by the Richmond Police Department in Richmond, Virginia. The container it's approaching drew suspicion this afternoon when an employee at the nearby grocery store noticed that the top was open and something inside was making noise."

The image cut to a taped interview with Kyle Jones, the grocery store employee. "It just seemed kind of weird, you know. So I went and got my boss."

Offscreen, a reporter from the local television station said, "Has it been here long?"

"Yeah. A couple days, I think. But I just thought it belonged to one of the other stores here. It's not the first time we've had one of those in back. But when this one started making noise, I knew something was wrong. My boss and I, we asked around. The other stores didn't know anything about it."

"So you called the police?"

"Yes, ma'am. Can't be too careful these days. You know, we're not too far from the capital. You never know what one of these terrorist <beep> might be up to. Oh, sorry."

"Did you take a look inside?"

"Are you kidding me? I wouldn't go anywhere near that thing. Roger, he works in produce, he walked over to check it out, but he couldn't see anything other than a few drops of water on the ground."

The image switched back to the robot as it rolled to a stop near the container.

Fredrick Price said, "In a move police say is strictly precautionary, residences in a four-square-block area surrounding the shopping center have been evacuated until it can been determined whether the container poses a threat."

THE OUTER BANKS, NORTH CAROLINA
5:32 PM EASTERN STANDARD TIME

TAMARA WATCHED THE PCN broadcast in disbelief.

She had been hoping Matt was wrong, and that this had all just been some big mistake. But the image of the robot approaching the shipping container erased all doubt. Project Eden had done the unthinkable.

She forced herself to look away from the TV and over at Bobby. He was sitting at the dining table, hunched over his laptop.

"So?" she asked.

"The links are still active."

"All of them?"

"Uh-huh."

That was a surprise. The video had been uploaded to a half dozen sites for over fifteen minutes. Usually Project Eden techs would have taken them down by now.

"How many views?" she asked.

"Around a hundred so far. I'm sending out links to anyone I can. As long as it stays up, I think we have a chance."

She tried to give him an encouraging smile, but failed. She turned back to the television.

Yes, maybe they would have a chance, but a chance at what? Saving a few thousand, or, if they were lucky, a few million? When weighted against the numbers of those who would die, it was a drop in the bucket. As scared as she'd been by what Project Eden represented, she'd always thought that the Resistance would find a way to stop them. That's what always happened in these kinds of situations, right? The bad guys might seem dominating, but, in the end, the side of good would come out on top? She'd been taught that from an early age, both in history and in books and movies.

Good *always* prevailed.

"Always," she whispered under her breath, hoping voicing it would make it come true.

YOUTUBE VIDEO

"MY NAME IS Tamara Costello. I am a former reporter for PCN. Last spring, during the Sage Flu outbreak, it was reported that PCN cameraman Bobby Lion and I were victims of the virus. As you can see, that was a lie. But it was not the only one.

"The outbreak was blamed on a rogue army officer, Captain Daniel Ash. While Captain Ash was present, he had nothing to do with it. The virus was released by an organization known as Project Eden, but it was merely a test, a very successful one. Project Eden's plan has always been to release the virus worldwide.

"This video is only being released because we have learned that is what's happening right now. We believe there will be dozens, if not hundreds, of different methods used to spread the disease. We have recently become aware of one that involves shipping containers loaded with the virus and moved into populated areas. If you are near one of these, it's probably already too late. For everyone else, I'm going to tell you what you need to do to stay alive…"

IM CONVERSATION TRANSCRIPT
BETWEEN DOUG MINOR, FREELANCE WRITER, AND
JOSE RAMOS, EDITOR FOR THE BEYOND BLOG
NETWORK
2:43 PM PACIFIC STANDARD TIME

DOUG MINOR: I'm starting to get a little freaked out: <link redacted>

<time break—27 seconds>

JOSE RAMOS: This has got to be some kind of

joke, right?

DM: I don't know. But that woman, I remember her. I looked it up and she *is* supposed to be dead.

<time break—5 seconds>

JR: Think I'll post this on a couple of our sites. Let people decide if it's a bad joke or not.

DM: Good idea. Look, going to run to the store and grab a few things, then come back home and lock myself in.

JR: Seriously? Think you might be overreacting.

DM: Hope so. But what's it going to hurt? I work here anyway. Are you at the office today or at home?

JR: Office.

DM: Maybe you should think about leaving.

<time break—18 seconds>

JR: Maybe.

13

OLIVIA'S PEOPLE HAD seemed indifferent to Ash, Chloe, Red, and Gagnon when they climbed aboard earlier, but they had at least allowed one of their people trained in first aid tend to Gagnon.

The pilot still had not regained consciousness, but, after being given a shot of morphine, seemed not to be in as much pain. The four of them were then taken to an unused stateroom that was barely large enough for the two single beds inside, and the door was locked behind them.

Exhausted, Ash and Red put Gagnon on one of the beds. Ash told Chloe she could have the other.

"And what are you two going to do?" she said.

"Stretch out on the floor," Ash replied, finding it hard now to keep his eyes open.

"Really?"

She looked at the ground and he followed her gaze. The space between the beds was narrower than the beds themselves.

"Move Gagnon all the way to the wall," she suggested, then glanced at Red. "You can share with him." Her gaze moved to Ash. "You can share with me as long as you don't try any funny business."

"Not feeling very funny."

"Good."

Ash barely remembered lying down beside her. The next thing he knew someone was shaking his leg.

"Get up," a male voice said.

Feeling no better than he had when he'd fallen asleep, Ash forced his eyes open. Standing at the end of the bed were two men.

"We need you to come with us," the closer of the two said.

Chloe stirred. "What's going on?" she asked, her eyelids barely parting.

"I guess I'm going somewhere," Ash told her, groaning as he sat up.

"Both of you," the man said.

With one of the men in front of them and the other behind, Ash and Chloe were guided through the ship to a room next to the bridge. Inside, a man and a woman were sitting at a long table.

Ash recognized them immediately. The Resistance had nicknamed them Adam and Eve, when the two were seemingly just innocent lovers who'd sneak occasionally onto the grounds of the Resistance's California facility known as the Bluff. Turned out they were really setting things up to rescue Olivia from the Bluff's detention level. Ash hadn't seen them with Olivia's people on Yanok Island, so they must have remained on the ship.

The two escorts stayed in the hall, shutting the door as soon as Ash and Chloe passed inside.

"Please, sit down," the woman said.

They did.

"You're Captain Ash, aren't you?"

"Just Ash," he said.

"Something to drink?" the man asked.

"Water," Chloe said.

The man retrieved two bottles of water from a cabinet along the wall and gave one to each of them.

"I hope you've been able to rest a little."

Ash shrugged while Chloe simply took a drink of water.

"We apologize for not waiting earlier," the man said,

sitting back down. "We didn't think anyone was left alive."

"We were actually surprised you were on the island in the first place," the woman added. "How did you get here?"

Ash remained silent.

"As we understand it," the man said, "you two were the last ones to see Olivia."

"That's right," Ash said.

"We'd like you to tell us what happened to her."

"She didn't make it out."

"That's not really an answer. Was it the explosion?"

"That certainly made it hard for her to leave," Ash replied.

Silence fell over the room for a moment, then the woman leaned forward. "Was she able to do what she had come to do?"

"You mean, did she release the Sage Flu virus?"

As one, the man and the woman straightened in their chairs, surprised.

"Release?" the woman asked.

"Isn't that why you were there? To initiate Project Eden's plan, while sending the Project itself into chaos? Well, congratulations. You succeeded."

"She *activated* the KV-27a virus?" the man asked.

Chloe leaned forward. "You didn't know she was going to do that, did you?"

The other two exchanged a look. The man pushed his chair back and stood up. "Thank you for the information. We'll let you return to your room now. If you get hungry, the kitchen is just down a few doors from where you're—"

"Hold on," Ash said. "You thought she was just going to take out Bluebird? She didn't tell you what she really had planned?"

"I'm sure you're still tired. We can talk more later."

"We can talk more *right now!*" Ash shot up onto his feet, and leaned across the table. "We're right, aren't we? You *didn't* expect this."

It was the woman who broke first, unable to keep the fear from her face. "She told us she just wanted to destroy them, and ruin their plans. That they deserved to fail for turning their backs on her."

"Well, she took them out, all right."

"Don't you see? The only place the release could have been activated from was Bluebird. If it had been eliminated without the virus being released, there would have been no way for anyone else to do it, and the Project would have died. But if she activated the virus, then the Project is still very much alive. It's far larger than just those who were at Bluebird. They've been working on this for decades. They've prepared for nearly every possibility. Just because the head's been cut off doesn't mean the body is going to die."

Ash stared at her for half a second. "We have to let people know." It was something that should have been done hours ago when he and the others had first come aboard the ship. He had been operating under the assumption that those on the boat had full knowledge of what Olivia was up to.

Precious time had been wasted doing nothing.

"And tell them what?" the man asked. "That they're all going to die? Them knowing what's coming isn't going to change that."

"I need to get in touch with the people who sent my friends and me here. They have plans in place. Things that will help. But the longer we wait, the less they'll be able to do."

Doubt clouded the man's eyes. "Whatever they have planned won't work. We told you, the Project is prepared for every possibility."

"I won't just do nothing!"

The man opened his mouth to speak again, but the woman touched his arm, stopping him. "He's right," she said. "We have to try."

THE COMMUNICATIONS ROOM was located at the back of the bridge. They all squeezed inside with the operator, a woman named Wetzler.

Because of the nature of the vessel, the room had been

equipped with gear that was specifically designed to work in extreme weather conditions and at very long ranges—a radio with an extremely powerful transmitter, two backups, and a specialized satellite phone that worked even through a thick cloud cover. The storm, though, would still make any connections tenuous.

They had to try the sat phone four times before Ash finally heard the other end ring.

A voice cracked through the static. "…is this?"

"Hello?" Ash said. "Matt, is that you?"

"…old…et him."

"Hello?" Ash said.

No response.

"Hello?"

He could only hear the hiss of the line, and was about to hang up so they could try again, when—

"…is Matt. Who's this?"

"Matt! It's Ash."

"Can hardly…ear you. Who are…"

"Ash. It's Ash."

"Ash? My God, where are…ou?"

"Doesn't matter. The virus. It's been set off."

"We know. Reports from…place. Doing what we can."

They were already on it. Which meant signs of the virus's dispersal must have shown up. "Matt, Pax and the others are stranded on Amund Ringnes Island. The plane's not going to be able to get them. It, uh, broke down." Telling him that it had crashed would only create unnecessary conversation.

"How ab…you?"

"We've been able to hitch a ride on a boat. Tell Brandon and Josie I'll be back as soon as I can."

There was silence on the other end, and Ash assumed whatever Matt was saying was lost in the connection. The Resistance leader then said, "Be careful."

"We will."

Ash hung up, and looked at the others. "They already know."

The room was silent. Until moments before, the release of KV-27a had been represented only by Olivia punching a code into a computer.

Now it was real.

THE BUNKER, MONTANA
4:06 PM MOUNTAIN STANDARD TIME

MATT HUNG UP the phone.

"That was Ash?" Rachel asked.

"Yes."

"Thank God he's all right. What about the others?"

"He didn't say."

She was quiet for a moment. "I think that's a good sign. He would have said something otherwise."

Matt nodded, though he wasn't as sure as she was. "He told me to tell his kids he was on his way back. I...should have told him about Brandon."

"No. You did the right thing. There's nothing he can do from where he is." She put her arm around her brother's shoulder. "Brandon's going to be okay." She squeezed him, and smiled. "I'll tell Josie her dad's on the way back. That'll make her feel better."

But Matt barely heard her.

He should have told Ash. If it had been Matt's son, he would have wanted to know.

He forced himself to focus, and turned to Christina. "Still no sign?"

Christina had been monitoring the security cameras in case the helicopters returned, or Hayes and Brandon showed up.

"Nothing," she said.

"Maybe I should send out a team," he said to himself.

"No," Rachel said. "It's too soon. The others may be waiting for us to show ourselves. You can't afford to risk everyone's life like that. Jon knows what to do. He'll take care of Brandon."

Matt grimaced, not wanting to hear the words, but knowing she was right.

14

BRANDON HAD KEPT a steady pace, stopping only briefly now and then to make sure he was still going in the right direction.

He knew he had traveled miles, but didn't know how many, or how many more he still had to go before he reached a town or road. It was becoming clear, though, that it wouldn't happen today.

The shade of the forest had dimmed considerably with the setting sun, and soon it would be too dark to travel. Off to the right, he spotted a downed tree that was caught in a tangle of other pines, creating a covered space underneath. He angled toward it, thinking it might be a good place to spend the night. After giving it a closer inspection, he decided it would definitely be better than sleeping out in the open.

He leaned wearily against the log and pulled off his backpack. The first thing he needed to do was eat. He opened a can of beans and scarfed them down in less than a minute.

The rumble in his stomach momentarily tamed, he gathered up loose pine needles and added them to the ones already under the dead tree to create a more comfortable surface to lie on. He untied his sleeping bag from the pack, and started to unroll it. As he did, he caught a whiff of something in the air.

Smoke?

He sniffed again. It was there for a moment, then gone.

He walked through the trees in a slow circle, testing the air until he reacquired the scent. It was definitely smoke.

Forest fire?

The thought made him tense, but he was pretty sure it was too cold for that. Or did fires not care about the weather?

He took in the odor once more. There was something comforting about it, something familiar.

A campfire. That's what it smells like.

It seemed to be coming from his left.

Could be a mile away, he thought, *just drifting on the wind.*

Or it could be closer.

A chill moved through his body. What if it was the people from the helicopters? Maybe a couple of them had been following him on foot.

He had a sudden urge to flee, to get as far away from the smoke as possible. Hurrying back to his gear, he rolled his sleeping bag back up, and reattached it to the bottom of his backpack. But then he paused.

What if it was someone else? Someone who could help him?

He stood there unmoving, staring into the darkness.

Just check, he thought. *They'll never know you're there.*

If he was careful and didn't get too close, he should be okay. Besides, whoever was out there—someone looking for him or someone who could help—it would be better to know than not.

With a final deep, decisive breath, he strapped on his pack and headed toward the smoke.

BRANDON ALLOWED HIMSELF to use the flashlight as he started out, but as the odor intensified, he became more and more nervous, and finally turned it off so as not to give himself away.

He was careful to keep the sound of his footsteps to a minimum as he watched the forest ahead for any sign of the campfire. So far, the darkness remained unchanged.

Maybe it *was* a mile away, he thought. If he didn't reach it in the next few minutes, he'd find another place to camp for the night, then look for the source of the smoke again in the morning.

He'd barely had that thought when he noticed he could see the sky up ahead above a large clearing.

He moved to the edge of the tree line and stopped. The clearing was probably twice as big as the one where Hayes had been killed, but its size wasn't what caught Brandon's attention. His eyes were fixed on something just the other side of center.

A house, spewing smoke from its chimney.

FOR THIRTY MINUTES, Brandon remained where he was, hidden in the trees. He shifted his gaze from window to window, watching for movement.

The house was two stories high, but small. He didn't think there could be more than two or three rooms on each floor. The fireplace was on the far side of the house, the chimney peeking up above the roof, silhouetted against the night sky.

There were three windows on the side facing Brandon, one on the first floor and two on the second. Because of the smoke, he knew someone had to be home, but the windows were all dark.

Still not comfortable enough to approach the house, he moved counterclockwise around the edge of the clearing to get a look at the rest of the structure. There were four windows on the new side—dark like the others—equally divided between the floors. There was also a door off to one side on the bottom floor. It had a set of three narrow steps that led down to the ground, and looked to Brandon like a backdoor instead of the main way in.

He kept going.

The next side was the one with the chimney—two windows here, one on each floor, and the stone chimney widening out to the back of a large fireplace.

There was also another building he'd been unable to see before. It was set off to the side about a hundred feet from the house, almost butting up against the trees. It looked to Brandon like a shed or garage.

Maybe he could find a way into it, and spend the night there. It would sure be better than sleeping out in the woods. After the sun came up in the morning, he could knock on the door of the house. Or maybe see if someone came outside first, and then decide if he should approach them.

He moved through the trees until the structure was between him and the house, and quietly slipped over to the building. Like the house, it had wood siding that had seen its share of bad weather.

He eased up to the corner and took a cautious look around it. Definitely a garage, he decided. The side he was looking at had a wide door that was more than large enough for a good-sized SUV to pass through. It appeared to be the kind of door that rolled up. If he could move it a foot or so, he should be able to slip underneath.

He sneaked over to the handle, and gently tugged it upward. The door barely moved a quarter inch before it stopped. When he tried again, the same thing happened.

Great, he thought.

It was probably operated by a remote control, like the garage his family had had once. No way he'd be able to open it on his own.

There's got to be another door, right?

He moved to the far corner and peeked around. The house was just a stone's throw away. From this angle he could see both the side with the chimney and what was obviously the front, given the small covered porch and door more appropriate for a main entrance. The windows there, like the rest of the house, were dark.

Slowly, he stuck his head out far enough so he could look along the side of the garage. There *was* a door.

He looked at the house again, studying the windows.

They're asleep, he thought. *They won't see me.*

94

He had to repeat this to himself a couple times before he got the courage to step around the side and sneak over to the door.

He placed his fingers on the handle and twisted it. Locked again, but the door was loose. He gently pushed against it, and could feel the bolt wanting to slip out of the latch. He thought for a moment, then pulled out Mr. Hayes's pocket knife. He couldn't get it all the way through the space between the door and the frame, but he was able to angle it in so that the tip touched the bolt. Working it like a lever, he pushed the bolt away from the latch until it was finally free.

Smiling in relief, he sent up a silent prayer wishing for nothing creepy to be inside, then pushed the door open, and quickly passed through.

The moment he closed the door behind him, the interior of the garage was plunged into darkness. He stood motionless, thinking he only needed a few seconds for his eyes to adjust, but as time passed the garage remained pitch-black. Not having a choice, he pulled out his flashlight and turned it on. The beam seemed impossibly bright, and he quickly put his free hand over the lens, cutting the illumination by more than half.

Worried that the light might have been seen from the house, he moved back to the door and placed his ear against it. After several quiet seconds, he began to breathe easily again, and allowed himself to take stock of his surroundings.

There was no SUV in the garage, but there was an old, faded Subaru station wagon. The amount of dust on the windshield indicated it hadn't been driven for a while.

Along the wall nearest the door was a workbench with tools packed neatly on the shelves beneath it. At the back end of the garage were larger shelves filled with boxes, each carefully marked to identify their contents—"Books," "Files 2010," and the like.

On the other side of the Subaru, between it and the wall, was a four-foot-wide area with only a few boxes at the back end. Plenty of room for his sleeping bag.

As he was taking off his pack, he glanced through the

95

windshield of the car. The backseat had been lowered, creating a long, flat open area.

He paused for a moment, thinking.

The interior surface would be a lot more comfortable to lie on than the cement. Given the dust, chances were the owners wouldn't be using the vehicle anytime soon. Besides, he planned to be up and out of the building before the sun rose, so they would never know he'd been here.

He opened the rear door of the station wagon and climbed in.

Three minutes later, as his sleeping bag warmed to his body temperature, he fell asleep.

A BEEP WOKE Lizzie.

She blinked her eyes, not registering the sound at first.

As she did most evenings, she'd fallen asleep in her favorite chair, the book she was reading—*The Age of Innocence* by Edith Wharton—lying open on her lap.

She was putting her bookmark between the pages when the beep sounded again.

She immediately snapped her head around to look at her computer on the desk by the window. The screen was dark, the computer still in sleep mode. What *was* on was the smaller computer sitting on top of the short filing cabinet. Her brother's computer. Even from her chair, she could see that the window for his security software was front and center.

She stood and whirled around, worried that someone had entered her house while she was asleep.

There was no one else in the living room, but that didn't mean they weren't somewhere else in the house. She listened for creaking floorboards and sounds of movement.

Nothing.

Still leery that an intruder was inside, she eased open the drawer of the end table, and pulled out the 9mm Glock pistol lying inside. There were guns hidden all over the house. Again, her brother's doing. At first she had planned on getting rid of them, but the longer she stayed in the house, the more she was comforted by their presence. The truth was, she was beginning to think her brother's concerns about the world weren't entirely off-base. Though she didn't have a television, she watched the news on her computer, and could see that the planet was falling apart.

Gun in hand, she tiptoed over to the computer. There was a warning flashing on the screen.

UNAUTHORIZED ENTRY—GARAGE DOOR #2

Not her house. Her garage. *Someone's trying to steal my car!*

She went over to the window next to the fireplace, and pulled back the blackout curtain just enough so that she could see the other building. The area between her house and the garage was empty, and the side door—garage door #2—was closed.

It would be, she thought, since they were already inside.

She let the curtain drop back down, and ran over to the closet by the door. She grabbed her jacket, gloves, and hat, and put them all on. Once outfitted, she traded the Glock for the Mossberg double-barreled shotgun from the rack on the wall. There was no need to check if it was loaded because it always was.

The final things she retrieved were in a box at the bottom of the closet. So far she'd seldom had any use for them, but they were her brother's pride and joy—a pair of ATN Generation II Night Vision Goggles with head mount. Three grand, he had told her they cost. She couldn't believe the expense at the time, but she was glad now he'd spent the money.

Instead of exiting through the front door in full view of the garage, she used the back, and made her way to the corner. There, she studied the garage long enough to be satisfied that no one was waiting outside. Then, keeping in the crouch, she ran toward it.

She was three-quarters of the way to the other structure when she heard a noise. Maybe a scrape or a step. One thing was for sure—it had definitely come from inside.

She paused in the no man's land between her two buildings, unsure what she should do. Despite the shotgun in her hands, she wasn't a violent person, and didn't know if she could shoot someone. Even if she could, she didn't know how many of them were there. One, she might be able to scare off, but two? Three?

This is our home. You can't just run away and hide, Owen's voice said. She didn't hear him all the time, but on occasion her brother would speak to her.

She nodded, and told herself he was right. She needed to protect what was hers, what was *theirs*. But she also had to be smart about it. She couldn't just burst into the garage without knowing what she was up against. At some point they would have to come out again. That's when she'd do something.

She angled toward the front of the garage. If they were going to steal her Subaru, they'd have to come through the big door. Just to play it safe, though, she found a spot where she could watch both the main door and the one on the side. She settled in to wait.

Ten silent minutes went by, then twenty.

What the hell were they doing in there?

When a half hour was gone, Lizzie decided to move in closer so she could hear better. She knelt down in front of the roll-up door and listened. Absolute silence. Thinking they might have heard her walk up, she stayed there for several minutes, sure she would hear something, but the garage remained deathly still.

She sat back up, frowning, and tried to make sense of things.

Maybe she'd been wrong about the noise. Perhaps it had come from the woods beyond the barn, a deer or an owl or something like that. Because winter was so late in coming, a lot of the local wildlife had been acting strange lately, like they didn't know what they should be doing.

The more she thought about it, though, the more she was sure the noise had come from the garage. Besides, the alarm *had* gone off.

You're going to have to check, her brother said.

"I know," she mouthed silently.

She moved around to the side door. As she reached for the knob, her eyes strayed to the ground. Footprints. One pair, it looked like, and not as large as she would have expected. *A woman?*

She listened again at the door, and again heard nothing.

You're stalling, her brother said.

"I'm not," she whispered. "Leave me alone and let me take care of this."

Then take care of it.

Not wanting to give him any other reason to doubt her abilities, she grabbed the knob and began turning it. Once the latch was free, she froze for a moment, then gave the knob a gentle push and let the door swing slowly open.

Both hands on the shotgun now, she tensed, fully expecting someone to start scrambling on the other side. But not a step or even a gasp of surprise.

What the hell?

If she didn't know any better, she'd think whoever had been there was gone.

She gave it a full sixty seconds, then, staying low, stepped inside.

She swept the room, her goggles more than adequate in the darkened space. No one was there. She leaned down and looked under the car, but was equally disappointed.

She looked around again, and paused on the shelves in the back. It was really the only good hiding place, so that's where her intruder must be. As she took a step in that direction, the Subaru creaked.

She turned quickly, thinking someone was coming around from the other side, but no one was there.

She took another look at the car, and leaned forward, surprised.

Someone was stretched out inside, tucked into a sleeping bag in the back of her car.

A boy.

15

WITH THE WORLDWIDE reach of satellite television, people across the globe were able to tune into PCN, CNN, and the other major news networks, and see coverage of the growing number of suspicious shipping containers in the US. Soon people in South America, Europe, and along the coasts of Africa reported seeing similar boxes, open and humming. According to reports, there had been several attempts to move them, but that had resulted in the boxes exploding and killing everyone in the immediate area.

Asia was just waking up, so few people had seen the stories. But as they sat eating their morning meals and drinking coffee and tea, their local stations brought them up to speed on the mystery.

A commentator on NHK in Japan went so far as to suggest that perhaps the government should order people to stay home until it was sure none of the containers were on Japanese soil. It was an idea that might have saved lives, but the government didn't heed the advice. At least not until they realized that they, too, had been targeted.

By then it was too late.

The government in Singapore was not nearly as slow on the uptake as the Japanese had been. By seven a.m., the entire country, including the extremely busy Changi International Airport, had been closed down, and a twenty-four-hour curfew put in place. Those who hadn't heard the news were stopped by roadblocks and roving police patrols and sent home. At first, people were not happy, but that quickly changed when they saw on TV that shipping containers, identical to the ones in the US and Japan, had been found at several places on the island.

The idea of the curfew was a good one. Unfortunately, the containers had already been spewing out the virus for hours, and those who had been out at night, a very popular activity on the small island nation, had already been exposed and carried the Sage Flu home to their families and neighbors.

Vietnam, Laos, Cambodia, Thailand, Myanmar, Bangladesh, and India all scrambled to check if they, too, had been the unknowing recipients of similar containers. While Thailand discovered a few in a couple of its port cities, the others were relieved to find that they were free of the boxes. Knowing it was not something they needed to worry about, several of these countries—plus many more in Africa—were able to turn their attention with pride to the mosquito-eradication program that started that very morning in all of their major cities.

The program had been touted as a cure for malaria by the company sponsoring it, Pishon Chem. Not only would it be eradicating the disease, but it had brought money into the communities by hiring thousands of locals to walk through the cities and spray the streets with the special liquid mixture.

Pishon was an old word. It was one of the rivers that had surrounded the Garden of Eden, and therefore an apt name for one of the Project's dummy companies.

In less accessible areas, where politics or geography had made the placement of shipping containers and the use of the malaria drug impossible, planes disguised as commercial aircraft dispensed the virus from above. The rate of initial infection from this method was calculated to be low, but low was enough. The Project knew the second round of infection—those getting it from the first—would initiate an incremental growth that would be impossible to stop.

There were other methods of exposure used here and there throughout the world. Misters in grocery stores designed to keep the produce fresh, free perfume and cologne samples being distributed at major international airports, and small bottles of "flavored water" being handed out at tourist sites in several major capitals of the world.

It was a massive effort that had taken decades to plan, and it was commencing nearly flawlessly. The previous directors of Project Eden would probably have been very proud, if it weren't for the fact they were all dead.

IMPLEMENTATION DAY PLUS ONE

FRIDAY, DECEMBER 23rd

World Population
7,176,607,708

Change Over Previous Day
+ 283,787

16

DESPITE HOW EXHAUSTED he'd been when he went to sleep the night before, Sanjay woke well before there was even a hint of daylight. His shoulders burned with tension, and he was finding it impossible to take anything but short, shallow breaths.

He lay that way for hours, trying to will himself back to sleep, but soon realized it was not going to happen. He wondered if he'd ever sleep well again.

If it weren't for Kusum, he would have gotten up and walked around, hoping that would drive the anxiety from his veins, but she lay in his arms, asleep, and he had no desire to subject her to the same hell he was going through. As it was, he could tell her sleep wasn't completely untroubled. Several times she'd twisted and jerked as her dreams momentarily took control of the rest of her body. A few times she'd even cried out.

He wondered, as she murmured what sounded like his name, exactly what she was dreaming about. Was he the hero or the villain in her nightmare? Or was it best not to know? He wasn't even sure which one he was to her in real life.

What if he was wrong? What if what he'd learned were lies?

When the sky in the east started to yellow, he knew he

could lie there no longer. He pulled his arm out from under her neck, and started to slowly move away.

"Where are you going?" she asked.

"Go back to sleep. I didn't mean to wake you."

"I've been awake for a while."

"Oh," he said, surprised. "I just thought I'd take a walk, see what's around."

She turned and looked at him for several seconds. "Were you lying to me yesterday?"

"No."

She considered him some more, then touched her arm where he'd given her the shot. "I don't feel any different."

"It was a vaccine. I don't think you are supposed to feel any different."

"I just thought…"

She didn't finish her thought. It took him a moment, but he finally realized that when she'd gone to sleep, she still believed he had drugged her.

"I told you. I have only been trying to save you."

"If what you have told me is true, what about my family?"

It wasn't the first time she'd asked that, and he gave her the answer he'd given before. "I only had the one shot."

"What about the one you took?"

That she hadn't asked before, and it surprised him. "I had to make sure it didn't hurt me before I could give it to you. Don't you see that?"

She sat up, suddenly determined. "We have to go back. You can get more for my family."

He rose quickly to his feet. "Impossible. I don't even know where I could find…" He paused. Yes, he knew where there might be more vaccine. The same place he had gotten it the first time. Still… "Today is the day they will spray the city. We can't go back there."

She stood and began wiping off the dirt that clung to her clothes. "We have to try."

"There is nothing we can do."

She stared at him, her face hardening. "Then I will go

without you."

She turned toward the road and started walking.

"Wait," he said, grabbing her arm.

She quickly twisted free, but didn't turn away. "If you care about me like you say, you will help me to save my family."

"By the time we get there, it may already be too late."

"I will not just wait here. I have to do whatever I can."

Again, she started walking.

"Kusum! Please!"

She didn't stop.

"Kusum!" She'd almost disappeared into the jungle. "All right, all right! I'll drive you back."

She slowed to a halt and looked at him. "Let's go."

THEY TRAVELED DOWN the rutted road toward the highway. In the first light of day, the jungle looked thinner and less menacing than it had in the dark.

It took them a full half hour to reach the blacktop road. Sanjay was surprised. He hadn't realized they'd ridden that far into the wilderness.

It wasn't long before he said, "We have to make a stop."

"Why?"

"The tank is almost empty. We would never make it all the way there."

He could hear her sigh, frustrated. "Okay, but as quick as we can."

A few minutes later, he saw a roadside stop that was selling petrol out of cans. While a young boy helped him fill his tank, Kusum went inside the hut that served as a shop, but she was only gone a few seconds before she rushed back out.

"Sanjay! Come quick!"

He looked at her, confused, but she'd already disappeared back through the door. He paid the boy for the fuel, and jogged over to the hut.

Inside were several tables full of food items for purchase, and two coolers stuffed with drinks. But Kusum wasn't

106

looking at any of them. She was standing near the back corner, staring at a TV on a table. Three other people were also crowded around, watching.

A BBC news anchor was framed in the center of the screen.

"…dozens of locations around the globe," the man said.

"What's going on?" Sanjay asked.

Kusum and one of the others shhh'd him, their attention never leaving the screen.

"Last evening local time, in the US state of Georgia," the anchor went on, "firefighters in the city of Athens attempted to relocate one of the boxes. This resulted in a fiery explosion that killed five firemen and three civilians. Several more similar incidents have been reported from elsewhere in the States and in Europe. Officials in most countries have now suspended all orders to move the boxes, and have begun evacuating persons living anywhere near suspected containers.

"There has still been no word on what the container's purpose might be, or who is behind them. Several helicopters—both news and police—have flown over boxes to get a look inside." The image switched to a downward shot of one of the boxes. It was rectangular in shape, large. While the top was open, there were two large circular areas side by side near the lip, each shimmering slightly. "Analysts have determined that what you are looking at are two exhaust-type fans that seem to be pushing whatever is inside into the air. Speculation has been focused on the possibility that the contents are biological in nature. Investigative teams in many nations have taken the precaution of wearing protective gear within a half-mile radius of the boxes.

"Several groups have put forward the suggestion that this is a hoax meant to send the message of what *could* happen. One Latin American organization is even taking credit for doing just that, but officials are saying the claim is baseless."

Sanjay couldn't believe what he was seeing. Mysterious boxes shooting something into the air? Something *biological*? Today? The timing was too coincidental. This had to be linked to the spray Pishon Chem was unleashing on Mumbai.

Kusum looked over at him. He could see in her eyes she believed him completely now, and was thinking the same thing.

"Come on," he said, grabbing her hand. "We have a long way to go."

"My family?"

"We'll try."

"Thank you."

They retuned to the bike, and raced west for Mumbai.

WITH EACH PASSING kilometer, the traffic seemed to be getting lighter and lighter. At first Sanjay didn't think anything of it, but when it got to the point where he and Kusum were only one of a handful of vehicles on the road, he began to wonder. It had to have something to do with the news—people captivated by the reports and staying home, worrying that the same containers would be found in the areas around Mumbai.

But while there *were* fewer people about as they entered the city, Sanjay did start to see many of the boys and men walking through neighborhoods spraying Pishon Chem's "mosquito-killing" poison. The public was so focused on the troubles abroad, it couldn't even see the one right under its nose.

Each time Sanjay saw one of the people doing the spraying, he was tempted to pull over and tell them to stop, but he knew no one would listen to him. More importantly, any delay getting to Kusum's family could be the difference between life and death.

They went directly to the fruit stand her parents owned, where Sanjay had first seen Kusum. But when they arrived, there was no fruit on display, and no one standing behind the cart. The stand was closed.

"No," Kusum whispered.

Without even looking at her, Sanjay knew she was thinking her parents and sister might already be sick. But the spraying had been going on for only a few hours, and even if her family had been exposed, Sanjay doubted there had been enough time for them to fall ill.

"It's okay," he said. "They've stayed home like everyone else. Look, most of the shops are closed."

He could feel her moving around on the back of the bike, scanning the area. "Yes. Yes, that must be it."

"Tell me where your home is."

ONCE MORE, AS they drove along the streets of Mumbai, they saw more of the army of sprayers delivering the deadly liquid, neighborhood by neighborhood.

I should be shouting, Sanjay thought. *I should be screaming for everyone to run*. But again, who would listen? *Save who you can*, he told himself, ignoring the question of how.

The building Kusum's family lived in was down a long, narrow alley. Thankfully, the closest Pishon Chem sprayers were nearly a kilometer away, and by the absence on nearby streets and sidewalks of the residual sheen from the spray, Sanjay knew they had not yet moved through this area.

"Where is everyone?" Kusum asked as they made their way down the alley.

He didn't have to ask her what she meant. Sanjay had seen hundreds of streets just like this one, usually teeming with people at this time of day. But they'd barely seen anyone, and those they had eyed them suspiciously while hurrying to some unknown destination.

"There," Kusum said after a moment, pointing over his shoulder at her building.

It was an old and tired-looking place, stained brown where water from the frequent rains had run down the sides for decades. Families would be stuffed inside, ten or more people in every two- or three-room apartment, doing what they could to collectively survive.

As soon as Sanjay pulled the bike to a stop, Kusum leaped off the back and raced for the door. He headed after her, passing through in time to see her running up a set of stairs. He tried to catch up but she was moving fast, and it was all he could do to keep her in sight. When he turned at the midway point between the second and third floors, where the stairs doubled back, she was gone.

"Kusum?" he called.

"This way!" she yelled, her voice coming through the door to the third floor.

Once he exited the stairwell, he spotted her three-quarters of the way down the hall, turning the knob on one of the doors. It seemed to be locked.

She knocked loudly and yelled, "It's me! Kusum!"

There was a momentary delay, then the door flew open, and her mother rushed out.

"Where have you been?" she asked. She touched her daughter's face, and pulled her into her arms.

"Kusum!" the voice of her father boomed out of the room. "Answer your mother's question. Where have you been?"

Kusum pulled back from her mother's embrace. "I…I…"

She glanced toward Sanjay, who had stopped several meters away. Her mother followed her gaze. Her father stepped into the hallway and did the same.

"You!" her father said. He started marching toward Sanjay. "What have you done?"

Her father was not a particularly large man, but at the moment he seemed like a giant to Sanjay. Fire raged in the man's eyes, and his nostrils flared in anger.

"I can explain," Sanjay said, backpedaling.

"I don't want to hear anything you have to say!"

As soon as Kusum's father was close enough, he grabbed Sanjay's shirt with one hand and struck him across the face with the other.

"You have ruined my daughter!"

"No!" Kusum told him. "That's not true."

She reached out to stop him, but her mother pulled her back.

"I have not," Sanjay pleaded. "I was only—"

"Shut up!" The man slapped Sanjay. "You expect me to believe your lies?"

Down the hall, a few doors opened and people peeked out, but none seemed willing to come to Sanjay's aid.

"Nothing happened," Sanjay said quickly. "I have done nothing to her. You can ask her."

As Kusum's father raised his hand again, Sanjay prepared to be hit once more, but the blow never came.

"Father, please." Kusum had broken free from her mother, and grabbed her father's hand. "Sanjay did nothing wrong. He was only trying to save me."

Her father whirled on her as if he'd hit her, too.

"No!" her mother yelled. "Don't."

"He was trying to save me," Kusum repeated.

Her father's anger seemed to lose a bit of focus, the tension in his upraised arm wavering. "Save you from what?" he said, his tone all but accusing her of trying to fool him.

Kusum's eyes moved past him down the hall toward their neighbors, who continued to watch the spectacle. "Please, Father. Let's go inside. We can talk there."

For a moment, it looked as if he wasn't interested in going anywhere, but then he took a deep breath and nodded. Yanking on Sanjay's arm, he shoved him toward the door. "You first."

The apartment was predictably small. The main room served as the kitchen, dining, and living area.

In addition to Kusum's parents, her younger sister Jabala was there, as were three others Sanjay didn't know. One was an older woman, and two were young children, a boy and a girl who were about five or six.

The most expensive thing in the room was the television. Like the one they'd seen when they'd stopped for gas, it was tuned to BBC International.

Kusum's father entered last and slammed the door behind him. "Saved you from what?" he demanded.

Sanjay pointed at the TV. "From that, I think."

Her father looked at him as if he'd lost his mind. "What do you mean?"

"Maybe we should all sit down," Kusum suggested. "Jabala, could you take Panna and Darshan into the other room?"

"I want to hear what you're going to talk about," Jabala said.

"I know," Kusum said softly. "I will tell you everything after, okay?"

Not looking happy, Jabala grabbed the hands of the two children and led them through the doorway at the far end of the room.

"Please, Father. Sit down," Kusum said.

After a moment's hesitation, her father did, and the others followed suit.

"I don't understand what you mean," her father said, looking at Sanjay.

Sanjay glanced at the floor, unsure how to begin.

"You need to tell them everything," Kusum said. "Just like you told me."

She was right, of course. It was exactly what he had to do, so it was exactly what he did.

If it weren't for the crisis playing out on TV, he was sure they would have dismissed his claims immediately.

"The malaria spray?" Kusum's father said when Sanjay finally finished, anger no longer underlining the man's voice. "Are you sure?"

"I am as sure as I can be. It's what was told to me."

"And your cousin?" Kusum's mother said.

"I saw Ayush with my own eyes." He paused. "By now, I am sure he is dead."

Both Kusum's mother and the old woman—her aunt—looked visibly shaken.

"Then why did you come back if you were trying to keep her safe?" Kusum's father asked. "You are saying they are spreading this…disease through the city right now."

"The vaccine will protect her."

"Are you sure?" Her father was starting to become angry again.

"Yes," Sanjay said. *About as much as I can be.*

Before her father could speak again, Kusum jumped in. "He didn't want to bring me back. I forced him."

"But why?" her mother asked. "If he's right, it's too dangerous here. You should have stayed away."

Kusum looked at her with surprise. "I came back for all of you. You are my family."

"And what could you possibly do for us?" her father asked.

"Warn you. *Save* you."

"Save us how?"

"We should all leave the city. Now."

"This disease, it will be everywhere. Do you have vaccine for us?" he asked, sounding as if he already knew the answer. "How are we supposed to stay alive?"

Sanjay leaned forward. "We don't have more vaccine. Not yet."

The others all looked at him.

"What do you mean, not yet?" Kusum's father asked.

"Do you have a car?"

"Do we look like we can afford a car?"

"But you can drive, yes?"

"Of course."

"Then we will steal one."

"Steal?" Kusum's mother blurted out. "We are not thieves."

Ignoring her, Sanjay said, "I have a plan that I hope will save all of you." *Plan* was probably a little generous. "Get a car and take everyone out of town." He looked at Kusum. "Do you think you can find your way back to where we were last night?"

"Yes," she said.

"Go there."

"What about you?"

He was silent for a moment. "I will go back to where I found Ayush. There might be more vaccine there."

Kusum brightened. "Do you think so?"

"There is a chance."

"I know where we can find a car," Kusum's father said,

no longer sounding as if their fate was inevitable.

His wife looked at him, wide-eyed. "You can't be serious."

"We're talking about saving our family. Of course I'm serious."

"What about Chandra and Rochi?" she asked.

Sanjay looked at Kusum, confused.

"My mother's brother and his wife," she whispered. "Panna's and Darshan's parents."

With a nod of understanding, Sanjay said, "You'll have to leave them behind."

"What?" Kusum's mother said.

"They've been through the city. There's a chance they've already been exposed to the spray. If they have, then they are as good as dead."

"We can't just leave them here."

"We can, and we will," her husband said. "We can call them, give them the chance to get away, but Sanjay is right. We cannot tell them where we are going. If they are alive when this is over, we will find them then."

Sanjay stood up. "You cannot wait here any longer. There is no telling how soon it will be before the sprayers arrive." He also had to get going himself. The sooner he finished, the sooner he could be back with Kusum and make sure she was all right.

"You should not go alone," Kusum said.

"It will be easier on my own."

She looked unconvinced.

"Don't worry," he said. "I will meet up with you by this evening. No later than eight, okay?"

She stared into his eyes for a second, then nodded. "Eight."

Sanjay gave her a reassuring smile, and turned for the door.

"Wait," she said. She disappeared into the other room. When she returned, she was holding a mobile phone. "Take it. Father has one, too. His is the first number listed."

"Thanks," he said.

She leaned forward and kissed him on the cheek. "Come back to me," she whispered.

17

A TOTAL OF fourteen suspicious shipping containers had been discovered within the five boroughs of New York City. The NYPD and NYFD had moved in quickly and cordoned off the areas surrounding the boxes. At first, the off-limits zones stretched for only a couple of blocks, but after news of boxes exploding elsewhere, they were increased to eight square blocks.

Unfortunately, there was not enough manpower to watch every inch of the boundaries around the restricted areas and continue basic services to the rest of the city. So unmonitored sections were unavoidable.

Joey Chin saw this as an opportunity.

Near the middle of the evacuated area was the building where Walter Natz lived. Joey had been trying to figure out how to get into Natz's place for weeks. While the guy was often away on business, his building had a doorman, at least ten roaming security guards at all times, and cameras on every floor, meaning any kind of incursion was next to impossible.

Until the evacuation, Joey had been unable to work up any viable options, and, understandably, his client was getting antsy. Four weeks and no visible progress had a way of doing that. The documents the man needed were inside a safe in Natz's home office. Joey knew he could get into the safe, no problem. It was getting to the apartment that was the challenge.

Until the evacuation order a few hours earlier. Officials had made it very clear there were no exceptions for anyone, security staff included. Best of all, Joey had found a vulnerable point in the boundary to the off-limits zone.

He had watched it for over an hour just to be sure, then simply walked across the darkened street, picked the lock on the door to a dry cleaner, and let himself in. As expected, the place had an alarm, but he quickly disabled it, and made his way through the building and out the back door.

From there, it was just a matter of working his way through the streets without being spotted by the helicopters that occasionally flew over the area. That was a piece of cake.

When he reached the block where Natz's building was, he gave it a thorough scan to make sure no one had secretly stayed behind. As expected, it looked deserted.

Of course, there were still the cameras, but those he could deal with.

He went around to the alley behind Natz's building, disabled the single camera covering the back entrance, and busted one of the low windows meant to allow light into the basement level. He knew the building's alarm system utilized touch plates at all doors and windows, but not the more sophisticated motion sensor that would detect a window breaking. He had identified that as a weak point right at the start, but the problem had always been the guards. The information he'd been able to obtain indicated one guard was always in the basement, which meant he would probably hear any breaking glass.

Not today.

Joey made his way to the utility room that controlled the power to the building. He had no intentions of killing all the power; that would make his job difficult. He was only interested in the power supply dedicated to the security system. The actual box was unmarked, designed to look like it was part of the larger electrical system. There were even dummy wires running from it to the main boxes. It was a good camouflage job. Someone not quite as experienced as

Joey would have continued looking elsewhere. Joey, though, had studied the true plans, the ones most people would never be able to get their hands on. That was part of the skill set he brought to any project—his contacts and ability to get whatever he needed.

Cover off, wires cut, job done. The offsite monitoring facility would wonder what was going on, but what could they do? It wasn't like they could send in cars full of security men. And even if they called the police, the NYPD had its hands full at the moment and would probably just hang up on them.

He headed for the elevator.

There were grander buildings in New York for sure, skyscrapers that allowed residents to live in the clouds. Natz's building was not nearly as tall as those. While he lived in one of the penthouse apartments, it only put him nine floors from the street.

Once Joey got there, he wasted no time opening Natz's door. As soon as he was inside, he glanced at the alarm and noted, with satisfaction, that the display screen was dead.

The only surprise was how warm the apartment felt. He went over to the thermostat and saw that it was set at seventy-eight degrees. He considered turning it down, but needed to limit his impact on the place so that his visit would remain undiscovered.

The door to the home office was closed, but not locked. The room was even warmer than the rest of the place. He guessed it had to be at least eighty-five degrees, if not hotter. While it had been only annoying at first, the temperature was now a problem. The last thing he needed was for any sweat to drip from his face to the wood floor, leaving a potential DNA sample that could be traced.

He looked around for another thermostat, but there was none in the room. Since the building was only nine floors high, the windows could actually be opened. He stepped over to the nearest one, flipped the latch, and pushed it out.

As he was bringing his hand back inside, something wet landed just above his lip. He wiped it off with his fingers, and glanced out the window, thinking it might be starting to rain. But he could see no clouds.

What he could see were several sets of bright lights illuminating a small lot two blocks away. He couldn't see all the way down to the ground from where he was, but he knew the lights had to mark the shipping container that was the reason he'd been able to get into the building.

Another drop of water blew in from outside, striking him on the bridge of his nose. Perhaps the clouds were above the building, just out of sight. If so, he hoped any storm they might bring would hold off until he was done.

Turning back to the room, he set to work.

Everything went as smoothly as he expected. An hour and a half later, he was back in the hotel room, the desired files in hand. At midnight, he would hand his client the prize.

But that wouldn't be the only thing he'd pass on.

RIDGECREST, CALIFORNIA
12:53 AM PACIFIC STANDARD TIME

MARTINA GABLE HADN'T intended to go to the party, but her friends Noreen and Jilly wouldn't take no for an answer, and had made her come along.

As she knew would happen, she ended up hanging in the back of the room, nursing a Coke and thinking about Ben. She liked how they just kind of got each other right from the beginning. The problem was, he went to school up in the Bay Area, and she was stuck down in L.A., limiting the time they were able to spend together.

Eventually Noreen and Jilly found her again, then a few of their old friends from their high school softball team joined them. At first it was the standard tell-us-what-you've-been-doing type of conversation, but it didn't take long before talk turned to the events that had dominated the news that day—the mysterious shipping containers.

"Just glad there's none of those things here," Jilly said.

119

"I heard they found one over by Walmart," a girl named Wendy told them.

"I didn't hear that," Jilly said.

"Neither did I," Noreen agreed. "Who told you?"

"A friend," Wendy said, her tone a bit meeker than before.

"Was it on the radio?"

She shrugged. "Maybe. I don't know."

The mood darkened as they spent several minutes guessing at what might be inside. Finally, they decided to hop into Noreen's Honda Civic and make sure there was nothing weird going on at Walmart.

Martina, being Noreen's best friend from high school, was assigned the front passenger seat, while the three other girls crammed into the back, but Walmart was a bust.

No police. No bright lights. No shipping container.

They ended up going to Carl's Jr., taking the same booth they'd often used back in their high school days, and sharing several bags of fries while they continued to speculate on the purpose of the boxes.

Finally, with a promise of getting together at least one more time before the holidays were over, Noreen took them back to their cars. Martina's was last.

"Really is good to see you," Noreen told her.

"Yeah. Same here."

Noreen tried to smile, couldn't pull it off.

"You all right?" Martina asked.

"I'm just a little, uh, freaked out," Noreen said.

"About what? School?"

"School's okay for the most part. It's just…" She looked up, a tear running down the side of her nose. "It's just this stuff today on the news. What the hell could be going on?"

"I don't know," Martina said. Though she'd been acting otherwise, it was kind of freaking her out, too. "It's probably nothing."

Noreen looked at her. "You think?"

"Sure."

"Then what is it?"

120

Martina put on her most comforting smile. "Nothing we need to worry about."

A few minutes later, they hugged goodbye, and both girls headed home.

In the strictest sense, Martina was right. She and Noreen didn't need to worry about the boxes. Their immunity ensured that.

But there would have been little comfort in that knowledge.

LONDON, UNITED KINGDOM
8:55 AM GREENWICH MEAN TIME

WITH ONLY TWO days left until Christmas, retailers had been anticipating that this would be one of the busiest shopping days of the season. The majority of customers on this day was also expected to be men. Typically, they were the ones who waited until the last minute, then rushed in and scooped up whatever they could find, no matter the cost. Savvy store managers made sure there were several items front and center specifically meant to catch the male eye.

Daniel Wheaton was such a manager, and he was in charge of one of the Marker's department stores. Marker's wasn't a large chain, only five locations throughout the UK, and it certainly wasn't high end, but it did fill a nice niche in the middle, and generated more than enough business to keep its doors open year after year.

During the Christmas season, Daniel all but lived at the store—going over receipts, making sure customers were being helped, checking inventory, and, in the words of most of the employees, doing anything he could to get in their way.

The one thing Marker's did not have was an electronics department. This made "catching the male eyes" a bit more difficult, but not impossible. It also meant that when the first news about the shipping containers appeared not long before closing the previous evening, no one in the store had any clue what was going on. Once the day's receipts had been tallied and the special last-minute displays were in place, it was nearly midnight, so Daniel took the tube home and went straight to bed.

That morning, his alarm woke him at five a.m. He was showered and on his way to the store before six.

The first sign that something was up came when he played the phone message for the automated office line and learned that two employees were not coming in. This was nothing more than an annoyance. He left messages on both of the affected managers' phones, asking them to call in whoever was next on their list. Once that was done, he promptly forgot about it.

In the next hour, though, six more employees left similar messages, and he began to wonder if there was some sort of mass sickout happening, maybe a coordinated effort to get more pay or something along those lines. But he thought someone would have approached him first before taking this kind of drastic action. He was so concerned about this possibility, it didn't even register with him that none of the employees had actually said anything about being sick, just that they wouldn't be coming in today.

Disturbed, he walked out of his office to see if any of the support staff had heard anything, and found only empty desks. Out helping the other employees get ready, he thought, trying not to jump to conclusions. After all, it was almost nine o'clock, nearly time to open.

He sauntered out onto the main floor, and was greeted by dead silence.

"Hello?" he called out.

The office was right outside women's wear. There should have been half a dozen employees making sure everything was in order, but the department was empty.

"Hello? Where is everyone?"

He walked briskly out into the main aisle, and did a quick circuit of the other departments. He was the only one there.

His jaw tensed. *Definitely some kind of protest*, he

thought.

This was going to be a disaster. Being closed two days before Christmas would be something that would affect them for months. He might even get fired.

He stormed back to the office, and put in a call to Edgar Keller, Vice President of Operations at Marker's headquarters. Instead of someone answering, the night system picked up. He punched buttons until he reached Keller's line. After the third ring, he was sent to voice mail.

Confused, he said, "Mr. Keller, this is Daniel Wheaton at London store number two. I seem to have a situation here. I have a feeling there must be an employee protest in the works. It's five minutes until we're supposed to open and no one has shown up. I was wondering if someone might have contacted you. Please call me back."

He hung up, and waited for a couple of minutes. When his phone didn't ring, he pulled out Keller's business card from his desk. On it was a mobile phone number, to be used only in the direst of emergencies. Losing a whole day's receipts, especially this close to Christmas, seemed pretty dire to Daniel.

He dialed the number. It, too, rang three times. He was afraid he'd be shuffled off to voice mail again, but then the line clicked.

"Edgar Keller."

"Mr. Keller, it's Daniel Wheaton."

"Wheaton?"

"London store number two, sir."

"Oh, right. Why are you calling me?"

Keller had always been a very busy man, but his tone was particularly brusque this morning.

"Sir, I seem to have a problem."

"What problem?"

"We're supposed to open…" He looked at this watch. It had just clicked over to nine o'clock. "Well, now. But none of my employees have shown up."

"And you find that surprising?"

Keller obviously did not, which made Daniel think there

was some sort of labor action underway. This was a relief. "What should I do?"

"I don't care what you do. Me, I'm staying with my family until we know what's going on. You might want to do that, too."

Staying with his family?

"I'm not sure I follow, sir."

When Keller said nothing more, Daniel realized his boss had hung up. He stared at the receiver, feeling very much like he was missing something. Finally, he put it down, and walked back out into the store to see if anyone had shown up. It was as empty as it had been before.

Even more surprising, there were no customers waiting outside the door. They *always* had customers who liked to get their holiday shopping done first thing in the morning. There should have been at least a dozen or more people peering through the window, wondering why the store was still closed.

He walked over to the main door, turned the lock, and stepped outside. Not only was there no one waiting, there were no pedestrians on the sidewalk at all. A few cars sped by, but at this time of the morning, the street should have been jammed.

Back inside, he made his way to Mrs. Norris's desk. The bookkeeper's small office was just a few doors down from his. There, on the credenza behind her chair, was the radio she liked to listen to while she worked. He turned it on.

As always, it was tuned to BBC Radio 1, but instead of Chris Moyles, the usual morning host, one of the news anchors was talking.

"...what steps to take. There has been no claim of responsibility, and most authorities around the world are unwilling to speculate."

Claim of responsibility? Had there been another terrorist attack? Maybe even here in the city?

"As a reminder," the anchor went on, "the Home Office has asked that residents in London and all other major cities remain at home today, and off the streets. This is a voluntary order at this point, but we are told that could change at any moment. If you're in the vicinity of what you believe to be one of the suspicious containers, you are advised to find shelter at least a mile from it, then report the container's location to local authorities. We will, of course, give you the latest information as it comes in.

"Right now we have a report from Russell MacLean in Edinburgh, where army special forces are attempting to disable one of the containers."

The sterile-sounding environment of the broadcast studio was replaced by the sound of wind and heavy equipment. "I'm here just outside the center of Edinburgh, where one of the devices seen around the world was discovered yesterday near a building that was undergoing restoration. Throughout the night, army officials…"

Daniel didn't even bother turning the radio off as he ran out of Mrs. Norris's office. He could hear the reporter in Scotland droning on, but the words no longer sunk in. He had to get home, away from the store. His branch of Marker's was located not far from Soho, an area he was sure would be a target for terrorists. His apartment, by contrast, was in a working-class residential neighborhood on the edge of the city, where it was surely safer.

He stopped just long enough to grab his jacket from his office, and raced out of the store, almost forgetting to lock the door as he left. His anxiousness stayed with him all the way to the Underground station, and throughout his mostly solo ride home.

As he climbed back to street level just a few blocks from his building, he finally allowed himself to relax. Soon he would be in the comfort and safety of his apartment, where he could sit in front of his television and get a proper sense of what was going on.

As he walked down the block, he felt moisture land on his face and hands. Clouds had been hanging over the city for days, but so far there had been no rain. It looked like today was going to be different.

Once he was in his apartment watching the news, he

never thought to look out his window. If he had, he might have seen that the clouds were far too thin to hold much water at all.

Of course, by then, he had forgotten all about the drops that had fallen on him.

18

IT HAD TAKEN Sanjay much longer than he anticipated to get to the building where his cousin had lain dying a few days before. The area was nearly surrounded by men spraying the streets with Pishon Chem's deadly mixture.

He wasn't worried about the vaccine not working. If that were the case, there would be nothing he could do about it, and he and Kusum would die like everyone else. What did concern him was unintentionally carrying the spray back to the others, and making them sick before he could inoculate them.

So he'd had to work his way around until he found a path that had yet to be sprayed, and then headed straight for the building. Only a few of the food vendors and shops that usually crowded Gamdevi Road were open, and most had no customers.

Sanjay's stomach growled, urging him to stop for a bite of whatever he could find. But he knew he couldn't risk it. What if the person working the stand had been exposed to the spray? Would he transfer it to the food, or even to his customers directly? Sanjay would just have to stay hungry.

He cut through the lighter-than-usual traffic, then turned off the road and drove right up to the building, parking his bike near the main door. His previous visit had been late at night, and he'd been forced to climb up to the rear balcony to the second-floor restaurant just to get in. But now, being the middle of the day, the front door was open.

In the lobby, a fat man in a tight suit sat behind a desk.

"May I help you?" he said.

Sanjay had not expected to have to deal with anyone. He hesitated for a moment before saying, "I'm with Pishon Chem. I've been sent to pick up something downstairs."

"They're all gone. No one is here."

"Yes, I realize that," Sanjay said, knowing that probably meant Ayush was dead. "Only picking up." He paused, then added, "Mr. Dettling sent me." Dettling was one of the European managers at Pishon Chem, and had been one of Sanjay's bosses.

"Mr. Dettling?" the man said.

"Yes. I'm sure you know him."

"Of course. Go ahead, then, but when you go back, tell Mr. Dettling he needs to send people to clean up. The rooms are unacceptable as they are now."

"I will be sure to let him know."

Sanjay skirted around the desk, and over to the door that led into the hallway running behind the elevators. A moment later he opened the door to the basement and raced down the stairs. If the people who had been there were truly gone, then it was unlikely he'd find more vaccine, but he had to check.

The door to the basement rooms Pishon Chem had been using was locked. He knocked, hoping there *was* someone present he could try to bluff his way past, but the door stayed closed.

He glanced down the hallway, his gaze zeroing in on the doorless room where he hid on his previous visit. Though it had been dark inside, he'd had the sense it was some kind of maintenance closet.

He ran to it, and felt along the inner wall for a light switch. When his fingers brushed against it, he flipped it on, and a weak bulb hanging from the ceiling lit up. Indeed, it was a maintenance closet. A couple of buckets, mops, brooms, cleaning supplies. There was also a chest of drawers that contained tools—wrenches, screwdrivers, and, best of all, a hammer.

He grabbed the last, returned to the door, and pounded at the wood until the locks finally gave way. The door swung open with a shove.

He moved quickly down the hallway to the room at the end where his cousin had been kept.

When he entered, he immediately could see why the man upstairs had wanted Pishon to come back. Everything was in disarray. Tables overturned, wiring and tubing on the floor, boxes of bandages and gauze and latex gloves thrown haphazardly around. The plastic wall that had divided the room in two was open in the middle, and the beds beyond, where Ayush and the others on his team had lain dying, were empty.

Sanjay stared for a moment at his cousin's bed, then shook himself out of it. He couldn't think about Ayush now. The living needed him. He could deal with the dead later.

The front half of the room, the part he was in, was where he'd previously found the nurses, and where he'd obtained the vaccine that he'd taken himself and given to Kusum.

He tried to remember exactly which of the cabinets along the wall it had been stored in.

The…center one.

The doors to all the cabinets hung open, the shelves inside mostly empty, their contents pushed to the floor. As he started going through everything, he already knew what he would find.

Nothing.

He grunted in frustration.

Returning to Kusum and her family without the vaccine was not an option. He was the only one standing between them and death. He *had* to get it.

He thought for a moment. There was one more place he could check. If the vaccine was anywhere, it would be there.

"What's going on here?" The man who'd been sitting upstairs stepped into the room. "What happened? The door is broken!"

"Sorry," Sanjay said as he pushed past the man.

"Sorry? *Sorry*?" the man said, waddling after him. "You have to fix that! You have to pay!"

"Pishon Chem will take care of it."

"Wait! You will stay here until I talk to them."

Sanjay rushed past the broken door into the common corridor.

"Wait!" the man called out, his voice growing farther away. "Wait!"

Sanjay didn't.

THE CAR KUSUM'S father had planned on using belonged to a man who owned a small shop about a kilometer away. Kusum's father had done some work there on and off, and knew the man hid the car keys under the dash near the steering column.

"I should not be gone more than an hour," he said. "I will push the horn three times. When you hear it, come down."

"No," Kusum said. "We all go."

"This is not up to you."

"I'm not trying to fight you. We should go together. It will be faster. You and I can carry Panna and Darshan. Jabala and mother can help *masi*."

Her tone was forceful and direct in a way she would have never spoken to her father before. But now was not a time to worry about what was appropriate. She kept her eyes locked on his, knowing he wanted to argue the point and put her back in her place, but instead he frowned and looked away.

"If you are all coming with me, why are you just sitting there?" he said.

They gathered what food they could carry, then left the apartment, not knowing when or if they would ever return. As they neared the end of the alley, Kusum's father set Darshan down, and moved ahead to look around the corner and make sure the area hadn't been sprayed.

After a moment, he waved at them. "Come on."

From that point on, he and Kusum would take turns scouting each intersection to make sure they were clear. Luck stayed with them until they were only three blocks from where the car was parked. That's when they saw some of the men spraying the road.

Panna, riding on Kusum's back, started shaking. Though she and her brother had not been in the room when Sanjay told his story, they'd overheard enough of the conversation between Kusum and her parents as they were walking to know there was something wrong about the men holding the sprayers.

"Don't worry," Kusum whispered. "We won't go near them."

"Are you sure?"

"I'm sure."

Panna fell silent, but she continued to shake.

Kusum's father studied the area for several seconds, then turned to his family and said, "This way."

Unlike Sanjay, who'd been able to find an untainted path to the building across town, the way to the car turned out to be completely blocked by the spray.

"What are we going to do now?" Kusum's mother asked.

"Let me think," her husband said.

"Think about what? We use another car," Kusum told them.

"What car?" her father said.

She swept out her hand, taking in the whole street. "*Any* car. We just need to get away."

Her mother looked uncomfortable, but instead of voicing her concern, she remained silent.

"We can't just take *any* car," her father countered. "We must be able to start it, and we must be able to get away before anyone notices."

One that started, yes, but Kusum didn't care if anyone noticed. As long as it would carry them, that's all that mattered.

For the first time since they'd left home, her great aunt spoke. "What about a taxi?" She gestured at two cabs parked along the side of the road in front of a restaurant. Each was empty.

"We don't have enough money for a taxi," Kusum's father said.

"Who said anything about paying?" Kusum's *masi* said.

Kusum looked at both taxis again, then set Panna down. After telling the girl to hold on to Jabala's hand, she headed across the road.

"Kusum?" her mother called out.

Kusum batted a hand at her, telling her to be quiet, and kept going. When she reached the other side of the street, she walked past each cab, glancing through the driver's-side windows. The keys to the second cab, the one in back, were just visible on the floor in front of the seat.

She glanced into the restaurant. There were two men at a table near the middle. They were the only customers, and their eyes were glued to a television on a shelf near the back. She was sure they were the drivers.

Looking back at her father, she motioned to the second cab, and moved her hand in front of her mouth in a broad gesture she hoped they'd understand to mean they needed to be quiet as they entered the vehicle. After her father nodded, she walked into the restaurant, and passed the table with the two men. There she stopped and looked up at the TV. The news was the same as it had been before, so while she pretended to pay attention, she wasn't really listening.

Out of the corner of her eye, she could see her family approach the taxi.

"Have they found anything here?" she asked, not having to fake a concerned tone.

One of the drivers looked at her, then back at the TV. "Nothing yet."

"You think they will?"

"I hope not."

A sound from the back of the restaurant caused her to look over. A woman wearing an apron and carrying two bottles of beer came out through a door and walked toward the occupied table. Kusum quickly repositioned herself to block the woman's view of the cabs out front. The woman set the beers down, and looked at Kusum.

"Sit wherever you want. I'll be back in a moment," she said.

"I'm, uh, just watching the TV."

A moment of displeasure crossed the woman's lips, but she shrugged and hurried back the way she'd come. Just before she passed through the kitchen door and out of sight, the woman coughed twice, deep and wet.

Kusum stared after her, momentarily frozen in place. She turned back toward the street, searching for any of the sheen from the spray, but there was none. Maybe the woman just had a cold.

Or maybe, Kusum thought, *she passed through an area that had been sprayed on her way to the restaurant.*

Kusum glanced at the taxi and saw that everyone was inside. Her father gave her a quick wave and a nod from the driver's seat, indicating they were ready. As casually as she could, she stepped back until she was no longer in the men's direct view. She then turned and hurried to the cab.

Jabala, in the front passenger seat, had left enough room for Kusum to squeeze in beside her. As Kusum reached the open door, her father turned the ignition.

"Go!" she yelled as she jumped in next to her sister.

Her father shoved the vehicle into gear and hit the gas.

"Hey!" One of the men in the restaurant jumped out of his seat. "Hey! Come back! That's my taxi!"

"Faster! Faster!" Kusum urged her father, sure the two drivers would get into the other cab and chase them down.

Her father turned from road to road, trying to mask their path. Whether it was because of that, or because the two men never left the restaurant, Kusum didn't know, but after several minutes it was clear no one was following them.

"Which way now?" her father asked.

"Northeast," she told him. "Out of the city."

THE AREA AROUND the Pishon Chem compound had not yet been sprayed. Perhaps they were saving it for the end, Sanjay thought. Or perhaps the managers were worried that even though they'd been vaccinated, the disease might still affect them.

Sanjay parked near the gate that led to the dormitories many of the workers, including him, had been using. As usual, there was a guard at the gate, a local, but not one Sanjay had seen before.

"Private property," the man said as Sanjay approached. "You cannot enter."

"I work for the company," Sanjay told him. "For Pishon Chem. I'm one of the coordinators. I have something I must talk to Mr. Dettling about."

As with the man at the building, the use of an actual manager's name caused the guard to relax. "Do you have your ID card?"

Every employee had been issued one. It had been a point of pride among the men. Sanjay did indeed have his ID in his pocket, but he was concerned all the guards had been given his name and told to detain him if he ever showed up.

"Of course I have one," Sanjay said. "But things were so busy this morning, I left it in the dormitory. I can bring it to you when I leave."

Though he was using all the right terms, he could see the guard was still hesitant to let him through.

"You understand how important today is, I am sure," Sanjay said. "Any delay could cause major problems, and if you do not let me go see Mr. Dettling, there *will* be delays. Do you want this to be your fault?"

"Maybe I should call him."

"Please, do it. Whatever will make this go faster."

"Your name?"

Sanjay gave him the name of one of the other coordinators, and the man disappeared inside the little hut that served as his only shelter from the sun. Sanjay could hear him on the phone, and knew before the man returned that the ploy had worked.

"Okay," the guard said. "You know where to go?"

"Of course."

"Mr. Dettling said he will be in the conference room."

"Thank you."

Sanjay headed in the direction of the building the managers used. Once he was out of sight of the gate, he cut down between two of the dormitory buildings, and around the side of the administration building so he could enter through the less-used back entrance.

There were a few people at the far end of the compound where the excess barrels of spray were kept. Their job, Sanjay knew, was to send full ones out to any zone experiencing a shortage. None of the men paid him even the slightest bit of attention as he opened the rear door and went inside.

The building was two stories. The top floor served as the living quarters for the managers, while all the business was done on the ground floor. The question was, where would they keep the vaccine? Surely there would be some on the premises just in case of an emergency. The top floor would keep it more isolated, which might be desirable to the managers. Then again, the first floor would make it more accessible in case they needed it in a hurry.

This being the day of the spraying, he figured that most, if not all, the managers would be downstairs in the work area, leaving the living quarters empty, so he decided to check there first.

Based on the vaccine he'd taken, he knew what he was looking for—small jars of slightly orange-tinted liquid. He was painfully aware there could be other things that looked the same, but there had been no label on the jar of vaccine he was given, so there was no way to identify it by name.

The stairway to the upper floor let out on a wide corridor. Every twenty feet or so, there was a door on either side. These would be the apartments, he guessed. Toward the middle was an open doorway that led to a dining area. Adjacent to this was a kitchen. Sanjay could hear the sounds of food being chopped up and dishes knocking together. He hadn't even thought about the fact there might be people working up here. He would have to be extra careful.

He slipped by the dining room and continued down the hall. More doors like before, all the way to the end. He frowned. He'd been hoping for a clearly labeled medical room or something similar. He didn't think they would store surplus vaccine in one of the private quarters. But, with the exception of the kitchen, there seemed to be only private apartments.

Downstairs, then, he thought.

As he walked back toward the stairway, he heard the distinctive sound of a door latch being disengaged. He looked around quickly, but there was nowhere to hide.

A door about twenty feet ahead of him opened.

All he could do was pretend he belonged there, so he walked with purpose toward the stairs, his head held up.

The man who came out of the room barely glanced in his direction, but Sanjay recognized him immediately. It was the senior manager, a gray-haired man Sanjay believed to be German.

Sanjay's muscles tensed with a sudden surge of rage. Here was the person in charge of the operation. The man had already taken Ayush's life, and now was trying to take those of the people Sanjay passed on the street every day, the food stall owners he visited, the men who'd been recruited, like him, to work for Pishon Chem. And, of course, Kusum's family.

Everyone.

A new plan quickly took shape in Sanjay's mind.

He slowed his pace so that he reached the senior manager just as the man was about to close his door.

"Excuse me, sir," Sanjay said. "I have a message for you."

The man looked over. "What message?"

"I was told to give it to you in private."

The manager glanced down the empty hallway. "I think we are private here."

"If you say so, sir." Sanjay paused, then said in a low, concerned voice, "There have been some deaths."

"Excuse me?"

"From the spray. Mr. Reiner said to tell you it's working too fast." Mr. Reiner was another manager, one who was supposed to be out in the field during the spraying.

The gray-haired man's eyes widened. "That's not possible," he said, more to himself than to Sanjay.

"There's more," Sanjay told him.

"What?"

Sanjay tried to look as uncomfortable as possible. "Are you sure you wouldn't rather hear this…"

It took a second, but finally the man pushed the door to his apartment open again, and said, "Come in."

He entered first, Sanjay coming in right behind him.

Once the door was closed, he said, "What else?"

The last time Sanjay had hit anyone, he was thirteen, but he had never forgotten what Ayush taught him after he lost that fight. "The elbow can be much more effective than the hand."

Sanjay's elbow proved the point as it slammed into the side of the man's head, and the senior manager dropped straight to the ground.

NOT KNOWING HOW much time he had, Sanjay quickly searched the room. In the nightstand next to the bed, he found a handgun. He'd never held one in his life, let alone used one. He took it anyway. The rest of the apartment seemed to only have what one would expect to find—clothes, a few personal items, toiletries. As far as he could tell, there were no little bottles of vaccine present.

Using the laces from a pair of shoes in the closet, he tied the man's hands together, then took a pillowcase off one of the pillows and tied it across the man's mouth. All the jerking around caused the manager to stir, and after a few more moments, his eyes opened to find Sanjay crouching nearby with the gun in his hand.

"You will do as I say, do you understand?" Sanjay asked.

The man tried to speak, but all he managed through the gag was a muffled jumble of sounds.

"Do you understand?" Sanjay said again.

The man's eyes narrowed, but he nodded.

"I know about the spray, and what it really is."

The man's expression remained unchanged.

"You are going to kill my countrymen with a disease like what happened in America."

This time one of the man's eyebrows twitched.

"If I could stop you, I would. But I know that's not possible. I don't understand how you can live with what you are doing, but I can't worry about that right now. You are going to help me."

A muffled huff.

"If you don't help me, I will kill you and find someone else who can." Though killing was against almost everything Sanjay believed in, he would be able to justify it in this one instance.

The man apparently didn't see the resolve in Sanjay's eye, because he laughed.

Without hesitating, Sanjay jammed the muzzle of the gun against the man's left shoulder and pulled the trigger. The sound was loud, but not as loud as he'd expected.

The man screamed through the pillowcase. His eyes squeezed shut for a moment, then opened again in disbelief as he twisted back and forth in pain.

"I will say it again. You are going to help me."

This time there was no laugh, just a nod.

"You will take me to the vaccine."

The man looked surprised.

Sanjay shifted the gun to the man's other shoulder. "You will take me to the vaccine."

The man nodded again, the look on his face pleading with Sanjay not to pull the trigger again.

THE GUNSHOT HAD not gone unnoticed.

When Sanjay opened the apartment door, he found two men standing in the hallway. Thankfully, they were not other managers, but Indians like him. Their aprons and grease-stained shirts identified them as the men from the kitchen. As soon as they saw the gun, they started to run.

"Stop!" Sanjay ordered.

138

They froze where they were, no doubt thinking they might get shot in the back.

"I am not going to hurt you."

"Then let us go," one of the men said.

"If I do, you will die."

"What is that supposed to mean?"

"Exactly what it sounded like."

"Please," the other man said. "We have families. Just let us go."

Sanjay knew the task ahead would be difficult to complete on his own, if not impossible. Who knew how many managers were still downstairs.

"Come back here. I promise I won't shoot you if you do," he lied. He had no intention of shooting them at all. They had done nothing but take work in a kitchen to support their families.

"Why should we?"

"Because there's something you need to know."

It took a bit more persuading, but finally the men came back to the manager's apartment. When they saw the injured man lying on the floor, gagged with his hands tied behind his back, they almost ran out, but Sanjay had already moved between them and the door, his gun convincing them to stay where they were.

"So what do you think we need to know?" the first man said.

As quickly as he could, Sanjay explained what was really going on with Pishon Chem and the spray. The men looked at him skeptically.

Sanjay stepped quickly to the manager and knelt down beside him. He pulled the gag off the man's mouth, and shoved the gun back into the man's uninjured shoulder. "Tell them."

"Tell them what?" the manager said defiantly.

"Tell them it's the truth."

"That there's a disease we're trying to distribute through Mumbai? That's crazy."

"Tell them!" Sanjay moved the muzzle of the gun over to

139

the man's wound, and shoved it against the bullet hole.

The man cried out.

"Tell them!"

The manager began panting deeply, his eyes flicking from Sanjay to the others. "He isn't…lying. It's true. But we're…only trying to make this a better world."

"By killing our countrymen?" Sanjay said.

"By killing everyone."

The last seemed to do the trick. The two other men looked horrified as the manager's words sunk in.

The first man turned for the door. "I need to get home. I need to save my family."

"Wait!" Sanjay called out. "The only way to save them is to help me."

The man looked back. "What are you talking about?"

ACCORDING TO THE manager, the remaining vaccine was locked in a storage closet near the main conference room on the ground level.

One of the two cooks went down the stairs first, checking to see if the way was clear. Once he gave them the signal, Sanjay, the other cook, and the manager joined him.

They could hear voices from farther down the main hallway. It sounded to Sanjay like the guttural language most of the managers spoke. Unfortunately, it was also coming from the same direction they needed to go in.

Every few steps, their captive manager grunted behind his gag in obvious pain. Sanjay didn't care what the man was feeling, but he did care if the noise gave them away.

"Quiet," he whispered.

Ahead, the hallway took a ninety-degree turn to the right toward the conference room and, just beyond it, the locked room where the vaccine was stored. Sanjay held up a hand for the others to stop, then leaned a few inches around the corner for a look.

While the corridor was empty, the voices were clearly coming through the open door of the conference room. Sanjay could make out at least four people.

"What are we going to do?" one of the cooks whispered.

Sanjay thought for a moment. The managers had never seemed particularly threatening to him—not physically, anyway—relying more on their leadership positions to get what they wanted from the men they'd hired. He had also never seen more than two or three guards patrolling the compound, all local hires. Since the public and the government had been more than happy to have Pishon Chem in India, the company apparently never thought it'd face a threat.

It was wrong, Sanjay thought.

Glancing back at the other men, he said, "Follow me."

He stepped around the corner, hauling the manager right beside him, and walked straight to the conference room. Just before he got there, he turned the manager over to one of the cooks, and moved into the open doorway.

There were five of the Europeans inside, not four. They were laughing at some unknown joke—something that caused Sanjay's anger to intensify—and it took them a moment to realize he was there.

It was the manager named Dettling, the man whose name Sanjay had been dropping, who spoke first. "Can we help you?" Before Sanjay could say anything, the man's eyes narrowed in confusion. "Sanjay?" Then those same eyes widened as he seemed to remember that Sanjay had gone missing after paying an unauthorized visit to his dying cousin.

"Mr. Dettling, you and your friends will stay here," Sanjay said.

"What do you mean, 'stay here'? What are you talking about?"

Sanjay lifted his hand so they could see his gun. "I would rather not hurt anyone else."

"What?"

Two of the men jumped up from their chairs.

"Sit," Sanjay ordered, pointing the gun toward them to emphasize the point.

The two men hesitated a second, then returned to their

seats.

"I don't know what you are thinking," Dettling said. "But whatever's going on in your head, you're wrong."

"Am I?"

Glancing to the side, Sanjay grabbed hold of the senior manager's shirt and pulled him into the doorway with him. One of the men in the room gasped.

"He's hurt," Dettling said, rising to his feet. "What have you done?"

He took a step toward the door.

"Stop," Sanjay said.

When Dettling took another step, Sanjay did something he would have never thought he was capable of doing—he pressed the thumb of his free hand against the wound on the old manager's shoulder. The man screamed, the gag barely blocking any of the noise.

Dettling stopped. "Don't hurt him."

Sanjay eased back on his thumb, but didn't remove it completely. "Who has keys to the room next door?"

A collective blank stare.

Sanjay pointed the gun at the man to Dettling's left. "The keys?"

This time there was a shrug or two. Then Dettling said, "I'm sorry. I'm not sure what you're—"

Sanjay pulled the trigger.

The man next to Dettling jammed backward against his chair and then tumbled to the ground.

"Who?" Sanjay asked, aiming the gun at the next person in line.

Two of the remaining men pulled sets of keys from their pockets and tossed them across the room.

"It's the silver one," one of them said. "With the J on it."

Sanjay shoved the senior manager back to the cooks. Then, without taking his eyes off the men at the table, leaned down and picked up one set of keys.

"Sanjay, please," Dettling said. He was holding his hands in front of him, his palms facing out, in an obvious attempt to show he meant no harm. "Why don't you put the gun down, and let us get medical assistance for our friends?"

Sanjay rose back to his feet, his eyes blazing. "And who will give medical attention to all the people of Mumbai when they become sick from your spray?"

"Whatever you think you've heard is wrong. The spray is only for—"

"What I've heard? Mr. Dettling, I have *seen* what your spray does. I have seen my cousin and the men he was working with dying from it. The Sage Flu. Are you going to tell me the nurse was lying?"

"Of course she was. Your cousin was only suffering from extreme exposure to the malaria spray. It was a very unfortunate event, but that's all it was."

Sanjay grabbed his captive and pulled him back. "And your senior manager here? He has confirmed that I am right. Are you saying he lied, too?"

"Yes. He was just telling you what you wanted to hear."

The worried look on the faces of the men behind Dettling belied his words.

"Then you are saying I won't find any of the vaccine in the room next door."

That caught the men by surprise. Even Dettling lost some of his composure before he recovered and said, "It's where we keep our medical supplies, so of course you'll find medicine in there. But a vaccine? I'm sorry. I don't even know what it would be for."

Sanjay wanted so much to pull the trigger again, and put a bullet right through the center of Mr. Dettling's chest, but that was a line his conscience was not yet willing to let him cross.

He looked over at one of the cooks. "Come here." When the man joined him, he said, "Take this." He handed him the gun. "Don't let any of them leave. Remember, they are trying to kill your family."

The cook nodded, his face hard and determined.

Sanjay motioned to the other cook to follow him, and bring the senior manager along.

"You're not going to find anything!" Dettling called out

as Sanjay moved away.

"Shut up," the cook with the gun said. "I am not nearly as nice as my friend."

Sanjay used the silver J key to open the closet door. The medical supply room was about the size of the main room in Kusum's apartment, and was cooler than the corridor, apparently having its own temperature-control system. Through the middle and along each wall were shelves filled with medical supplies.

He pulled the gag out of the old man's mouth. "Where is it?"

The manager gasped several times.

"Where?" Sanjay repeated.

"Over there," the man said, his voice weak. "In the glass cabinets."

Sanjay dragged the man across the room.

The cabinets were built into the shelving unit. There were two of them side by side, each about Sanjay's height, and two meters wide. Inside were boxes and bottles of varying sizes.

"Which one is it?" Sanjay asked.

"In there," the man said, pointing at the second cabinet. "Those bottles on the third shelf down."

Sanjay opened the cabinet, pulled out one of the small bottles, and raised it to the light. The liquid inside was clear, not tinged with orange like what he'd been given.

"You're lying."

"Why would I do that?"

"This isn't the vaccine."

"Of course it is."

"Then you take it."

"I've already been vaccinated."

"I don't care."

Sanjay spotted a box full of prepackaged, ready-to-use syringes on a nearby shelf. He opened one, and stuck the needle through the rubber cap on the bottle. He drew in the same amount the nurse had given him and, in turn, he had given Kusum. He moved the needle toward the manager's arm.

"No," the man said before Sanjay could plunge it in.

Sanjay held the needle just above the manager's skin. "Why not?"

"I…I made a mistake. That's not it."

"Then what is it?"

"I don't know," the man said, though Sanjay was willing to bet the man did know.

Instead of asking him again where the vaccine was, Sanjay searched through the bottles, looking for the orange tinge. Finally he found two boxes of bottles sitting together in the first cabinet that matched his memory of the vaccine.

He held one in front of the man. "This is it."

By the defeated look on the man's face, Sanjay knew he was right. He added the box of syringes to the two boxes of vaccine, and headed to the door where the cook was waiting. Stopping just inside, he took a quick look around. There were no windows in the supply room, and the only way in and out was the single door.

"Stay here," he said to the manager, and went out into the corridor.

Sanjay and the two cooks escorted the other managers individually into the medical supply room. The only exception was that they allowed Mr. Dettling to help his injured colleague.

After making sure they'd taken all the mobile phones from the men, they shut the door and jammed a chair from the conference room under the handle. It wouldn't keep them inside for too long, but it would be enough for Sanjay and his new friends to get away.

He gave each cook a few of the needles and several bottles of vaccine, then instructed them on how to administer it.

They thanked him, and left as fast as they could.

Before taking off, Sanjay found a bag in one of the rooms, put the remaining vaccine and needles in it, then hurried from the building.

"Your identification," the guard said as he walked by the

gate.

"Oh," Sanjay groaned. "I totally forgot. Look, you can call Mr. Dettling again while I wait, if you want. But please hurry. He told me I needed to deliver this across town as soon as possible." He held up the bag.

The guard frowned, then shook his head and waved him through. "Next time, don't forget."

"I won't," Sanjay said. "Thank you."

Less than a minute later, he was speeding away from the compound, barely believing he'd actually done it. He had the vaccine, more than enough for Kusum's family. He couldn't wait to meet up with them again, sure that they were already out of town and nearing the rendezvous point.

They weren't.

19

THE WHOLE NIGHT had been a nonstop race through the woods. The monsters, faceless but always close, hounded and teased Brandon as he tried to get away, but every time he thought he was free, he would hear them again.

The forest seemed to go on forever. He knew there had to be a road somewhere, something that would lead him to others who could help protect him from the creatures hunting him.

A howl. Not a wolf, but something else, and so, so close.

"No!" he yelled. "No! No!"

His eyes shot open as the final shout woke him from his sleep. For several seconds, the terror of the woods clung to him as if it were the real thing, then it began to fade and the world came back into focus.

He was momentarily confused by how low the ceiling was above him. So low, in fact, he could reach up and easily touch it. But the air was freezing, and the last thing he wanted to do was pull his arm out from under his...sleeping bag?

The fire at the Ranch. The helicopters. Mr. Hayes. Oh, God, Mr. Hayes. The endless hours of trekking through the forest. The house. The garage.

The old station wagon.

Now he remembered, and wasn't sure which was worse—the nightmare or reality.

Though he hadn't wanted to expose himself to the frigid air, he had to check the time. If it was late enough, he needed to head out to the safety of the forest. Using the flashlight, he checked his watch.

Eighteen minutes to six a.m. Definitely time to get out of there.

He was about to turn the flashlight off when he realized something was wrong. The door to the car was open. He had shut it when he climbed in. He was sure of it. Had he woken at some point and opened it but didn't remember? He didn't think so. He'd never been the kind of person who'd get up during the night and forget about it like a sleepwalker in a movie.

He played the light through the door but didn't see anything there. Feeling a bit of the panic he'd experienced in his dream, he scrambled out of his sleeping bag and scooted through the car door. He spun around, shining the flashlight through the room. It was exactly as it had been earlier.

Relax. Maybe you just didn't shut it all the way and it swung open while you were sleeping. Just get your stuff together and get out of here.

After allowing himself another few seconds to calm down, he pulled his sleeping bag out of the car, rolled it up, and tied it to the bottom of his pack. He thought about eating a little bit, but decided that could wait until he was back among the trees.

He pulled his pack over his shoulder and headed for the door, but when he turned the knob the door only opened an inch before stopping. He tried again, and got the exact same results. Something was keeping it from moving any farther.

He looked through a sliver of space between the door and jamb, but it was still too dark outside to see much of anything. Putting his hand over the lens of the flashlight, he aimed it through the opening near the ground and moved it upward, looking for the cause. He found it at about eye level. A closed hinge held in place by a padlock.

He immediately shut the door and stepped back.

They know I'm here.

Whirling around, he looked toward the roll-up door. It was his only option.

There had to be a switch inside somewhere that would open it. It would make a lot of noise, but he didn't care. He just needed to get out of there.

Usually the switches were near the door people used to walk in and out, in this case the one that had been padlocked. He moved the flashlight beam over the wall near it, but there was nothing that looked even close to what he thought the switch would look like.

He turned in a circle, desperate to find the button. Then, as his gaze passed over the car, he realized he was being an idiot. There would be a remote in the station wagon.

He pulled the driver's door open and searched around. With a "yes!" he found the device tucked down next to the seat. He climbed back out of the car, and moved as close to the door as possible so he could make a quick escape.

He pointed the remote at the shadowy form of the motor hanging from the middle of the ceiling, and pushed the button.

Nothing happened.

He pushed again, then hit the back of the remote in case the battery wasn't sitting right. That's when he noticed the tiny green light next to the button. When he pushed, the light lit up. Apparently the remote was getting power, but it wasn't turning on the motor.

The only possibilities would be either the motor was busted, or the power to the garage was off. It didn't matter what the answer was. The problem was the same.

Wait, wasn't there something about remote doors? Something his father had told him once?

He shined the light on the motor, and saw the wooden handle dangling from a rope a foot below it.

The emergency release!

After dumping his pack on the ground, he climbed onto the roof of the Subaru and stretched as far as he could, but his fingers just barely missed the handle. He hopped down and went to the storage area at the back. Half a minute later, he found a box that he was sure could handle his weight. He lugged it over to the car, and manhandled it onto the roof. Once he climbed back up, he scooted it until it was directly under the handle, and stepped on top.

This time he had no problem reaching the piece of wood. He pulled it down as hard as he could. There was a groan and a pop, then the door moved upward an inch or so.

Relieved, he jumped down and raced to the exit. Putting his hands underneath the door, he was able to easily raise it enough to get out. The noise was loud, but probably less than it would have been with the motor.

He pushed his bag outside, snaked through the opening, and stood up.

Keep moving. Get to the woods!

He picked up his pack and started to pull it on.

"You're pretty smart for a kid."

The voice belonged to a woman who couldn't have been more than twenty feet away. Brandon turned slowly toward her, but all he could see was a shadow where she stood.

"Find everything in there you wanted?"

"What?" Brandon said. "I didn't take anything. I was just—"

"Right. You left *everything* there."

"Check for yourself. The only things I have are what I came with. I just wanted someplace where I could get out of the cold and sleep."

"Then why didn't you just knock on our door?"

"Because it was late," he said quickly. "I didn't want to disturb you."

"Because you wanted to see what was in the garage."

"No! I told you. I just wanted to sleep."

The flashlight beam swayed just enough to the side that he could see the barrel of a rifle.

"Please," he said. "I'm just trying to get to the highway, that's all. I didn't take anything from you. Please, just let me go, okay?"

"Not okay," she said. "Before we *let* you do anything, we need to make sure we get all our stuff back."

Brandon took the pack off and held it out toward her.

"You want to check? Okay, check. There's nothing there."

"Oh, we'll check. But first we need to do something about you."

ARCTIC OCEAN
7:03 AM CENTRAL STANDARD TIME

SOMETIME DURING THE night, the icebreaker Danus Marko moved out from under the storm into a slightly less rough, open sea. Ash was unaware of this, though. After his radio conversation with Matt, he'd been given a meal and had fallen back into a deep sleep from which even the rising and falling and rolling of the ship couldn't wake him.

When he finally opened his eyes, the ship seemed to be barely swaying at all, the vibrations of the heavy-duty engines cut back to a level that was almost unnoticeable. He pushed himself up, confused.

Chloe lay on the bed across from him, her eyes still closed. Their hosts had decided not to treat them as prisoners anymore but as guests. They had been given a second room next to the one they'd been sharing with Red and Gagnon.

Ash checked his watch and was surprised to see it was already after seven a.m.

"Chloe," he said.

No movement.

He sat up. "Chloe."

She rolled onto her back, but her eyes remained shut.

Ash rubbed his face, and ran his fingers through his hair. Stretching his neck, he rolled his head from side to side, then stood up and gave Chloe a shake.

"Wake up."

A groan, then lids parting. As soon as she focused on him, her eyes shot open all the way. "What's wrong?"

"I think we might have stopped."

"Stopped?" She sat up.

"I'm going to go check."

"Not alone."

They stopped first to check on Gagnon and Red. Both were still out. Ash checked Gagnon's temperature and was encouraged by the coolness of the man's brow, and the color that had returned to the pilot's face. Seeing no reason to wake up Red yet, they headed for the bridge.

There were four people present when they arrived—three crew members and Gleason, the male half of Adam and Eve. Out the window Ash could see lights, maybe a mile or less from the ship. Not lights from another vessel, though. The way these were strung out, they could only be on land.

"Where are we?" Ash asked.

Gleason looked over, surprised. "You're up. Good. We can get going."

"Get going?"

Gleason nodded out the window. "We're dropping you off here."

"And where is here?"

"Grise Fiord. Thought it might be where you wanted to go."

Ash looked toward the lights again, his turn to be surprised. The small, isolated village of Grise Fiord was the location from which Ash and his team had left on their flight to Yanok Island. It was also at Grise Fiord where they'd left the Resistance's private jet with its crew, waiting for them to return.

A way home.

"There is a little problem."

"What problem?"

"We've been in radio contact with authorities on the island. They're not exactly in a welcoming mood at the moment."

"What do you mean?"

"Apparently the world has gone a little paranoid in the last twenty hours or so."

"They know about the virus?" Ash asked, hopeful. If people knew what was going on, maybe there was a chance to limit the damage.

152

The look on Gleason's face was not as optimistic. "People know something's going on, just not what, exactly. There've been rumors, apparently bolstered by a video that showed up on the Internet, telling people what they need to do. But from what I understand, nothing official has been determined. The people at Grise Fiord apparently don't want to take any chances."

"Then how are we going to get there?"

"We'll move in some, then you and your friends can take one of the Zodiacs in."

"That still doesn't mean they won't try to stop us."

Looking tired, Gleason said, "You'll have to convince them not to."

Ash stared at him for several seconds. "Where are *you* going?"

Gleason shook his head. "I don't know yet." He paused. "Unfortunately, my people and I haven't received the vaccine. So isolation seems like a good idea, but we'll take a vote. This isn't a decision for one person to make."

"I'll get my people ready," Ash said, turning for the door. "You get us as close as you can."

As he and Chloe walked back to Red and Gagnon's room, Chloe whispered, "There's vaccine on the jet. We could have bartered that, maybe gotten them to take us all the way in."

"These are the same people who raided the Bluff and freed Olivia, who killed almost everyone there. Do you really think they deserve to be inoculated?"

She frowned. "Okay, maybe not. But it would be safer coming into the dock in this than a small boat."

He made no reply.

She sighed. "I hope you know what you're doing."

So did he.

MONTANA
6:23 AM MOUNTAIN STANDARD TIME

PALE HORSE

THOUGH THE WOMAN had never pointed her rifle directly at Brandon, the double-barreled gun had always been aimed at a spot nearby. He'd had no choice but to do everything she ordered.

The first thing she had him do was return the box he'd put on the roof of her car to its shelf, then she'd marched him across the yard to the house. He'd been terrified to go inside, but he had no other options. She directed him to a set of stairs that led down to the basement, and locked him in a room crowded with canned food and bags of grain.

At least she'd left the light on. And, he reminded himself, she hadn't shot him. Yet.

Trying to think like his father, the first thing he did was check to see if there was any other way out of the room, but the only exit was the door he'd come through, and that wasn't budging.

Exhausted, terrified, and not sure what to do next, he sat down on a large bag of rice and did his best not to cry.

"I should have just stayed in the woods," he told himself. "I should have just kept going."

If his dad had been there, he would have probably said something like, "Don't deal with should haves. Deal with what is, and staying alive."

But how was he supposed to do that? He was locked in a cellar. If he'd had his bag with him, he might have found something inside to use as a weapon, or something to force the door open. But as far as he knew, his bag was still sitting in front of the garage.

Wait. Maybe there was something in the room he could use.

He jumped up and took in every inch of his makeshift jail cell. His gaze fell on the shelf against the far wall. Stacked four high and five deep were cans of Campbell's soup. Apparently the woman was fond of cream of mushroom.

He thought for a moment. A soup can had some weight to it, and would fit nicely in his palm. A nice fastball into the woman's leg might at least knock her down or stun her enough so he could make his escape.

Buoyed by this idea, he grabbed one of the cans and tossed it up and down. Not quite the baseball he and his dad played catch with, but it would do.

He figured the best place for him to stand to guarantee he wouldn't miss would be about five feet straight back from the door. The problem with that was, it would also give her enough time to see what he was up to. The smart place to be was off to the side. He wouldn't necessarily see her as soon as she opened the door, but she wouldn't see him either, and would be forced to take a step inside. As soon as she did, he could let the can fly.

The only wild card was that he assumed there was at least one other person in the house. The woman had said *we*, so she wasn't alone. It would be horrible if he disabled the woman, only to be stopped by other people who lived in the house.

He went back, picked up a second can he could take with him, and returned to the spot near the door. Once settled, he focused his attention on the creaks of the floorboards above him. It sounded like there was only one person moving around—the woman, he assumed—so maybe her friend was on the second floor. If whoever it was stayed there, Brandon thought he should be able to get out of the house before the other person even knew he'd escaped.

Suddenly, he heard a door open and steps moving downward, the sound now coming through his cell door instead of the ceiling.

He tensed.

This is it.

The can in his throwing hand began to feel slippery. He quickly set it down, wiped his sweaty palm on his pants, and picked the container up again. That was better.

As the steps approached his door, he cocked his arm back, ready to throw.

But instead of opening it, she stopped just outside. "What's your name?" she asked, her voice not as strained as it had sounded when she first found him.

Come on. Just come in.

"I asked you a question," she said. "What's your name?"

"Please, just let me out," he yelled. "I didn't mean to cause any problems. I...I have someplace I need to go."

"And where would that be?"

"Uh...home. My family. They're waiting for me."

"So you're telling me you live around here?"

"Yeah. A few miles away. I went out for a walk and got lost."

"You're packing an awful lot of stuff for someone just out for a walk."

He had no idea how to reply to that.

"What's your name?" she asked again.

He hesitated. "Brandon."

"Well, Brandon. You want to tell me what you were really doing in the woods?"

Please open the door.

"Brandon? Why were you out there?"

"I...I was being chased." The words left his lips before he even realized what he'd said.

"Chased? By who?"

"They were in helicopters," he said. Now that he had started, he couldn't stop. "And they had guns. They killed my friend, the man who was helping me. Please, I was just trying to get away."

The door opened, but Brandon had already dropped the hand holding the soup. It wouldn't have mattered anyway. The woman remained out of view.

"Why were they chasing you?" she asked.

How did he explain that? "I don't know."

Silence.

"We heard those helicopters," she said. "Yesterday. They were a long ways off, though. Ten, fifteen miles at least. Are you saying that's where you were?"

"Yes." His voice almost a whisper.

"Yeah, yeah, I know. I'll ask him." Her words were almost a mumble.

"I'm sorry?" he asked.

Ignoring him, she said, "You're from over the big ridge, aren't you? From that valley with that big building, and the airstrip?"

She'd seen the Ranch?

"Well?" she asked.

"Yes."

"Owen told me about it. Some kind of militia place, isn't it?"

"I don't know what that means." Was Owen the other person in the house?

"Private army. Anti-government. Racists, maybe? Religious zealots? Both?"

"No. Nothing like that."

"Then what is it?"

Again he paused. He'd never been good at lying, so he was sure she'd see through him if he tried now. "The Resistance."

"The what?"

"Resistance."

She was silent for several seconds. "What exactly are you *resisting*?"

"The, um, end of the world."

He heard her mumble again, but this time couldn't make out what she was saying. It went on for nearly a minute, with pauses here and there, like she was listening. Finally, she stepped into the doorway, the barrel of her gun leading the way.

"Are you just a bunch of brainwashed crazies? Or are you telling the truth?"

There was something in the way she asked the questions that made Brandon think she was inclined to believe him. Like she knew something. Like—

Oh, no. "It started, didn't it?" he asked. "That's why the helicopters attacked us."

"What started?" she asked.

He tried to recall everything he had overheard and learned while he was at the Bunker. "The shipping containers."

157

"What shipping containers?"

"They're all over the place. They've been turned on, haven't they? Is it on the news?"

Her face twisted in confusion. "The news?"

Her response caught him off guard. Maybe it *hadn't* happened.

Before he could say anything more, she shut the door on him. A moment later, he could hear her go upstairs and across the floor. There was a loud scrape, maybe a table being moved or a chair, then nothing for several minutes.

When the floor creaked again, she was walking faster than she had previously. In no time, she was down the stairs and opening the door to his room again.

"Come with me," she said, disappearing into the main part of the basement.

Confused, but hoping this might be his opportunity to get away, he followed her. Once they reached the main floor, the woman crossed over to the sparsely furnished living room, and stopped in front of a plain wooden table with a computer sitting on it. He could hear what sounded like voices coming out of it, but he couldn't see the screen.

Brandon's eyes strayed to the front door. If he moved quickly, he could get outside before she'd be able to do anything.

"Over here," she ordered.

Now, he told himself, *go!* But instead, he walked into the living room, the power of what might be on the computer drawing him forward.

On the screen was the website for one of the cable news networks. It was playing a live feed.

The room around Brandon seemed to disappear as he was sucked into the reports of the strange containers that had been found in dozens of countries, emitting some kind of mist. Authorities were doing everything they could to keep the public away from the boxes, but Brandon was sure that wouldn't matter.

After several minutes, the woman looked at him. "You knew."

He nodded, his eyes not leaving the computer.

"Then tell me what's going to happen next."

"Almost everyone is going to die."

GRISE FIORD
7:41 AM CENTRAL STANDARD TIME

A SPOTLIGHT CUT across the water, lighting up the Zodiac.

"That's far enough," a voice boomed over the electronic megaphone. The speaker was standing on the dock not far from the light, surrounded by several others.

Ash backed off on the Zodiac motor, but didn't bring the small boat to a full stop. He had no intention of using the dock, but he had to get by it to reach the beach closest to the airstrip.

"We just want to get to our plane," Ash yelled back, not sure if they would even be able to hear him.

Something hit the water next to the boat. A split second later, the sound of a rifle shot echoed through the air.

"Any closer and the next one will go through the side of your vessel," the man on the dock announced.

Ash cut the engine.

"Please," he called out. "There's nothing wrong with us. We just need to get to our plane."

No response.

He looked over at Red, who was sitting up front next to Gagnon. "Pass me the radio."

Red tossed it to him. The device was a handheld walkie-talkie with eleven different channel options. They had tried it several times on the way in, but hadn't been able to reach anyone. This time, Ash held it in the air so those on the dock could see it, and yelled, "Channel Four! Channel Four!"

There was movement on the dock, several of the men clustering together in discussion. Finally one of them broke from the crowd and jogged to the shore. They watched his progress until he disappeared into one of the buildings.

"We really need to get Gagnon someplace warm," Red said.

The pilot, whose condition had been improving, had lost a lot of the recently regained color in his cheeks.

There was a pop over the radio, then, "This is Grise Fiord calling party on boat."

Ash pushed the transmit button. "This is Daniel Ash."

"Mr. Ash, I regret to inform you you're going to have to leave. We can't have you here."

On shore, the man who'd gone into the building reemerged, holding what was undoubtedly a portable radio in his hand.

"All we need to do is get to our plane so we can leave."

"Plane?"

"The jet parked on your strip. That's ours."

"Hold on."

They watched the man run down the dock to the others. There was another conference, then a different man broke from the crowd and headed to shore.

"Listen," Ash said into the radio. "We'll go directly to the airstrip. We won't come near anyone."

"Just stay where you are," the man said.

Several minutes passed before the person who had left returned with someone new. When they reached the group, the radio crackled to life again.

"Ash? Is that you?"

"Harlan?"

"Yeah, it's me." Harlan Pinto was the pilot of their private jet. "Where's the seaplane?"

"No time right now. Tell the men there with you we just want to get to the jet and that's it."

"They understand that, but I'm told they're not comfortable with you coming ashore at all. Everyone's freaked out about what's going on in the rest of the world. The news have been showing the video Tamara Costello made telling everyone it's a biological attack. People here have created a kind of reverse quarantine zone."

"Let me talk to the man in charge," Ash said. "But you stay close and listen in."

"Okay. Just a second."

A pause, then, "This is Gerald McKay."

"Mr. McKay, you're in charge of Grise Fiord?"

"That's right." McKay had a rough, smoker's voice.

"I can make you a deal, and guarantee that no one in your town will ever get sick by what's happening elsewhere."

"So can I. That's why we can't allow you to come ashore."

"My guarantee works no matter who comes ashore, now or in the future."

"And exactly how can you do that?"

"By providing you all with a vaccine."

McKay fell silent. In the lights on the dock, Ash could see the men talking to each other. They seemed to be directing much of their attention at Harlan.

When things settled down, McKay came back on. "How is it you have a vaccine for a disease some terrorists just released in the last twenty-four hours?"

"It's not just any disease, Mr. McKay. It's Sage Flu." He paused, letting the reality of that sink in. "We've had the vaccine ready for some time now, knowing the day would come when these terrorists tried it again. We'd hoped to stop them, but…"

"Bullshit. You're just saying anything to get us to allow you ashore. You know so much about this, maybe you're already infected."

"What do you have to lose? Harlan will get it for you. You can choose to take it or not after that. But I'd take it if I were you."

"Maybe it's water, or even poison. Hell, it could even be a vitamin shot. You think we're going to believe you'd show up *right now* with a cure for something we're not even sure exists yet?"

Ash would not get through to them. He could see that.

"Hang on," he said to Chloe and Red.

He restarted the engine.

"What are you doing?" McKay asked.

Ash tossed the radio on the floor, gunned the motor, and headed around the end of the dock in an arc he hoped would make them harder to hit.

"You'd better be going back out to sea! You're not wanted here!" McKay yelled at them.

Once he cleared the dock, Ash aimed the boat at the spot on the shore that would put them just below the road leading to the airfield.

"They're heading off the dock," Chloe said. "You want to share your plan?"

"Get to the plane."

She smirked. "Brilliant. But I guess it's better to die from a gunshot than freeze to death out here on the water."

"I'd rather not do either."

As they drew closer to the shore, Red said, "Ice ahead, all the way to the beach."

"How far does it come out?" Ash asked.

"Looks about twenty-five feet."

"All right. Let's hope this thing rides the ice better than Gagnon's plane did!"

"Seriously?" Chloe asked.

"You have a better idea?"

She stared at him for a moment, then shook her head.

Ash opened up the motor as fast as it would go, building up speed while he still could.

"Here it comes!" Red yelled.

At the last second, Ash killed the motor and pushed it down, so that the propeller end lifted out of the water instead of jamming into the ice and stopping them cold.

The boat skidded across the surface, slewing left and right, then turned until they were sideways to the beach, with only their momentum keeping them headed in the right direction.

"Bump!" Red said.

With a loud thump, the boat jumped up and slammed back down. Ash shot out a hand and grabbed Chloe, barely stopping her from flying over the side.

As they passed from the ice onto the rocky beach, there was a rip followed by the loud hiss of air, and the inflatable sides of the boat began to collapse.

Ash was the first out. He grabbed Gagnon's legs and said, "Come on. We've got to keep moving."

With a grunt, Chloe crawled out after him. Red shook his head as if he were dazed, then took a hold of Gagnon's shoulders. The two men lifted the pilot out of the boat, and followed Chloe up to the road.

From that point, it was just over a quarter-mile to the small airfield. They headed toward it as fast as they could go, but made it only fifty yards before they heard running feet behind them.

"Stop!" a man yelled. It was McKay's voice, though unaided by the radio now.

"Keep moving," Ash whispered.

"Dammit, stop!"

They didn't even pause.

There was a double crack of gunfire and two bullets screamed by them, one on either side. They still didn't slow.

"Don't make us shoot you!" McKay yelled.

"We're not making you do anything," Ash called out.

Another gunshot, this bullet sailing over their heads.

Red looked over at Ash, worried.

"Keep going," Ash told him.

There were three more shots before they reached the plane, but none hit them. As they neared the aircraft, the side door opened and Barry Kincaid, the copilot, looked out.

"Ash!" he said, surprised. "You made it." Then he noticed the others coming behind them with guns. "Oh, shit."

"Get the plane ready for takeoff," Ash ordered.

With a nod, Barry disappeared back into the plane.

"You first," Ash told Red as they reached the short stairway to the entrance. As soon as they got Gagnon inside, Ash passed the man's legs off to Chloe, and headed back toward the door.

"Where are you going?" she asked.

"Get him comfortable and warmed up. I'll just be a

163

minute."

A few feet past the door was a storage compartment. He opened it, pulled out a two-by-ten-inch blue box, and climbed outside.

As his feet hit the ground, the plane's engines growled to life. Gathered in a line about fifty feet away from the plane were the men who'd been on the dock. There were nine of them, ten counting Harlan, whom they were holding back.

"What the hell do you think you're doing?" McKay's voice came out of a red-bearded man standing near the middle of the group.

"Leaving," Ash said.

"You shouldn't have come ashore. You may have exposed us all."

"Lucky for you, I didn't." Ash leaned down and set the box on the ground.

"What's that?"

Ash kept his eyes on McKay and nodded toward Harlan. "Let my friend go, and I'll tell you."

McKay looked over at the jet's pilot. "Larry, let him go."

The man holding Harlan's arm looked confused. "But don't we need—"

"Just let him go," McKay said. "What are we going to do? Keep him prisoner?"

The other man reluctantly let go of the pilot's arm.

Harlan wasted no time getting back to the plane.

"Go inside and get ready," Ash whispered as he neared. "We leave as soon as I get back on board."

"You got it."

As soon as Harlan was safely on the plane, Ash pointed at the box. "Inside is the vaccine I was talking about. There are instructions for dosage. No needles, though. You'll have to provide those yourself."

"How can we believe it's really a vaccine?"

Ash shrugged. "I guess you can't. Either take a chance or don't. But as I said before, I'd take it if I were you."

He turned and climbed aboard the plane. After the door was shut, he checked to make sure the others were ready, took a seat next to a window, and turned on the intercom to the cockpit.

"You guys set up there?" he asked.

"We're ready," Harlan replied.

"Then let's go."

"Where to?"

"Home."

20

PEREZ HAD ONLY slept four hours since waking at six a.m. the day before. After the video conference call with the executive committee, he had spent much of his time gathering and analyzing the latest observations on how Implementation Day was proceeding.

It had always been believed that panic would set in once people realized that the shipping containers weren't isolated events. The quarantine areas around the containers were also foreseen, but the Project had been overly generous when it predicted how quickly they would be implemented. The reality turned out to be much slower, allowing considerably more of the KV-27a aerosol to find suitable hosts.

Monitoring software indicated a total of twenty-seven IDMs were non-functioning. Three of these had failed to start up in the first place. Eight had suffered some kind of internal malfunction during the delivery process. And sixteen had been destroyed when their self-destruct systems kicked in, either by the box being moved or someone trying to get inside.

The produce sprayers that had been installed in hundreds of grocery stores across North America and at a few chains in Europe would, Perez surmised, prove to be less effective. While they were working fine, the panic was keeping most people at home, and many of the markets had closed.

On the success side was the Pishon Chem malaria project. He'd been concerned that the fear created by the shipping containers might cause some of the nations involved to call off the spraying, but it had done just the opposite. Many governments, he realized, were hoping that the "miracle" formula would not only kill malaria-bearing mosquitoes, but also neutralize whatever the shipping containers were belching out.

Perez couldn't help but allow himself a smile. If the virus worked as it was supposed to, and with the coverage they'd been able to achieve so far, the Project's planned mop-up of survivors might be scaled back.

With everything going well, Perez turned to consolidating his power. There was no question that the only way the Project would truly succeed was to have a single leader—him. The committee would no longer be necessary. However, that didn't mean *a* committee couldn't be useful, perhaps one to help guide policy, though in reality, he would be the one steering everything.

Easily doable. In fact, most of the current committee members would be fine additions to the new one. Dr. Lassiter would be a pushover, and Perez was confident he could make Tolliver and Halverson see things his way, too.

Nakamura, on the other hand, was a problem.

Perez had met people like her before. They liked to be part of the in-crowd, and would feverishly defend their exclusivity whether it was a logical move or not. They were the kind of people who always thought they knew better though they seldom did.

The kind of people who would never be helpful to the cause.

How Nakamura had reached the position she had, he didn't know. In his opinion, someone had made a mistake, and as a revamped Project Eden set about creating the new world, there would be no room for mistakes.

Perhaps if she had been located in Europe or Asia, he'd have given her a pass—for a little while, anyway—but the fact that she was at NB89 near Seattle made dealing with the situation so much easier.

He thought it was important to not just delegate the task to someone else, but to also be a part of it. After all, in his past life—the life that had ended when Bluebird fell out of contact—*he* had been the one sent out to handle these kinds of issues.

The phone rang right on time.

"Yes?"

"Your conference call is ready, Mr. Perez," Claudia said.

"Thank you."

He hung up and turned to his computer. A moment later he was looking at Patricia Nakamura sitting smugly in her office.

"Mr. Perez, I'm not sure what you want to discuss, but it seems to me anything we need to talk about should be done in one of our committee meetings."

"Of course it would seem that way to you."

"Excuse me?"

"You perceive the world through an unfortunate filter."

"I don't know what you're talking about. I think we're done here."

She reached for her keyboard to cut off the call, and hit the appropriate key, but, as Perez knew would happen, their connection remained live.

"What's wrong with this?" she said to herself.

She hit the keyboard over and over but nothing happened.

Perez touched the cell phone sitting on his desk. On it was a prewritten text:

NOW

He hit SEND.

"Be careful you don't break that," he said.

"Shut up," she told him.

She reached for the monitor, going for the button that would turn off the screen. Once more, she was stymied.

Frustrated, she stood up and leaned toward the monitor,

her head moving out of sight as she undoubtedly searched for the power cord.

"I wouldn't do that," he said.

"Try to stop me," she shot back.

It was the perfect cue, and though the door didn't open for another couple of seconds, it worked well enough.

She looked up. "Who are you?"

Sims walked in with two of his team behind him.

"Ma'am, please have a seat," he said.

"What is this? What's going on?" Nakamura looked back at the monitor. "This is *your* doing, isn't it? Tell these men to leave. They have no right to be here."

"Actually, you're the one without any rights now," Perez said.

One of Sims's men pushed Nakamura back into her chair.

"Hey!" she yelled. She started to get back up, but changed her mind and reached for the phone on her desk. She punched in a number before she raised the receiver to her ear. When she did, she looked at the monitor again. "Dr. Lassiter will deal with you."

Perez gave her a halfhearted smile.

After a moment, she looked at the phone, used her finger to disconnect the call, and listened again. The anger on her face intensified. "It's not working! What did you do to it?"

Perez leaned forward. "Ms. Nakamura, the Project thanks you for your service, but regrets to inform you that you are no longer necessary to its future success."

"The *Project* thanks me?" While there was still anger in her voice, it was now tinged with fear. "You're not the Project. You don't get to make that kind of decision."

"That's where you're wrong. I *am* the Project, and your failure to realize that is the reason my men are there now. But know this. When the trigger is pulled—"

"Wait! No!" she blurted out, her voice full of fear and desperation.

"—it's not being pulled by the man there with you. It's being pulled by me."

"Mr. Perez, I...I'm sorry. I didn't understand the sit—"

"That's right. You didn't."

Perez nodded once. Behind Nakamura, Sims raised his gun, put it to the back of her head, and removed her from the Project.

21

SOMEONE WAS SHAKING Martina's shoulder.

With a groan, she tried to turn away. It was much too early, she was sure of it. By the time she'd gotten home and fallen asleep the night before, it was after two in the morning. She had promised herself she really would sleep as late as possible today, noon if she could manage it.

"Martina, come on. Wake up."

She opened her eyes, surprised. Her father was standing over her. He *never* woke her up.

"What's going on?" she asked, her voice still full of sleep.

"Get up, get dressed, then come downstairs."

She glanced at the clock by her bed and groaned. She had barely slept six hours. "Did I forget something? Are we supposed to be somewhere?"

But her father was already heading out the door. "Just get ready and come down." With that, he was gone.

She sat up and blinked several times, trying to shake the sleep from her system. As she swung her legs off the bed, she noticed that several drawers of her dresser were open. She hadn't left them that way the night before. When she got up and walked over to shut them, she was surprised to see they were empty.

What the hell?

She checked the other drawers. Several pairs of pants were missing, and her sweaters, too. Then she noticed that someone had laid some clothes out for her on her desk chair.

More confused than ever, she pulled them on and hurried downstairs to find out what was up.

A cold wind was blowing in through the open front door. Out the living room window she could see her father and brother over near the garage, putting something in the trunk of the car. Above them, high gray clouds dimmed the day.

Something banged in the kitchen.

"Mom?"

Martina stepped off the last tread of the staircase onto the cold tile floor and walked to the back of the house.

Her mother was near the kitchen sink. On the counter in front of her were boxes and packages of food. It looked to Martina like everything from inside the cabinets had been pulled down. Her mother was going through it all, sorting them into groups.

"Mom, what's going on?"

Her mother jerked around with a start. "Oh, Martina. I didn't hear you come down." She attempted to give her daughter a smile, but quickly gave up. Her eyes strayed down to Martina's feet. "Where are your shoes?"

"Where I left them when I took them off last night," Martina said, as if it should have been obvious.

"Well, hurry and put them on."

"Why? What's going on?"

"Just do it!" her mother said sharply.

Martina took a step back, surprised by the intensity of her mother's tone. "Okay. No problem."

Her mother closed her eyes for a moment. "I'm sorry. Please, just…put them on, okay?"

"Sure. I'm putting them on."

Martina retrieved her shoes from the entryway, slipped her feet inside, and laced them up. From a peg by the door, she grabbed her zip-up hoodie and headed outside.

Her dad and brother were still at the back of the car. They had lowered the hood of the trunk, but it looked like there was too much inside for it to close all the way.

"Donny, grab me some rope," her father said.

Her brother ran into the garage.

"Dad, would you please tell me what's going on?" Martina said.

Her father glanced over. "Good, you're dressed. There are some water jugs in the garage. Can you put them in the backseat for me?"

"Dad!"

He looked at her again, and finally seemed to register her earlier question. "Did you see the TV?"

"The TV?" She shook her head. "It was off."

He stepped over to her and put his hands on her arms. "I don't want you to panic."

"You mean like you guys already seem to be doing?"

"The shipping containers they've been finding all over the place? The rumor is it's some kind of biological attack."

"What?" She pulled away from him, her mind assaulted by memories of the outbreak that had almost killed her. That, too, had been a biological attack.

"I said, don't panic."

"What is it? Who did it? Do they even know for sure?" The questions jumped out rapid fire.

"The government's not saying anything yet, but that doesn't matter right now. What we need to focus on is getting out of here."

She grew still. "Getting out of here? Did they find one in town?"

"No," he said quickly. "But they're all over Los Angeles, and some in Bakersfield and Las Vegas."

They were surrounded.

"I don't want to be here when someone who's been infected shows up," he explained.

"But where are we going?"

"The Fullers' cabin. They went back east for the holidays, so no one's there."

The Fullers' cabin was in the Sierra Nevada Mountains, not that far away. Martina and her family had borrowed the place for a week just that past summer.

He looked her in the eye. "I really need your help. Are you going to be okay?"

The person she'd been before the previous spring would have probably argued with him, saying he was overreacting, and that they should just wait and it would probably turn out to be nothing. But coming so close to death changed all that.

"I'll get the water," she said.

"Thanks, sweetie."

THEY TOOK THE back way to the cabin, using one of the winding roads that went up through a steep valley on the desert side of the mountains. When they'd taken the same road in the past, it had always been sparsely traveled. This time, there were dozens of vehicles, all heading up.

"Looks like other people were thinking the same thing," Martina said.

Her father barely nodded in acknowledgment. He had a tight grip on the wheel, and his mood had darkened every time he glanced at the cars behind them. She knew he'd been hoping they'd be alone.

At the top of the canyon, the road crested over a pass into a high plain, where the desert gave way to the thin fringes of a forest that thickened with every passing mile. Here and there were small patches of snow, a few inches deep at best. That might change soon, Martina thought. The clouds that had been hanging high above their desert valley were much lower here, and were dark and heavy with moisture.

"You brought the tire chains, right?" she asked.

"Of course we did," Donny said. "They're in the back. What do you think? That we're stupid?"

He was fourteen and in that wonderful phase that made Martina want to be nowhere near him pretty much all the time. Still, she held back the response that wanted to jump from her lips. It wouldn't serve any purpose, and he was just being a kid anyway. The restraint was a grown-up move on her part, one she would have patted herself on the back for if she wasn't so scared.

"Maybe we should try the radio again," her mother suggested. She reached over and flipped the radio back on.

The narrow valley they had driven up from the desert had blocked the signal to their satellite radio, so they had kept it off. On again, it tried hard to reestablish a signal, but there were just too many trees and mountain peaks getting in the way.

"We'll check again at the cabin," her mother announced, turning it off again. "I'm sure it will work there."

In a way, Martina was happy they weren't able to pick up anything. When they'd listened to the news before they lost reception, there had really been nothing new, just the same reports and speculation over and over again. It had started to drive her crazy.

The old highway through the forest had several intersecting roads branching off from it. Here and there cars would turn off, heading to whatever destination they had in mind. When the Gables finally reached the turnoff for the Fullers' cabin, there were only two other cars left behind them.

Though the new road was unpaved and bumpy, Martina's father seemed less tense.

The change didn't last long. A few minutes later, his disposition reverted back to what it had been at the beginning of their trip. They were skirting the edge of a large meadow that allowed them to see a good portion of the road behind them. There, about a quarter-mile back, was one of the cars that had been on the main road.

"Relax, Ken," Martina's mother said to her husband. "There are a lot of places out this way."

He grunted, but said nothing.

A few seconds later Donny said, "Isn't that the Webers' car?"

Martina looked back at the other vehicle. It *did* kind of look like the Webers' car, but there were probably about a thousand other models they could have said that about.

Mr. Weber worked in the same building as Martina's

dad. He and his wife had three kids, a set of twins who were high school seniors this year, and a younger girl who was either a sophomore or freshman. The Webers were part of the same bridge club her parents were in, and the families had occasionally done things together in the past.

The meadow fell away as they reentered the woods, and the car—the Webers' or not—disappeared with it. As soon as it was out of sight, Martina's father increased their speed.

Her mother grabbed the dash. "Ken, please. You're going to get into an accident."

The car vibrated as it bounced over the road, but Martina's father didn't slow down.

"Ken!"

As the road bent to the left, the back end of the car fishtailed for a second before it came back under control.

"For God's sake! We're not going to have to worry about whatever's happening everywhere else. *You're* going to kill us!"

He leaned forward, his chin nearly touching the wheel as he gripped it more tightly.

"Ken!"

After a couple seconds, he let out a breath and settled back against the seat, slowing the car.

Martina's mother looked at him, her eyes wide. It appeared as if she was going to yell at him, but, like Martina had done earlier with her brother, her mother held her tongue and turned back to watch the road.

They almost missed the turnoff to the Fullers' place. It was Donny who pointed just in time at the tree with the missing branch that marked the road. Martina's father slammed on the brakes, kicking up a small dust cloud, and made the turn.

The dirt road was really just a long driveway that led across a portion of the twenty acres the Fullers owned. The rains from the previous spring had created a wash down the middle that had unevenly eroded the dirt surface. Martina's father had to slow the car down to a crawl several times, and even then couldn't avoid scraping the undercarriage.

The cabin was tucked within the trees, so it appeared almost out of nowhere after a leisurely curve to the left. There were no lights on inside, and no other cars parked out front.

As soon as they pulled to a stop near the front door, Martina's father said, "Let's get everything inside right away," and climbed out.

Donny jumped out after him, and Martina reached for her door handle to do the same, but then she realized her mother hadn't moved.

A sniffle. Low, as if it wasn't supposed to be heard.

"Mom?" Martina said.

Her mother shook her head. "Go help your father," she said quickly.

Martina leaned forward between the seats. "Mom, are you all right?"

"I'll be fine."

Martina knew that wasn't true. Her mother's eyes were wet, and a few tears had already traveled down her cheeks. Martina put her arms around her, hugging her as best she could with the seat between them. "It's going to be okay, Mom. We're safe here."

"I know…it's just…it's not a great day for any of us, I guess."

"Yeah, I've had better."

"Me, too," her mother said.

They looked at each other, then Martina grinned, and they both laughed softly.

"I'm fine, I swear," her mother said. "Come on. We should help."

Martina gave her one more squeeze, and they both got out.

The lid of the trunk was open, so Martina couldn't see her dad or brother. As she walked to the back, she realized the lid hid one more thing.

Stopped at the spot where the driveway widened into the area in front of the cabin was the car that had been following them. Now that it was this close, she could see her brother had been right. It *was* the Webers' car.

PALE HORSE

Mr. Weber was behind the wheel, his wife in the front passenger seat, and their three daughters in back. Martina knew the twins. She liked Riley but wasn't fond of Laurie. For twins, they were nothing alike. She didn't know the youngest girl, Pamela, very well.

Martina's father was staring at the other car. In his hands was a rifle. She knew he had a few guns he'd inherited from his brother who'd passed away a few years before, but it had never crossed her mind that he'd bring them along. It was logical, she guessed, but surprising.

"Ken, what are you doing?" her mother said as she came around from the other side of the car.

"You and the kids, get in the house," he said.

"Put that down. You're going to hurt someone."

"If I have to, I will."

"You're talking crazy, Ken. That's the Webers. They're our *friends*."

Just then, the door on the other car opened, and Mr. Weber climbed out. He held up his hands to show he had nothing in them. "Hey, no need for a gun," he called out. "Just looking for a place to hide out, like you."

"This place is taken," Martina's father said.

"This is the Fullers' place, isn't it? I've heard them talking about it."

"Get back in your car, Mark. Find someplace else."

"Be reasonable. It's just me and my family. We're scared like you. Wouldn't it be better if we worked together? Make things easier."

"There's not enough to take care of both us and you."

"You mean food? That's not a problem. I've got a whole car full of food. We just need a roof to sleep under. Someplace where we can stay warm."

"It's a small place. There's not enough—"

"Just the floor. We can sleep there. Come on, you don't want to do this."

"He's right," Martina's mother whispered. "This isn't the type of people we are. And if they've brought food, that will help us, too." She touched her husband's shoulder. "There's enough room inside for all of us."

"You followed us up," Martina's dad said to Mr. Weber.

"Not on purpose," Mr. Weber said. "At least not until we reached the mountain pass and I realized you guys were ahead of us. I just thought it would be good to stick with friends."

"Ken, just let them join us," Martina's mom said. "You're not going to shoot them, for God's sake. They'll freeze out here if they don't find shelter."

Martina's father remained rigid for several more seconds, then his shoulders sagged. He lowered the rifle so that the barrel was pointing at the ground. "All right. You can stay. But if anyone else comes, we turn them away."

"Sure," Mr. Weber said. "Sure, of course."

He brought his car over and together the families started unloading the two vehicles. They were only halfway done when the snow started to fall, so they rushed to get the rest inside.

"For a minute there, I was afraid your dad would shoot us," Riley Weber said to Martina as the two of them made hot chocolate for everyone later.

"He was just trying to protect us, that's all."

"Yeah, I know. Still, it was kind of freaky."

"Sorry," Martina said.

Riley shrugged. "It's okay. Dad's been pretty crazy himself. When they started reporting about the shipping containers yesterday, he called my mom and told her she needed to get home right away."

Martina looked at the other girl. "Where was she?"

"Christmas shopping. Down in L.A."

Martina felt a chill run down her arms.

"Hey, don't worry," Riley said. "I know what you're thinking, but it's okay. There weren't any of those things anywhere near where she was."

"How do you know?"

"She didn't see any and there weren't any reports of them on the news. Look." Riley glanced over at her mother in the living room. "She's fine."

Martina followed her gaze. Mrs. Weber did, indeed, look

fine. If she'd been exposed, it had happened almost a day before, and surely she would have shown signs of something by now. Still, shouldn't Martina say something to her parents, just in case?

She decided to tell her mom; she'd know what to do. Her dad would just panic.

"I think it's ready," Riley said.

Together, the girls poured the hot chocolate into mugs and carried them out.

As soon as she found a moment, Martina took her mother aside and told her what Riley had said. Her mother was concerned, but not overly worried.

"Should we tell Dad?" Martina asked.

Her mom patted her on the arm and smiled. "He's under a lot of stress right now. Best I'll have a little talk with Mrs. Weber. For now, we'll just keep this to ourselves."

In that, Martina's mother was right.

22

"WE'RE SWITCHING NOW to our Pentagon correspondent, Brian Keeter."

The image of the anchor, Carl Morgan, cut to a split screen, with Morgan on the left, and Brian Keeter on the right, standing in front of a wooden paneled wall that had several flagpoles in front of it.

"Brian," Morgan said. "What's the latest from there?"

"Carl, while spokesmen here are not saying anything official at the moment, sources have told us that scientists working at the US Army Medical Research Institute have been able to confirm that the substance being released by the shipping containers is consistent across all the locations they've been able to test."

"Biological?" Morgan asked.

"Again, nothing on the record, but yes, Carl. My sources say the institute has been able to precisely identify the biolo—"

The screen with Keeter's image suddenly went black. Morgan looked momentarily confused, but quickly regained his composure.

"Apparently we're having some signal problems with the feed from the Pentagon. We'll go back to Brian Keeter as soon as we're able to reestablish the link. In the meantime, we've received word that the planned test destruction of one of the boxes has been delayed. No reason has been given, but our experts speculate…"

THE MEDIA REHASH CENTRAL BLOG
NEW POST
1:16 PM EASTERN STANDARD TIME

NOT SURE HOW many of you were watching PCN a few minutes ago, but something I would classify as odd just occurred. Resident PCN talking head Carl Morgan was having a discussion with field reporter Brian Keeter when Keeter's feed was suddenly cut off (Keeter was the reporter who broke the Martin Hills bribery story back in August).

I don't know about you, but it sure sounded like he was about to reveal what these shipping containers are spitting out on everyone. He was able to at least report that it *is* biological, not that that's a big stretch. We've all been presuming that. Still, I think it's the first time anyone has said it as definitively as he did. Well, other than the woman purporting to be Tamara Costello in the viral YouTube video.

Morgan played it off like it was a satellite issue. I call bullshit. I think Keeter's feed was cut at the source.

Oh, did I mention? He was broadcasting from the PENTAGON!

WHITE HOUSE BRIEFING ROOM FEED
CARRIED LIVE ON ALL MAJOR BROADCAST
AND CABLE NETWORKS WORLDWIDE
1:20 PM EASTERN STANDARD TIME

LOWER THIRD GRAPHIC over man walking to podium:

WHITE HOUSE PRESS SECRETARY LIONEL SCHULTZ

SCHULTZ: I have a brief statement, and will be taking no questions after.

(Groans from crowd, and shouts of complaint.)

SCHULTZ: Please, settle down.

(Noise diminishes, but crowd restless.)

SCHULTZ (reading from sheet of paper): Progress has been made in identifying the nature of the threat to our nation and our friends around the world, and steps are being taken to mitigate the problem.

PAUL LUNDEN, REPORTER, ABC NEWS: What steps?

SHEILA BLACK, REPORTER, ASSOCIATED PRESS: What's the nature?

SCHULTZ (still reading): The president has been apprised of every new development, and remains focused on dealing with this issue head-on. At two p.m. eastern time, he will address the nation.

MARY WHITMORE, REPORTER, BBC: Will he be in here?

KYLE NORRIS, REPORTER, PCN: Will he be taking questions?

SCHULTZ (looking at the press pool): The president will be addressing the nation from the Oval Office, and no, there will be no questions. Thank you.

(As Schultz heads off stage, pandemonium breaks out.)

TRANSCRIPT
PRESIDENT'S ADDRESS
2:03 PM EASTERN STANDARD TIME

MY FELLOW AMERICANS and citizens in nations throughout the world, over the last day and a half, we have all watched as signs of what we now know is a massive, unprecedented terrorist attack have appeared. The shipping containers we have seen on our televisions have been found in hundreds of cities around the globe. We have been working in conjunction with other governments to 1) determine exactly what the threat is, and 2) figure out how it can be stopped.

I wish I could bring you better news. Scientists working at both the US Army Medical Research Institute and the Centers for Disease Control have been able to isolate the bio-agent and identify it. With the exception of a few minor variations, it resembles the Sage Flu virus that devastated the Mojave Desert area of California last spring, and caused a minor outbreak in St. Louis less than a week ago. It is believed that while quarantine measures have helped isolate many of these viral bombs, enough of the virus has already been released to cause catastrophic problems.

As you know, moving the containers has not worked,

nor have attempts to disassemble them. We had hoped to destroy them, and, in fact, tried to do just that several hours ago. Unfortunately, much of the virus was not destroyed, and instead was carried off in the wind.

We continue to try to find methods of shutting the containers off, but I will not lie to you. We believe it will be too little, too late.

Because of this, I have ordered a complete shutdown of all nonessential government agencies, and all private and public businesses. I've also just signed an executive order declaring a nationwide state of emergency and instituting a twenty-four-hour curfew. Military personnel will be joining local law enforcement to see that everyone remains safe.

Contact with people outside your home should be avoided. To that end, we ask that you all go home, seal your windows and doors, and remain there until it can be determined that it's okay to go outside again.

We continue working on solving this crisis. Once we do, we will then focus on bringing to justice those responsible.

Until that time, may God save us all.

THE MEDIA REHASH CENTRAL BLOG
NEW POST
2:09 PM EASTERN STANDARD TIME

I'M NUMB, AND if anyone is actually reading this, I have no doubt you are, too. My first thoughts after listening to the president was to think back over the last thirty-six hours, and remember all the places I've been and people I've talked to.

There've been a lot. It also doesn't help that I live in New York City, where I've lost count of how many containers they've found. I'm pretty sure I'm screwed.

I received an email from a loyal follower right after the president's address. He said, "He [the president] didn't say it, but what he's done is declare martial law. I'm not sure he has the right to do that. We need to challenge this. Our personal liberties are at stake!"

Normally, I would agree. You all know me well enough to know that anything that encroaches so blatantly on our rights would be more than enough for me to raise the alarm.

But, brother, I've got to tell you, on this one you're an idiot. What the president was saying is that we are going to get hit, and hit HARD. He's just trying to save whatever lives he can. If that means we need to hermetically seal ourselves inside steel drums, then that's what we should do.

This is about survival now, not our rights as citizens.

I'm going to take a break, see how this all plays out. And I'm also going to turn off comments because at this point, what's there really to say? Hopefully, I'll be back when it's all done. If not, well…

23

ALL WORK IN the Bunker came to a standstill as the president spoke.

"It's not going to work," Rachel said once the short speech was over.

"It could save some lives," Matt said. "It all depends on how long the virus stays active. If someone can wait it out, they'll have a chance."

"For now, maybe. But we both know it will come back, like flu does every year. It'll become part of the biosphere. If it doesn't kill them now, it'll kill them next time."

"We'll just have to get them the vaccine first."

She stared at her brother. "And how are we supposed to do that? We only have a limited supply."

"At the moment," he corrected her. "We'll continue making it."

"It still might not be enough."

"Or it *might* be."

"We've been doing all we can for years, Matt, and what did that get us? We failed. The Project won. They're going to get their restart, and we can't stop it."

For the first time he noticed the circles under her eyes. "When was the last time you slept?"

She glared at him, then whipped around and half ran toward the door.

"Rachel!" he yelled. He tried to follow her, but with his leg, he could only go so fast. "Rachel!"

Just before he got to the door, Christina called out, "Matt, I've got the men at the emergency tunnel on the phone. They've got the door open and are about to go through. They want to know if you still want to go with them."

Matt paused. If he kept after his sister, it would just make her more upset. What she really needed was sleep, not talk. Reluctantly, he said, "Tell them I'm on my way."

THE ONLY WAY out of the Bunker now was via a long tunnel that exited through a hidden hatch in the woods. Similar to the other two entrances, both of which were now unusable because of the fire, a large blast-like door had been slid into place when they went to full cover, sealing off the underground facility from the tunnel and the world above.

While closing the massive door was easy, the built-in safeguards made opening it again considerably more difficult. It had taken the team over an hour to slide it open wide enough for people to pass through. When Matt arrived, all six of them were standing by, geared up and ready to move.

"Let's go," he said, not wanting to waste any more time. Brandon and Hayes had been out there for over twenty-four hours now, and he would not relax until they were found.

One of the team members handed Matt a coat and a pistol. One by one, they passed through the opening into the tunnel.

The air grew colder as they approached the far end. When they reached the hatch, Matt toggled his radio.

"We're ready to go up," he said.

"All clear," Christina replied through his earpiece.

The lead man, Miller, released the lock on the hatch and carefully lowered the unhinged edge, revealing a metal plate above covering the hole. On top of the plate would be a layer of dead needles and loose branches providing the perfect camouflage to anyone looking for it on the other side. Working with two of his men—Reubens and Barlow—he maneuvered the plate up and to the side, clearing the way.

As soon as they were all out of the tunnel, they headed down the road toward the barn. Hayes and Brandon had been heading back to the Bunker from there when the helicopters were spotted, so that was the logical starting point for Matt and his men.

"I've got footprints," Miller called out several minutes later.

Matt limped over, his knee bothering him more than he was willing to admit. Miller was kneeling down, studying several prints.

"Theirs?" Matt asked.

"Must be," Miller said. He pointed at the ground. "There's a big set and a small set."

"This is as far as they got?"

"I think so."

"Then they must have headed into the woods from here."

"I'm not so sure about that."

"What do you mean?"

"Looks to me like they headed back toward the barn."

"Back to the barn?"

"Yeah. See?" Miller stood, pointed at some more tracks, and followed them down the road a dozen feet before stopping. He glanced at Matt. "They keep going."

"Then we follow them."

Why in the world would Jon take Brandon back to the barn? Matt wondered as they headed down the road. He had told Hayes to go into the forest and find one of the emergency supply stashes before hiking out to the highway. Going to the barn would have been extremely risky. The helicopters would have surely checked it.

As they neared the barn, two of the men ran ahead, while the rest continued following the footprints.

Miller stopped, still watching the ground. "It's kind of a mess here. Tracks going to the barn and to the woods over there." He pointed to the right.

The men who'd gone to the barn jogged back up.

"Well?" Matt asked.

"No one's there, but someone was," one of the men said. "All the stalls are empty, and the horses are gone."

Matt looked past the two men at the barn, searching for any sign of the animals, but none were around.

"Could they have ridden away on one of them?" Barlow asked.

That thought had crossed Matt's mind, too, but it would have been a huge risk. The attack team from Project Eden could easily have spotted them on a horse, and chased them down with one of their helicopters.

"I think they went into the woods on foot," Miller said. He crouched down next to the footprints. "These leading toward the trees? They're on top of the other ones, so they're the last ones made."

"They could have doubled back to the barn on the grass," Barlow argued.

Miller shrugged, conceding the point, but not seeming to buy into it.

Matt looked at the barn, then at the woods. "I think the horses were only a diversion. Jon wouldn't have risked taking one. We go into the woods." He touched the transmit button on the radio. "Christina, what's the closest emergency supply location from the barn?"

There was a pause, then she said, "There are three within a two-mile radius. One is a mile and a half northwest of you, one almost due west three-quarters of a mile, and one is northeast just over half a mile. I can send you all of their coordinates, if you'd like."

Matt looked down at the prints Miller had found. The set on top was heading east. It was also the only logical direction to find civilization.

"Just the last one for now," he said. "We'll check there first."

THERE WAS NO question that the emergency stash in the east was the one Jon and Brandon had visited. It was half uncovered, and many of the supplies were gone.

Matt shone his flashlight into the tube. Per procedure, all the empty bags from the supplies they had taken had been put back inside, but, oddly, they had all been scrunched toward the bottom, like someone had crawled into the tube and stamped them down with their feet. An unnecessary step. Also, why had Hayes left the top half off? He should have replaced the metal plate and pushed the loose ground cover back over it.

The men from the team were scattered around the area, searching every square inch for any clues.

"Anything?" Matt called out.

"They walked in together from over there," Miller said, pointing in the same direction they had come from. "I also found two sets of prints heading away. They're both going in the same general direction, but they're not on the same path."

"You mean they split up?"

"Or left at different times. Which is pretty much the same thing, I guess."

The team broke into two groups—Matt, Barlow, and two of the other men following Brandon's prints; and Miller and the other two following Hayes's. It wasn't long before the two sets of tracks diverged enough that the groups were no longer in sight of each other.

There was only one reason Matt could think of for Hayes and Brandon to split up. Someone from the Project Eden team must have been in the area. That also could explain the compacted bags in the storage tube. Perhaps Brandon was hiding inside.

Matt could see the hint of a clearing ahead. Just before they reached it, the radio came to life.

"Matt," Miller said. "You need to come here."

"Where are you?"

"There's a clearing. It's pretty much straight northeast of where—"

"We're just coming to it now," Matt said.

"You'll see us once you get here."

As soon as Matt stepped out from the woods, he spotted the others. Miller and the two men with him were hunched over something on the ground. It wasn't until Matt was a few feet away that he saw the legs of a man.

"Oh, Jesus," he said.

Miller turned. "It's Hayes."

"Dead?"

Miller nodded. "Shot in the back."

Matt knelt down next to Miller and looked at the body. Hayes was lying on his back, part of his chest blown out.

"You turned him over?" Matt asked. If Hayes had been shot in the back, he should have been lying on his stomach.

"No. He was already like this."

So it was either the person who killed him who turned him over, or…

God, let me be wrong.

Matt struggled back to his feet. "We need to look for Brandon," he said loudly enough for all of them to hear. "Spread out. Check everywhere."

After twenty minutes of searching, the only thing they discovered were depressions in the meadow where a helicopter had landed.

That troubled Matt even more. Had they taken Brandon?

They carefully checked the area around where the helicopter had been, but the ground was a mixture of dead grass and leaves, so no footprints had been left behind. No way to know who might have boarded the aircraft.

"Miller," Matt called out. When the man came over, he said, "I want you to do a circuit just outside the clearing. See if you can pick up Brandon's trail again and figure out which way he went."

"No problem."

As Miller started to turn away, Matt said, "Look *very* hard."

24

BRANDON HAD TOLD the woman what he could. The Ranch and the people there, he said nothing about. When she wondered how he knew what he did, he'd kept his mouth shut. He was confident she believed him, though; he could see it in her eyes.

Once she had finished asking him questions, she'd let him get some food from the kitchen, where he noted the back exit out of the corner of his eye. She then ushered him back down to the room in the cellar.

"Take an inventory," she told him, pointing her gun at a clipboard hanging on the wall.

His face scrunched in confusion. "What?"

"Check to make sure everything on that list is still correct."

"Wouldn't you already know that?"

Her mouth tightened into a tense, straight line. "Just do it," she said. She slammed the door closed and locked it again.

Having no intention of counting cans and jars, he had spent most of the morning thinking of ways he could get away. They all came down to the same thing—if the opportunity presented itself, he would just run.

A good enough plan, except for one big problem: the gun. Would she actually take a shot at him? He didn't think so, but it was hard not to remember the hole in Hayes's chest.

PALE HORSE

While he'd been thinking, he could hear the woman walking around upstairs. She seemed to be in constant motion, moving from room to room, pulling open doors, scraping across the floor. She was still alone, though, so maybe the person she lived with wasn't home. He hoped so.

After a while, the woman turned up the volume on her computer so loud that he could hear the *wah-wah-wah* of the voices on the news resonating through the floor. Occasionally, he could even make out a word here and there, but mostly had no idea what was being said.

As the time passed, he started thinking about that coming evening. He didn't want to spend it in the cellar. He wanted to be away from there, as far as possible. He paced back and forth, his anxiety increasing.

Finally, he stopped himself, knowing he needed to distract his mind so he wouldn't wind himself up so much.

He caught a glimpse of the clipboard.

It's better than nothing.

So, despite his earlier decision, he began checking the woman's supplies. In addition to the cans of cream of mushroom soup, there were hundreds of others containing pears, apricots, baked beans, lima beans, peas, pineapple chunks, Spam, and beets, just to name a few. The jars, with the exception of seventy-two containing Ragu spaghetti sauce, were all labeled on the lid and filled with things he guessed the woman had jarred herself—cherry preserves, apple sauce, pickles, stewed tomatoes, and the like.

After a while he started to get hungry again. Checking his watch, he saw that it was already past noon. If she didn't come soon, he might be tempted to open one of the jars. The applesauce looked pretty good.

He was halfway through the final section when he heard the woman coming down the basement stairs. He turned as the door opened, prepared to hand over the inventory, hoping that if he seemed to be cooperating, she might ease up on him a bit.

The look on her face made him forget all about the clipboard in his hand. Her eyes were wide and her mouth slightly open. Stunned was the only word to describe her. It was then that he noticed she wasn't holding her rifle.

"Come," she said. She turned, leaving the door open.

By the time he reached the stairs, she was already at the top. He raced up the steps, and into the kitchen. The woman wasn't there, but he could hear her around the corner in the living room. He looked to the left, taking his first good glimpse of the rear door to the house.

Go!

He started to take a step, then froze in surprise. His backpack. It was sitting by the door, just off to the side.

Run.

This time, it wasn't the sight of his bag that stopped him, but the voice coming from the computer in the other room.

"…again. As the president finished his speech, we received a release from the Department of Homeland Security. A three-hour grace period will start at the top of the hour to allow people to get home. After that, anyone outside without proper authorization will be in violation of the curfew and subject to arrest. The release also lists in detail what you can do to protect yourself and your family in your home. We have posted the document on our website, and will be going over the points in just a few minutes. But first, we're going to replay the president's speech in its entirety."

By the time the news anchor finished speaking, Brandon had moved into the living room. The woman was standing in front of the computer, her eyes glued to the screen. The image on the monitor changed to a familiar one of the president sitting at his desk in the Oval Office.

"My fellow Americans and citizens in nations throughout the world, over the last…"

Brandon listened as the president spoke of the Sage Flu and the measure to stop it that hadn't worked.

Before the president finished, the woman looked over. "You can't fake this. That's really the president. This is really happening."

It was as if at that very moment, the full reality of it hit her. She staggered forward, grabbed for the desk chair, and sank to the floor.

Run! the voice in his head yelled again.

He spotted the rifle. It was clear across the room near the front door. He could easily make it outside before she could grab it.

Still, he hesitated. She hadn't moved since she'd fallen to the floor. Maybe he should help her. She'd probably just been scared when she found him in the garage.

Run!

Instead, he took one step toward her. "Do what they tell you," he said. "I'm sure you'll be all right."

She turned toward him in slow motion. He had expected to see shock and fear on her face. What he saw were unfocused eyes and a strange, crooked smile. She stared at him for a moment, then slowly turned away.

He backed out of the room, and passed quickly through the kitchen. She wouldn't come after him. He knew that now. In fact, he'd be surprised if she moved from where she was before the sun went down. Still—

Run!

He picked up his pack, opened the door, and did just that.

25

SEAN O'BRIEN FELT the sweat running past his ear. He wanted nothing more than to wipe it off, but the biosafe gear he was wearing made that impossible. He looked over at Ryan Dunne and wondered if his partner had the same problem. Ryan, though, looked as calm as ever behind the faceplate of his hood.

"Remind me to talk to whoever designed these things," Sean said. "Would be nice if it had something built in to cool us off."

"Stop complaining."

"You can't tell me you're not hot in there, too."

"What I'm feeling doesn't matter."

They made an odd pair, Sean and Ryan. Sean was the joker, the guy always telling the stories at the pub, while Ryan was all business all the time. But this had translated into a surprisingly strong partnership, and they'd worked well together for the five years they'd both been part of the Protection Branch of An Garda Síochána, Ireland's national police.

While many of those in their branch were geared more toward liaison work with other agencies, Sean and Ryan were situational specialists, called in when something delicate needed handling. Which was why they'd been chosen to try to deactivate one of the shipping containers that had shown up in the city. This particular one was just outside Trinity College, and had been belching out, for hours and hours, what the Americans had just confirmed was a virus.

An area of over half a mile around the box in every direction had already been evacuated. Unfortunately, the residents had fled in a near panic, leaving cars strewn haphazardly throughout the neighborhood. This meant Sean and Ryan had been forced to walk in, wearing the less-than-comfortable suits, instead of riding in most of the way in the back of a truck.

Because neither destroying nor moving the boxes had worked elsewhere, Sean and Ryan were tasked with finding out if they could just be turned off. The fact that this had also been unsuccessfully attempted elsewhere didn't faze their bosses. The men were told to get in there and find a way.

"I could use a pint," Sean said.

"Maybe you can suggest that to the suit designers, too, and they can put in a feeding tube."

"Oh, a joke. What's gotten into you, Mr. Dunne?"

Sean could see Ryan shake his head, but his partner didn't reply.

It was weird to be walking down streets that were usually teeming with students and locals at this time of the evening. It felt like a ghost town. Sean almost expected a tumbleweed to roll across the road, and some eerie organ music to start playing.

But the only unusual sound was the hum, increasing in volume with every block. They knew from overhead surveillance that it was generated by two large fans at the top of the box. They had expected to hear it, but it was still unsettling.

They turned the final corner and stopped as they had their first direct view of the container. According to the reports, a considerable number of the boxes had been found near construction sites. Theirs was no different. It was a block and a half away, sitting in front of an old apartment building in the process of being torn down.

Even from this distance, they could see the slightly

distorted air above the container where the vapor was being pushed out.

"Let's get this done," Ryan said.

Sean turned on the microphone to the radio. "Dani, you have our visual?"

Dani, more formally known as Danielle Sullivan, was handling communications back at the checkpoint.

"Your cameras are working fine," she said. Both men had micro cameras attached inside their hoods at the base of their faceplates. "You're clear to move in."

"Proceeding to the container now."

The two began walking toward the container. Sean wasn't sure what Ryan was feeling, but for him every step took renewed effort, as if the road itself were melting around his feet and holding him down. It didn't help that several droplets of the liquid from the box had landed on his faceplate.

Much too quickly for his taste, they reached the box. Up close, its dark blue metal siding looked worn and in need of fresh paint. With the exception of the roof that shouldn't have been open, it looked like a normal shipping container.

Ryan put a hand on the side. Reluctantly, Sean did the same. The hum that he heard matched the vibration coming through his protective glove. There was no way to describe it other than it felt evil. He could leave his hand there for only a couple of seconds before pulling it away.

"I'll go this way," he said to Ryan, nodding to his left. "Meet you on the other side."

Heading in opposite directions, they circled the container, looking for a way to gain access to the inside. The only thing Sean found were the doors at the short end. Like the other containers in the reports they'd received, the doors had an odd-looking lock system. No one, apparently, had been able to break through it yet—at least not without setting off the explosives inside.

"Anything?" he asked Ryan when they met up in the back.

"Nothing that I could see."

"I'll give the door a try, just in case, but we'll probably have to go in through the top."

"I agree," Ryan said.

"Dani, you got that, right?"

"Got it," she said. "Just be careful, okay?"

"If we were careful, we'd be sitting out there with you."

"Be as careful as you can, then."

While Ryan scoped out the easiest route to the top, Sean went back around to the door on the short side. He gave the handle a try first, but it didn't move. He examined the lock next, hoping to discover some way of disengaging it. As he ran his hand along the backside of the device, the hum and vibration began to fade.

"What did you do?" Ryan asked.

Sean jumped back from the container. "Nothing. Just trying to open the door."

The hum dropped lower and lower in both tone and volume.

"What's going on?" Dani asked.

"It, uh, sounds like it's shutting down," Ryan told her.

"You mean, you did it?"

"We didn't do anything," Sean said. "I tried the door, but others have done that, too, and nothing happened then."

"Maybe our container's different," she suggested.

"I guess it could be," Sean said, but he didn't believe it. Why would it be?

Ryan popped around the corner. "Help me get up on top. I want to take a look inside."

"Use the door," Sean suggested. With the brackets and hinges, it was as close to a ladder as they could get.

Ryan climbed up and looked over the side.

"Yeah. It's off," he said, not hiding his surprise. "I don't know how, but it is."

Sean wanted to see, too, so he climbed up at the other corner.

The two big fans sat side by side, aimed at the sky. Their blades were spinning more and more slowly until they came to a full stop.

BRETT BATTLES

"I think I can get down there," Sean said.

If he was careful, he could maneuver through the blades. Below them on his side was an empty area more than wide enough for him to fit in.

"Not sure that's such a good idea," Dani said.

"Not sure it is, either," Sean said, "but under the circumstances, if I can find out what happened, maybe we can use that to turn off the other ones."

The radio remained silent for a moment, then Dani said, "You're clear to go in."

He glanced at Ryan. "You'll have to help me."

Ryan stretched out along the edge above the door, and held out his hand. Sean grabbed it, and lowered himself through the fan. For a second he worried that it would turn back on and cut him in half, but it remained as dead as it looked. Once his feet hit the bottom, he let go of Ryan and took a look around.

Most of the container seemed to be filled with large barrels that must have held the virus. He tapped on one and was surprised by the echo. It was empty.

Well, of course, that made sense. The box had been dispersing its contents for quite a while now, so some of the barrels would have to be empty. He knocked on the ones next to it. They, too, echoed back.

Frowning, he examined them for a moment, then used a small pair of cutters from his belt to hack through the tubes connected to the top of the first barrel.

"What are you doing?" Ryan asked.

Instead of answering, Sean cut the final tube, and tried to rock the barrel back and forth. Because of all the barrels on the other side, and the two metal straps that ran across the width of the container on his side, it didn't move much.

"Hand me your bolt cutters," he said.

"Why?"

"Just pass them down!"

Ryan handed him the large cutters. Sean got the tool's jaw around the edge of the upper strap and bit into it. It took him a few minutes, but he was able to cut the strap in two. He bent the sides out of the way. The lower strap proved easier to slice through, and he was able to part it in about half the time.

No longer restrained, he yanked the barrel into the open space where he was standing, and squeezed around it into the spot where it had been. From there, he used the cutters to knock on all the barrels in the second row. Once he finished, he moved things around until he could reach the third row, then the row after that, and the row after that.

When he was done with the final row, he took a deep breath.

"Dani," he said. "I know why it turned off."

"Why?"

"It wasn't anything we did. The damn thing is empty."

THE CONTAINER IN Dublin was not the first to shut off, nor was it the last. The first occurred in Wellington, New Zealand, in the parking lot of a small shopping center, precisely fifteen minutes before the one in Dublin. The last was twenty-seven minutes after Dublin, in Hawaii on the island of Oahu, just four blocks away from Waikiki Beach.

A few of the containers had experienced misfires on certain barrels. The operating software had been designed to skip over these and move on to the next. For the most part, though, the contents of each IDM had been delivered in full.

26

PEREZ WAS NOT surprised by anything in the president's speech.

The nature of the virus was bound to be discovered. But so what? No one would live long enough to develop a vaccine, let alone mass produce it in the quantities needed. And when the president said they would continue to try to find a way to turn off the IDMs, it might have sounded good, but in reality it meant next to nothing. By then, ninety-five percent of the virus had already been released, more than enough to achieve the Project's goals.

And now the containers were all off, causing even more concern and speculation around the world.

As far as he was concerned, the more panic the better.

Perez had shaken his head at Homeland Security's list of suggested safety measures—seal off doors and windows, avoid contact with anyone not in the home with you, take frequent showers and wash hands every thirty minutes, and on and on and on. Measures that, along with the twenty-four-hour curfew that would be nearly impossible to enforce, might have worked if they'd gone into effect *before* the IDMs went active.

But not now. The end was coming.

There was a single knock on his door, and Claudia stuck her head in. "Dr. Lassiter would like to speak with you."

Perez smiled. *Excellent*. The doctor had saved him the effort of making the call himself.

"Video?"

"Yes."

"Thank you, Claudia."

As she left, he activated the video chat on his computer.

Dr. Lassiter looked stressed and tired.

"Good afternoon, Doctor. How can I help you?" Perez said.

"I've been trying to get ahold of Patricia Nakamura for several hours with no success. The last time I called, a man I've never seen before came on and told me she was no longer with NB89. *With*, not at. Do you know what he's talking about?"

"Of course I do."

The doctor waited, but when Perez didn't add anything, he said, "Then you need to tell me. I'm the acting chairman of the council."

"Patricia Nakamura is dead."

"What?" Whatever explanation Dr. Lassiter had been expecting, that was not it.

"She was a problem and had to be removed."

"You had her *killed*?"

"An unfortunate necessity, but one my men handled efficiently."

"Your men?"

"Project Eden Security."

"Those are our men. *My* men!" He paused. "Mr. Perez, I am placing you under arrest. You are to go to your quarters and—"

"Dr. Lassiter," Perez cut in. "I think I need to correct you on something you said earlier. You are no longer acting chairman of the council. That position has been dissolved, and the council itself has been transitioned into an advisory role for the Project's principal director."

"The principal director? He's alive?"

Perez smiled. "Yes. I would say the director is alive and well."

"Oh, thank God."

"But I believe you're confusing things again. The former PD that you're thinking of is undoubtedly dead. I, on the other hand, am not."

"You? Don't be ridiculous. You're not the PD and you never will be."

"That's where you're wrong, Doctor. I've been in contact with nearly every Project facility, and it has been decided that this part of our plan needs a strong leader. A role, I'm sorry to say, you are not fit to fill. They have all agreed with my decision to take over." It wasn't completely true. While he had been in contact with most bases, he hadn't actually asked for any endorsements. He just told them he would be the one running this phase of the Project, and they had gone along with it, as he knew they would. When it came time for the next phase and he was still in charge, they'd go along with that, too.

"I don't believe any of it," the doctor said. "You are to step down, and break off all contact with the rest of the Project."

"Now, Doctor," Perez said, his voice dripping with faux compassion, "I think you're forgetting that the security forces answer to me now. And if I tell them to, they will pay you the same type of visit they paid to former council member Nakamura."

"You wouldn't," the doctor said, but the look in his eyes was not confident.

"You do have another choice," Perez said. "It would please me if you serve on the advisory council. People would still see you as a person of influence. Now, of course this means you would back any decision I make, but that seems preferable to a bullet in the back of the head, wouldn't you say?"

"I...I..."

"I have a team within five minutes of your location. I could call them now, if you'd like."

"No," the doctor said quickly. He stared at his keyboard for several seconds. "Can I...can I at least think about the offer?"

"Of course. I'll give you sixty seconds."

It took the doctor only twenty-one.

27

CONTRARY TO WHAT Martina's mother had thought, their satellite radio was just as ineffective at the cabin as it had been when they were driving up the ravine. They had also tried the regular broadcast radios—the one that was part of the old '70s-era stereo in the cabin and the one in the Webers' car—but all they picked up was static. Cell phones were useless, too, not even a single bar of signal, so the two families were completely cut off.

The afternoon had been spent taking stock of what they had, then playing a tense game of Monopoly organized by the two moms to distract their children. But after only thirty minutes, everyone gave up. There was no ignoring what was going on.

"How long are we going to have to stay here?" Laurie, Riley's twin sister, asked.

"There's no way to know that yet, honey," her mom said.

"We'll stay as long as we need to," her father added in a voice sharper than needed.

"This place is so…boring. What are we supposed to do?" Laurie asked.

"Sweetie, it'll be okay," her mother told her. "You can read, play games, go for a walk."

"That's probably not a good idea," Martina's father cut in. "We don't want others to know we're here."

"Ken, a walk won't hurt," Martina's mother said. "There's probably no one within a mile of us."

"We can't know that for sure, and we don't have any more room for anyone else." His eyes strayed to Mr. Weber as he finished.

"So we have to stick around the cabin? That's even worse!" Laurie said. Unlike Riley, she was more social, and used to hanging out with her friends, talking about stupid things Martina had never been interested in.

"That's enough," Mr. Weber said. "You know why we're here. I don't want you causing any problems."

"I *don't* know why we're here," Laurie countered. "Because of some stupid things on TV? Seriously, Dad, I bet we're all going to look like idiots."

"Enough," her father said again.

She glared at him, her lips pressed tightly together, then stood up. "Not talking about it doesn't mean it's not stupid!" She disappeared down the hallway that led to the bathroom and the cabin's two bedrooms.

"I'm sorry," Mrs. Weber said, an embarrassed smile on her face. "She's just…"

"A teenager?" Martina's mom suggested.

Mrs. Weber looked relieved. "Yes. Exactly."

"Hey, we're teenagers, too," Pamela said.

Her mother patted her on the leg, and said in a low, conspiratorial voice, "Yes, but you all understand what's going on and can deal with it."

"I'm going out to get some fresh air," Riley whispered to Martina. "Wanna come?"

Martina nodded, and the two girls climbed to their feet.

"Where are you going?" Mr. Weber asked.

"To check out the snow," Martina said.

Donny jumped up. "Hey, I want to check out the snow, too."

"It's going to be cold."

"I don't care."

Martina glanced at Riley, who shrugged that it was okay with her.

"All right," Martina said to Donny. "Come on. Anyone else?"

There were no other takers.

As they were putting on their shoes and jackets, Martina's father said, "Stay close to the cabin."

"We will," Martina told him.

Night had settled over the mountains, and the snow that had been falling since not long after their arrival had created a blanket of white over the ground at least half a foot thick.

"It's so quiet," Riley said.

Martina had noticed it, too. The cover of snow seemed to have absorbed all the sounds of the woods, leaving behind only a peaceful hush.

"Whoa," Donny said. "This is awesome."

He started to run out from under the covered porch.

"Hey, hold on," Martina said. "You can play in it in the morning."

"Forget that!"

She grabbed the back of his jacket, stopping him. "Donny, if you trip over a rock buried under the snow and break your arm, what do you think Dad's going to say?"

"I'm not going to break my arm," he scoffed.

"Ugh," she said, and let go. "Your funeral if you do."

He ran out into the snow and promptly fell down, skidding for several feet.

"Woo-hoo!" he yelled, laughing.

"Boys," Riley said, smirking.

"Brothers," Martina corrected her.

"Yeah, I don't have to worry about that."

"No, just a twin that's a jerk."

Riley smiled. "At least she makes me look good." She pulled a set of keys out of her pocket. "Come on."

"Hold on. We can't go anywhere."

"I know that," Riley replied as she jogged over to her family's car. The doors were unlocked, so she got in on the driver's side and motioned for Martina to get in on the other. As Martina opened the door and slid into the seat, Riley reached into the back and pulled a cloth bag off the floor. She fumbled around inside it for a moment, then pulled out a computer cable. From her pocket she retrieved an iPod, and used the cable to connect it to the radio.

"I downloaded the new Patrolled by Radar album yesterday. Have you listened to it yet?"

Martina had heard of the band, but didn't know their music. "Not yet."

"It's great."

Riley stuck the key into the ignition, and turned it so that the electrical power came on. As soon as the radio lit up, she reached over to punch the button for the auxiliary input.

"Wait!" Martina said, grabbing her friend's hand.

Riley looked at her, confused.

"Listen." Martina turned the volume up.

Static filled the car, but within the pops and snaps there was a voice. It would come in clear for a few seconds, then fade to almost nothing for a few more before cycling up again.

"...homes. So far there...arrests, most in connection with looting at... reiterated the importance of obeying the curfew...said the majority of the people seemed to...have also responded to several reports of gun...five deaths since the president's speech this morn...listening to the voice of San Francisco on..."

When the voice faded away this time, it didn't immediately return. Martina's hand shot to the dial to try to regain the signal, but she couldn't tune it back in. She moved up the dial, searching for anything.

A signal suddenly came in loud and strong. "...out of Washington confirms that the terror boxes have ceased working around the world. Several of the boxes are now being examined by experts, but no new information is available. The Department of Homeland Security has reiterated the need for all citizens to adhere to the nationwide curfew, reminding those who are thinking about violating it that they will be arrested and detained for the duration of the emergency."

"Holy shit," Riley said.

"I'm going to get the others."

Martina threw open her door and rushed back to the cabin.

"The radio!" she yelled as she entered. "It's working now!"

"What?"

"How?"

Mr. Weber said something about nighttime atmospheric conditions as everyone in the living room donned their jackets and hurried out to the car. Donny had already joined Riley. The only one missing was Laurie, presumably still pouting in one of the back rooms.

For an hour they crowded around the open car doors and took turns sitting inside as they listened to the news and a replay of the president's speech. When the newscaster started reading information they'd heard twice already, Martina's dad reached over and turned the ignition off.

"Dad!" Martina said.

"We've heard enough," he told her. "We should all go in and get some sleep. It's been a long day."

"He's right," Mr. Weber said. "Come on, everyone. Let's go."

Martina was at the head of the pack, so she was the first to see Laurie standing on the porch near the front door. The girl's eyes were wide in shock, and she was absently chewing on her lower lip.

"Were you able to hear the reports?" Martina asked.

Laurie gave her an almost nonexistent nod, but her lip remained sucked between her teeth.

"Good thing we came up here, I guess."

Mrs. Weber walked over and put an arm around her daughter's shoulders. "Come on, honey. Sleep will do us all some good."

Laurie allowed herself to be turned and ushered back into the house.

Fifteen minutes later, the lights were out and everyone was lying down—the kids in the living room, and each set of parents taking one of the bedrooms. Try as she might, Martina couldn't fall asleep. Her mind spun with the possibilities of what the next day might bring.

Several hours later, when she was finally beginning to drift off, she heard someone go outside. A moment later a car door opened, and she could hear the faint muffled sound of the radio.

Her dad, probably, or Mr. Weber.

She was tempted to go join whoever it was, but her eyes closed once more as sleep finally took hold.

She'd been the last awake, except, of course, for the person who'd gone out to the car.

Who was neither her father nor Mr. Weber.

28

MATT HAD BEEN forced to call off the search for Brandon as sundown neared. He couldn't risk losing anyone else as the cold night took over.

The biggest problem was that there had been no clear indication of which direction Brandon took. The best they could do was split up again and follow the paths Miller thought were the most likely. But as the afternoon wore on and there had still been no signs of the boy, Matt couldn't help thinking it was more likely that those in the helicopter had taken Brandon.

Once back in the Bunker, he'd gone straight to the control room and had Christina bring him up to speed with what had been happening elsewhere. It turned out that most of Europe and Asia, and several countries in Africa, had jumped on the curfew bandwagon. Pretty soon the whole world would be on lockdown.

Maybe it would be enough, he thought. *Maybe the virus will be stopped before it can even get started.*

But he didn't really believe that.

"Have there been reports about anyone getting sick?" he asked Christina.

"Not yet."

Though no one in the control room would say it, they all knew that was odd. During the original Sage Flu outbreak, the time between exposure and first signs of infection was often less than half a day. The containers had started launching the virus into the air a day and a half earlier. There should have been some people already sick. Hell, not just some, but a lot. Even the deaths should have started.

For the first time, he began to wonder if maybe something had gone wrong. Perhaps prolonged exposure to the air had killed the virus. Or perhaps the virus itself had mutated into a nonlethal bug without the Project realizing it.

The president had said that "with the exception of a few minor variations," it resembled the Sage Flu virus.

Maybe the variations were unanticipated flaws that would cause the Project to fail.

"Matt?"

With a start, he pulled himself out of his thoughts.

Rachel was standing in the doorway to the control room, still looking as if she were single-handedly carrying the weight of humanity on her shoulders.

He walked over. "How are you feeling?"

"Did you find Brandon?" she asked.

He hesitated, then shook his head. "We'll start up again in the morning."

"Josie's been asking about him. I've tried to reassure her, but…"

He put a hand on his sister's arm. "I'll talk to her."

As he started to walk out of the room, she touched his back. "I'm…I'm sorry about before."

"You shouldn't be."

"I didn't mean what I said. I was just—"

"Tired? Frustrated? Angry?" He smiled. "I know. And if you need me to say it, you're forgiven, but you weren't saying anything the rest of us hadn't already thought."

There were thanks in her eyes.

He pulled her into his arms and gave her a hug. "I'd better go find Josie."

He located her down the hall in the cafeteria, sitting at a table by herself.

"Is it true?" she asked as he sat down.

"Is what true?"

"I heard Mr. Hayes is dead."

Matt hesitated, then said, "Yeah. I'm afraid it is."

"And Brandon's still out there?"

"Yes."

"So he's alone?"

"He'll be fine."

"If he's still out there, why did you come back?"

"It's dark. We could walk right by him and not see him."

"But you might also find him."

"Morning will be easier," he said. "For him, and for us. He's a smart boy. I'm sure he's tucked away somewhere safe."

"You can't let him stay out there. That'll be *two* nights!"

"I know you're concerned. I'm just as worried about him as you—"

She pushed herself up. "No, you're not! You don't care! You're leaving him out there by himself while we're all safe in here. He's just a kid!"

Matt felt what energy he had left drain away. "I need my team to get a few hours of sleep at least. Then we'll go back out."

"Before the sun comes up," she said. Not asking—telling.

"Yes, before the sun comes up."

"All right," she said, still not looking happy. "Maybe I should come with you. If he hears my voice—"

"Absolutely not," he said. "It's not safe."

She opened her mouth to argue, but before she could, Christina's voice came over the intercom system. "Matt, return to the communications center immediately."

Josie said, "I could help."

"You could also get lost, and I'd have to look for two children," Matt told her.

"Matt," Christina said over the intercom, "you need to come back now!"

Josie's brow creased as she narrowed her eyes. "I'm not a child."

Instead of debating the point, he stood up and said, "You're staying. If you try to follow us, we *will* turn around and come back. Is that understood?"

He stared at Josie until she nodded, then he hurried back to the communications center.

"What is it?" he asked as he entered the room.

"The jet," Christina said. "They've just called in."

"Our jet?"

She nodded.

"Where are they?"

"They're requesting permission to land."

THE FLIGHT SOUTH to Montana would have taken Ash and the others about six hours if they'd been able to fly direct, but due to a shortage of fuel at Grise Fiord, they'd been forced to make a stop at Baker Lake, the same place they'd landed on the way north.

Even then, it shouldn't have taken more than an hour to refuel and get back into the air. But it did, due to Implementation Day.

"Permission denied," the person manning the control tower had radioed back as they neared Baker Lake. "The airport is closed."

"We have a fuel emergency," Harlan explained.

"I'm sorry, you'll have to go somewhere else."

"There's nowhere else close enough for us to land before we run out!"

This time there was no response.

"Baker Lake? Baker Lake, do you read me?"

Harlan glanced over his shoulder at Ash, who was hunched behind him. "What do you want me to do?"

"Do we have a choice?" Ash asked.

"If we're lucky, we might be able to make it to one of the outposts along Hudson Bay, but it'll be a close call."

"That doesn't sound like a choice to me. Take her down."

Harlan nodded. As he and Barry set to work getting the

jet onto the ground, Ash returned to the passenger cabin, and grabbed one of the guns before retaking his seat.

Chloe eyed him suspiciously. "Trouble?"

"Same problem we had at Grise Fiord."

With a nod, she unbuckled her belt and retrieved two guns, giving one to Red before sitting back down.

The landing went as smoothly as always, and as soon as the wheels touched down, Ash returned to the cockpit.

"They've been yelling all the way in for us to abort," Harlan said.

"What did you tell them?"

"Nothing."

Harlan maneuvered the plane onto the taxiway and headed toward the fueling area.

"We've got company," Barry said.

Sitting across their route were a police car and a small fire truck. Standing in front of the vehicles were several men holding what appeared to be rifles.

Harlan flipped a switch on the dash, and the controller's voice came over the speaker. "...made an unauthorized landing, and are ordered to immediately take off. Do not open your doors or attempt to leave your aircraft."

"Tell him we're—" Ash began.

Harlan raised a hand, stopping him. "I got this." He activated his radio mic. "All right, if that's what you want. But I should tell you I've only got just enough fuel to get us in the air, which means we'll be coming back down pretty damn quickly. I'll probably only have time to bank the plane to make sure it takes out the center of your fine little town."

There was no reply for several seconds, then, "You are ordered to stay where you are. Do *not* open your doors. If you do, we will shoot."

"We just need some fuel."

"Stay where you are. We will contact you with further instructions."

Harlan pulled off his headset and leaned back. "Okay, I guess we wait."

It wasn't long before one of the men at the roadblock

climbed into the police car and drove off toward the tower. As soon as he left, the fire truck repositioned itself so that it was more in the center of the taxiway.

Four minutes later, a new voice came over the radio. "This is Officer Thomas Belford, RCMP. You have violated a direct order not to land at Baker Lake. This is both a territorial and federal offense. If you do not get your plane back into the air, you *will* be placed under arrest."

"My turn," Ash said to Harlan.

Harlan nodded at Barry, who handed Ash his headset.

"Officer Belford," Ash said. "I'm sure your superiors would not be fond of planes falling from the sky because they were denied landing rights."

"I don't care."

"You don't care?"

"The citizens of Baker Lake have voted unanimously to close the town to avoid any outbreaks here. No one gets in."

"We're not trying to get *in*," Ash said. "We just want to refuel."

"I'm sorry. I can't allow you to leave your plane."

"Fine. We'll stay on board. One of you can do it for us."

"No one is getting anywhere near your aircraft."

"Then what exactly do you expect us to do?"

"I already told you that. Get yourself back in the air."

"I believe we explained to your friend in the tower what will happen if we do that."

There was silence for a moment before Belford said, "You are to remain right where you are."

"And then?"

"Just stay there."

Ash frowned.

"So?" Harlan asked.

Ash looked out the cockpit window. About another hundred yards beyond the fire truck was the fueling area. So close. He thought there might be enough room to skirt around the edge of the truck, but that was only if it didn't move back in the way and the men with the guns didn't shoot.

Ash keyed the mic again. "Officer Belford, let me give

you something else to think about. If you just leave us sitting here, at some point we *will* try to get out. Maybe you'll shoot us, maybe you won't. Either way, if we're carrying the virus, it'll be out there potentially infecting you and your men. Wouldn't it be in your best interests to help us get on our way?"

The silence that followed made him wonder if his message had been heard. The answer finally came thirty minutes later, when the men standing in the road climbed onto the fire engine.

As the truck pulled away, Belford's voice came back over the radio. "You are to proceed to the fueling station, but remain in your aircraft. At no point are you to even touch the handle on your door. Do that, and we will burn your plane with you in it. Understood?"

"Yes," Ash said.

It was another hour before they were in the air again. They were just beginning to relax when Ash was called back to the cockpit.

"What is it?" he asked as he entered.

Harlan pointed out the window to his right, then the one on the left. Pacing them about one hundred feet to either side were two military fighter jets.

"Have they tried to contact you?"

Harlan nodded. "Wanted to know where we're headed. Told them back to the US from one of the research stations up north."

"And?"

"Said they're going to make sure we make it through their fine country with no problems."

The jets paced them until they were within a quarter mile of the border before finally peeling away. Ash expected to be greeted by two more aircraft, with US Air Force markings, as soon as they were back in the States, but the sky was empty.

From where they crossed, it took them only another hour to reach the Ranch. Not wanting to draw attention from anyone else, they waited until they were almost ready to descend before radioing in. Unlike at Baker Lake, they were given immediate permission.

At first, as they swooped down toward the ground in the early evening, the darkened valley seemed unchanged. It wasn't until they were almost on the ground that Ash sensed something was wrong. They should have been able to see the lights of the Lodge and the dorm, but everything was dark.

Ash returned to his seat and buckled in just before the wheels touched the ground. As soon as Harlan taxied the plane to the parking area, and the engines began to wind down, both Ash and Chloe headed straight for the door. She beat him there by a step, and was the first one out. When he stepped out onto the tarmac beside her, he was surprised to find no one there to greet them. Granted, they had just radioed in, but there should have been plenty of time for someone to drive the half mile down from the Lodge.

"Not exactly excited to see us, I guess," Chloe said.

Ash jogged over to the road, and looked in the direction of the Resistance's headquarters. No cars coming as far as he could tell, just the night filling the void.

"Where is everyone?" Red asked from the plane's doorway.

"Don't know," Chloe said. "Ash, you see anything?"

"No. Just—" He stopped. From somewhere not far down the road, he heard a noise. "Hello?" he called out.

There it was again. Steps, he realized.

"Hello?"

"Captain Ash?" a voice called back.

"Who's that?"

Out of the darkness emerged the shapes of four men. "Captain Ash. It's Ross Miller."

Ash didn't allow himself to relax until he saw the man's face and was able to confirm that Miller was indeed who he said he was. "Where is everyone?"

"In the Bunker," Miller said. He looked past Ash at Red. "Tell Harlan to shut everything down and go dark."

"What's going on?" Ash asked.

"Let's get you all inside first. Matt'll brief you."

Ash frowned, wanting to know now, but held his tongue.

"We have an injured man. Is someone bringing a car?"

"Sorry. None available at the moment." He turned to the men who'd come with him. "Tony, radio in for a stretcher, then meet them halfway to escort them in."

One of the men, who must be Tony, nodded and ran back in the direction of the Lodge. But Ash wasn't content to wait for him to get back.

"Red," he called out. Red stuck his head out the doorway again. "Stay here with Gagnon until help shows up."

"Will do."

Ash looked at Chloe. "I'm heading to the Bunker. You coming?"

"Hell, yeah," she said.

"I'll have to guide you," Miller said.

"We know how to get in," Ash told him.

"Actually, I'm pretty sure you don't."

Ash narrowed his eyes. "What the hell is going on?"

"This way," Miller said, and started down the road.

Ash and Chloe shared a quick look before taking off after him.

Halfway to the Lodge, Miller veered off the road into the trees.

"Where are you going?" Ash asked.

"Back door."

"Why the back door?"

Miller paused, and looked back. "Because the front door is blocked."

"By what?"

"The remains of the Lodge after it burnt down."

"What?" both Ash and Chloe said.

Instead of following Miller, the two of them ran down the road. When they reached the spot where they could see the Lodge, they stopped.

Though the moon wasn't out yet, their eyes had had time to adjust to the night. What remained of the Resistance's headquarters was a disorganized mound of debris. There was no need to go any closer. The building was completely destroyed.

221

Ash heard Miller jog up behind them. "How did this happen?" he asked without turning.

"We went to full cover," Miller said.

"Why?"

"We were attacked by the Project."

Ash whirled around. "My kids. Where are they?"

"Please. Let's just get inside."

Ash grabbed Miller by the arms. "Where are they?"

"Captain Ash, please let go of me."

"Tell me," Ash said.

Miller hesitated. "Your daughter's in the Bunker."

"And Brandon?"

Another pause. "He was caught outside during the attack."

A bitter freeze rushed through Ash's arms and chest. "What…happened to…"

"We're not sure what happened to him. One of our men was with him. They hid in the woods."

"So they got away?"

"Please. Matt has all the information."

"Tell me what you know!"

This pause was the longest of all. "We have no idea where your son is."

Ash stared at him, unable to speak.

"What about the man who's with him?" Chloe asked. "Can't we get ahold of him?"

"Jon Hayes was with him, but…"

"But what?" Ash whispered.

"We found his body this afternoon. He'd been shot."

"But Brandon?"

"No sign of him."

Ash finally let go of Miller. "Take us in."

WHEN THEY EMERGED from the tunnel and passed around the large, thick door that was used to seal off the Bunker, Josie Ash rushed forward and threw her arms around her father.

222

Sobbing into his shoulder, she said, "It's my fault. I'm sorry. I'm so sorry. I didn't know he'd gone outside. If I'd known he was planning to, I wouldn't have let him. I'm so sorry."

Ash stroked his daughter's hair. "Sweetie, it's okay. Not your fault. Don't ever think it is. I'll find him. Don't worry."

"I'm sorry. I'm sorry."

If he could have held her until the sun came up, he would have, but he needed to get moving and find his son. He looked over at the small group waiting to greet them, and saw that Matt was there.

"Josie," he whispered in his daughter's ear. "Go with Chloe for a moment, okay? I need to find out all I can about your brother."

"I'm sorry, Dad."

He kissed her on the forehead. "I told you, not your fault. Now go with Chloe."

Josie sniffled as she nodded, then stepped over into Chloe's embrace.

Ash walked directly to Matt. "We need to talk. Right now." Without waiting for a response, he headed down the hallway, and soon heard Matt's distinctive gait following him.

When he reached the shooting range, he opened the door, checked to make sure no one was inside, and entered.

As Matt followed him in, Ash said, "Shut the door."

Matt did, then said, "I know you're upset, but—"

Before Matt could get anything else out, Ash slammed him against the wall. "*You* were supposed to watch them! You promised me they would be safe!"

Matt put up no fight. "You're right. I did. It's my fault he's out there."

"Damn right, it's your fault!"

Ash held Matt tight against the wall, seething.

"Have at it. Whatever you want to do to me, I deserve," Matt said.

Ash glared into Matt's eyes, and came close to slamming his fist into the side of the Resistance leader's face. Finally, his breathing began to slow, and he took a step back, dropping his hands to the side.

"Tell me what happened. Everything."

Matt did exactly that.

"We're not sure if he's out there or if the men in the helicopter took him," Matt said as he wrapped things up. "As soon as the search teams have had a little sleep, they'll head out again."

"One of them is going to head out right now with me," Ash told him.

"They're tired. They need rest."

"And my son needs me." Ash headed for the door. "Have whoever it is meet me at the tunnel entrance in fifteen minutes."

IMPLEMENTATION DAY
PLUS TWO

SATURDAY, DECEMBER 24th

World Population
7,176,892,851

Change Over Previous Day
+ 285,143

29

SANJAY COULD NOT find Kusum or her family anywhere.

After stealing the vaccine and leaving the Pishon Chem compound the previous afternoon, his plan had been to head straight out of the city to the rendezvous point. Only getting out was not quite so easy.

More and more streets and neighborhoods had been sprayed with the virus. By the time he found a clean route to the outskirts of town, the sun had dipped below the horizon.

As far as he could tell, there were no spraying efforts in the countryside. That didn't prevent the paranoia about what was happening in the rest of the world from spreading beyond the limits of Mumbai. Many of the roadside restaurants and stalls that had been thriving the night before, when he and Kusum had ridden by, were closed and dark now. The few people Sanjay saw seemed to be in a hurry, and when they heard his motorbike, they would look at him in fear.

At first he took the lack of traffic to be a good thing, as he was making up for some of the time he'd lost in the city. But then, after he'd been in the country for about half an hour, something whizzed by his head. He slowed, surprised by the sound. This caused the noise of the bike's motor to decrease so that when a second object flew past him, he heard the crack of a gun and realized someone was shooting at him.

He twisted the accelerator as far as it would go and sped down the road. Glancing over his shoulder, he could see the headlights of a car about half a kilometer back. He wasn't sure if the shots were coming from it or not, but he wasn't going to take a chance. At the next road, he turned right, then right again behind a closed shop, and killed all power to the motorcycle.

Scared out of his mind, he waited for the car to pass. Instead, he heard it slow at the same road he'd turned on, and pull to the side and stop, idling.

He could hear voices, indistinct but angry. Then the car started up again, this time turning around and heading back where it came from.

While he waited to make sure it didn't return, he felt around until he found the wire running into the back of his headlight and yanked it out. He did the same to the taillight. This was one time, he thought, when driving in the dark would be safer.

It was nearly ten p.m., two hours after he was supposed to be there, when he reached the place he and Kusum had spent the night before. No one was there.

All sorts of thoughts flew through his mind, most ending with something horrible having happened. *No*, he told himself. *Remember how long it took you to get out of Mumbai. It's the same for them. They'll be here soon. You just have to wait.*

But when midnight came and went, and they had still not shown up, his terrible thoughts returned. Maybe they *had* run into trouble. Maybe they had been shot by the people who shot at him.

Maybe they would never show up at all.

The last, he refused to believe.

I need to find them in case they need help.

He began searching in an ever-widening arc from the spot where they were supposed to meet, but as the sun came up, he was still alone.

His eyes felt like someone had dumped handfuls of sand

in each, and it was becoming harder and harder to focus.

Go back to the meeting place, he thought. Maybe he'd missed them somehow and they were there waiting for him, wondering where *he* was.

He was lucky that he was on the small rough road leading to the rendezvous point when he fell asleep. If he'd still been on the highway, he would have been traveling at a much higher speed and would have most likely died.

The bike veered to the left, the front tire slamming into a rut. He woke in midair, flying over the handlebars. His mind was still trying to figure out what was happening as he slammed into the ground.

Dazed, he lay along the side of the road for several minutes before trying to sit up. That's when the pain kicked in. His left shoulder was the worst. He touched it with his right hand and realized it was sticking out in a way it was never meant to.

Dislocated.

There were other pains, too, scrapes and bruises on his face and arms.

Then he forgot about it all, even his shoulder. *The vaccine!*

He struggled to his feet, his left arm dangling uselessly at his side, and searched for his bike. It had traveled for another fifty feet before spinning off the road.

He could see at first glance that he wouldn't be using it again. The fork holding the front wheel was bent to the side, while the wheel itself was skewed at an odd angle. The back didn't look much better. He moved around it, looking for the bag containing the bottles of vaccine, and found it still strapped to the back of the seat where he'd put it.

He fought with the straps with his good hand, until they gave way and he could get the bag off. He sat on the ground and opened the top. Immediately he saw that the boxes holding the vaccine were wet.

"Please, no," he said as he opened the first lid.

This was the box from which he'd given several bottles to the cooks at the compound, giving the remaining bottles plenty of room to smash into each other. Of the seven that had been there, only two were still intact. He checked the other box, the full one, and sighed in relief. Three bottles along the side had been destroyed, but that was it.

His focus no longer on whether the vaccine was okay, his injuries forced themselves back to the forefront, screaming for attention.

He knew he had to get his shoulder back in place, otherwise the pain would render him useless. He tentatively pushed at it with his right hand. The pain intensified, but the bone barely moved from its unnatural position.

This wasn't something he could do with his hand. The angle wasn't right, so he wouldn't be able to generate enough strength. But pushing was the logical thing to do.

Once more, he worked his way back onto his feet, and staggered over to the nearest tree. Gingerly, he placed his dislocated shoulder against it.

"Don't think," he said out loud. "Just push."

He took a breath, cleared his mind as best he could, then shoved.

He didn't realize he'd screamed, nor did he feel it when he hit the ground after he passed out from the spike of pain as his joint slipped back into place.

IT WAS LIKE Kusum was a stranger in her own country.

The half-deserted streets were unsettling, of course, but it was the people she *did* see that made her feel this way. Most were in other cars, and while those who usually drove in Mumbai were often creative in the ways they weaved around each other, now even those methods seemed tame.

She and her family had seen over a dozen accidents, nearly half of which happened not far in front of them. They had been rear-ended twice, but neither her father nor the people who had hit them even considered stopping.

It was as if India had gone insane.

The spray carrying the deadly disease was also a

problem. At first, the men with the tanks on their backs seemed to be everywhere, swarming the city like the mosquitoes they were supposedly there to kill. But it was clear that some were deserting their jobs when they noticed the city around them behaving unusually. Still, a large number of the men continued their task, no doubt unwilling to do anything that might jeopardize the much-needed money they were promised. They blocked her family's route so many times, Kusum began to wonder if it would be possible to avoid the virus's path.

When her father drove them through West Mumbai into Thane, they had no choice but to stop. Traffic was jammed in front of them, perhaps thirty or forty cars deep. Though they could not see the exact cause, they could see a column of black smoke rising above the road.

Kusum's father turned his head to look out the back window. "Out of the way," he commanded. "I can't see."

The four in the backseat leaned to the sides as he put the taxi into reverse. The car began to move backward, then suddenly stopped.

"Move, move!" he yelled. This time, his words were intended not for those inside the cab, but for the cars Kusum could see arriving behind them. He waved his arm back and forth. "Clear the way!"

But the cars paid no attention. It wouldn't have mattered anyway. As soon as the new arrivals pulled to a stop, more came behind them, blocking them in, too.

Kusum's father cursed and shut off the engine. "We walk," he said.

They grabbed their bags and piled out of the car.

"Stay close," he told everyone, and started walking toward the smoke.

"There is a problem up there," his wife said. "Maybe we should go another way."

"That's the way we need to go," he replied without turning around.

Most of the people caught in the jam were heading away from the fire. They pushed and shoved past Kusum's family, not caring if they hurt anyone. But soon, Kusum and her group were past the bulk of the crowd and were able to pick up their speed.

The cause for the stoppage turned out to be four cars piled into each other, blocking the road. One car had flipped on its side, while the others were all twisted and tangled against each other. That wasn't the worst of it, though. There were bodies, some still in the cars, and a few on the road. All were bloodied and torn and unmoving.

Though it had been at least ten or fifteen minutes since the accident occurred, there were no police, no ambulances, no emergency personnel at all.

"Don't look," Kusum's mother said, putting a hand over young Panna's eyes.

Kusum did the same for Darshan.

"I want to see," her cousin said.

"No," Kusum told him. "You don't need to see this."

"I've seen dead bodies on TV."

"This is not TV."

Her father led them around the edge farthest from the car that was still on fire. That's when Kusum heard it—a moan, long and painful, coming from the sedan on its side.

"Keep moving," her father said.

Kusum looked at her sister. "Take Darshan."

Jabala kept walking as if she hadn't heard her.

Kusum grabbed her sister's arm. "Hold on to Darshan. Make sure he can't see anything."

As if in slow motion, Jabala finally looked over. Kusum could see how scared she was.

"Jabala, it will be okay, but I need you to watch him. Can you do that?"

Her sister blinked, her eyes focusing on the boy. "Yes," she said. "I...I can."

Kusum pushed Darshan over to her, and headed for the wreckage.

"What are you doing?" her father called out.

"Someone's hurt," she yelled back.

"We don't have time! We need to keep moving!"

231

She wanted to shout back, "We need to help if we can," but she knew she would just be wasting her breath. She ignored him and continued on.

The moan was definitely coming from the sedan. She looked through the back window but could see nothing, so she ran around and looked through the front.

There was a woman slumped against the door that was pressed against the ground, blood pasted across her forehead. Kusum could see no movement, and thought it unlikely she was the one making the noise.

"Hello?" she called out. "Is someone in there? Are you hurt?"

The moan started up again, this time becoming a word. "Help."

It had to be coming from the backseat.

Frowning, Kusum looked around. She thought if she was careful, she should be able to climb on top of the closest wrecked car, and look into the back of the sedan through the passenger window facing the sky.

As she mounted the other car's hood, her father yelled, "Kusum, get down from there right now!"

"There's someone who needs help," she said.

"I don't care."

"I do!" The words slipped out of her mouth before she even realized it. Talking back to her father was something she had never done until today. But running for her life was something she had never done, either. Maybe she had gone just as crazy as the rest of the country, but there was no way she could just ignore someone in need.

She half crawled onto the top of the car, and moved over to the edge where it had slammed against the perpendicular sedan. Getting onto her toes, she leaned over the sedan's roof and looked in through the half rolled-down, rear passenger window.

At first, all she saw was a jumble of cloth and bags and baskets. Then she realized that within the chaos was an old woman.

"I'm here," Kusum said. "How badly are you hurt?"

The old woman's head turned, and her eyes flicked open. "Help," she said, her voice weak. "Nipa."

Is that her, or the woman up front? Kusum wondered.

"Don't move. I'll come down and help you." Though how she would do that, Kusum wasn't sure yet.

"Nipa," the woman said again. "Help Nipa."

So it was the name of the woman in front. Kusum had no way of knowing for certain, but she had a strong feeling the other woman was dead.

"Let me help you first," she said. "Then I will do what I can for…Nipa."

"No. Nipa first."

With great effort, the old woman pushed out of the way some of the items that had fallen around her.

Kusum stared down in surprise. Nipa was not the driver, either. She was a child, no more than a year old, tucked against the old woman's side. The baby was awake and looked scared to death.

Kusum looked over to where the others had stopped to watch.

"Get down! Now!" her father yelled. "You're putting the rest of us in danger."

"I need help," she said. "There's a baby here."

"What?" her mother said, stepping out from the group. Without waiting for a response, she turned back to the others. "Jabala, come with me."

"But Darshan," Jabala said.

"Leave him. Darshan, Panna, you stay with *masi.*"

The two children nodded.

As Kusum's mother and sister passed her father, he said, "Where do you think you're going?"

"To help," her mother said. "And you're coming, too."

Knowing they were on the way, Kusum climbed onto the side of the sedan, reached through the half-open window, and found the handle. Quickly, she rolled the glass the rest of the way down.

The opening was now more than large enough for her to fit through. The trick now was to do it without dropping onto the old woman and the baby. She slipped her legs in first, and eased herself down until only her shoulders and head were not inside the car. She stretched out her foot, caught the top of the front seat, and used it to guide her all the way down.

Kneeling, she found herself closer to the woman behind the wheel than the older one in back. Not really wanting to, but knowing it had to be done, she put her fingers against the driver's neck. She wasn't really sure about the right spot to check for a pulse, so when she didn't feel one, she moved her fingers around, but still found nothing. She looked at the woman's chest. It wasn't moving. If the driver was still alive, it was by the thinnest of threads, and there was nothing Kusum could do for her.

As she moved over into the back part of the car, the child, Nipa, looked up at her and tightened her grip on the old woman.

"It's okay," Kusum said. "I'm here to help you."

"Save her," the old woman whispered. "Please."

"I will save both of you."

The woman tried to smile, but ended up coughing. This caused Nipa to start crying.

"It's okay," Kusum said, touching the girl's cheek. "Everything will be fine."

"Nipa first," the woman managed to say between coughs. She moved like she wanted to hand the girl to Kusum, but she had little strength.

Kusum reached out and put her hands under the baby's arms. As she started to lift the girl away, Nipa panicked and tried to grab the old woman again.

"Don't worry," Kusum said, pulling the girl to her. "I won't hurt you."

She hugged the baby to her chest, but Nipa turned her head so she could look at the old woman and continued to cry.

"It's okay, it's okay," Kusum said over and over.

After several seconds, she heard a noise above, and her father's head appeared in the open window.

"Hand her up," he said, once he'd taken a look at the situation.

234

Kusum stood as best she could and raised the girl toward his outstretched hands. Nipa screamed in protest.

"She's just scared," Kusum said.

"Of course she's scared," her father replied as he grabbed hold of the baby. "I raised two girls, remember? I have seen scared before."

As he pulled Nipa out of the car, Kusum knelt back down next to the old woman. "Your turn," she said.

The old woman didn't move.

"Hey. Come on. Time to get you out of here."

No response.

Worried, Kusum put her fingers on the woman's neck. This time she did feel a pulse, though it wasn't strong. She put a hand on the woman's chest to check her breathing, and instantly pulled it up again, looking at her palm. Blood covered the pad at the base of her thumb. She pulled back the cloth that had fallen over the woman's midsection, and stifled a cry.

The tip of a piece of metal was sticking up right below the woman's ribs. Blood was soaked into the clothes around the wound.

"Kusum," her father said.

She looked up.

"There is nothing we can do for her. We can't move her and we can't stay."

"Take care…of Nipa," the old woman whispered. "I will stay here with my…daughter."

Kusum fought back the tears of frustration that had suddenly gathered in her eyes, knowing her father was right.

Carefully, she covered the wound back up, and wiped her palm on the cloth.

"Rest now," she said. "I will take care of Nipa."

Though the woman's eyes were closed, she seemed to relax.

"Come," her father said. "Let me help you up."

With a nod, she stood and took his hands.

PALE HORSE

DARKNESS FELL BEFORE Kusum and her family reached the edge of the city, which meant they were still a very long way from where they were supposed to meet Sanjay.

They had checked every abandoned vehicle they passed, but soon discovered each had been left behind for a reason. As for traffic, it had dwindled to a trickle, and the cars they did see never once slowed as they passed Kusum's family walking along the side of the road. Unless they found another ride soon, there was no way they would reach Sanjay that evening.

"You want me to take her?" Kusum's mom asked.

Kusum held the sleeping Nipa against her chest, the girl's head lying on her shoulder. They had barely restarted their journey when Nipa insisted that Kusum carry her. The girl then clung to her like she was afraid Kusum would disappear at any second, until she finally passed out.

"I'm okay," Kusum said.

In truth, she liked holding the girl. She had promised to keep Nipa safe, so that's what she would do until they could reunite her with her family.

That task would not be easy. She'd realized not long after they left the accident that she should have grabbed the old woman's—and perhaps the driver's—identification. That way she would have had information about Nipa's family. But by the time she'd thought of it, they were too far away.

Once everything is back to normal, I'll go to the police and tell them where the accident occurred. Surely, they'll have information about who was involved.

The good thing was that Nipa appeared to have suffered only a few scratches and bruises in the accident. How the incident would affect her mind, only time would tell. Of course, given the situation they were all going through, the girl wouldn't be the only one mentally bruised.

"They're still there," Jabala whispered a few minutes later.

Kusum glanced over her shoulder. Sure enough, the three figures that Jabala had first noticed over an hour ago were passing beneath several lights about one hundred and fifty meters behind them. At first Kusum had dismissed them as just being others trying to get away from the city, but the distance they kept never changed, even after Kusum's family stopped for a few minutes to rest.

"Who do you think they are?" Jabala asked.

"I don't know."

The shortest of the trio was probably a child, but the distance made it hard to tell whether they were men or women, let alone what age they were. Really, the only important question was, were they trouble or not?

"Do you think you can take Nipa without waking her?"

Jabala eyed her suspiciously. "Why? What are you going to do?"

Kusum nodded toward the people following them. "Find out who they are."

"You could get hurt. You don't—"

"They won't see me. Don't worry, okay? Here, take her." Kusum gingerly lifted Nipa from her shoulder and put her in Jabala's arms.

"What's going on?" their father asked, glancing back.

"I'm going to find out who those people are," Kusum said.

"You are *not*."

"I am. We need to know."

"You're my daughter. You will stay with us."

"Someone needs to check. If you had a son, you would let him do it. You have none. Who are you going to send? Darshan?" She waved at her young cousin, who was clutching tightly to Kusum's mother. "I'm the only one."

"I'll do it."

"No," Kusum said. "You need to watch over the others. *I* will go."

She could see the conflict in her father's eyes. After a moment, he reached into the bag he was carrying and pulled out a sheath holding a four-inch knife. "Here," he said, handing it to her. "Don't use it unless you have no choice. Be very careful."

"I will."

Before he could change his mind, she slipped between two closed roadside stands and into the brush behind them. Looking back, she could see her farther hesitating, wanting to follow her.

"Keep moving," she said in a harsh whisper.

Reluctantly, he turned in the direction they'd been headed and said, "Come on, everyone. Let's go."

She watched them for a second to make sure her father didn't change his mind, then found a good spot where she could see the whole road, and settled in. It wasn't long before she heard the footsteps of those on the road behind them. One was walking faster than the others. *The child,* she thought, working twice as hard just to keep up.

Though she knew there was no way they'd see her, she crouched down a bit more. The sound of the steps increased until finally the trio came into view.

The smallest was definitely a child, a boy probably no more than Darshan's age. What was surprising was that the other two were children also. Taller, yes, but their faces gave away their age. Kusum thought they couldn't have been more than eleven or twelve. They were both girls, the taller of the two holding the hand of the boy.

She looked to see if any of them was carrying weapons, but the only things they had were their well-worn clothes and each other. Kusum considered what to do next, and decided on a course of action her father would have disapproved of.

She waited until they passed, then silently moved out from her hiding place and onto the road behind them.

"What are you doing?" she said.

All three jumped, the smaller of the girls letting out a brief scream. As they looked back, Kusum could tell they wanted to run.

"Don't move," she said, showing them the knife.

"Please don't hurt us," the smaller girl said.

"Then tell me why you're following us."

The girls exchanged a glance. The tall one, who Kusum could now see was a few years older than the other, said,

"We're not following you."

"You've been following us for the last hour and a half."

"We're just using the same road. You can't stop us from doing that."

Though the girl was smaller than Kusum, she had donned a tough front, going so far as to move in front of the other two.

"Where are you going?" Kusum asked.

"To visit our family," the girl said quickly.

It was a transparent lie. Kusum was sure they'd grown up in the streets, and doubted they even knew who their families were. She didn't even think any of the three were related to each other, as none shared any similar physical traits.

She stared at the older girl for several seconds, then put the knife back in the sheath and held it at her side. "When was the last time any of you had anything to eat?"

"We ate just a few hours a—" the older one began.

"Yesterday," the boy said. "In the morning."

Kusum frowned. "Come on, then." She walked through the middle of them, and started down the road toward her family. After a moment, she looked back. "I said, come on. Unless you're not hungry."

The boy was the first to move, but the girls weren't far behind him.

With that simple invitation, Reva, Induma, and Adesh joined Kusum's family.

They would not be the last.

30

LIZZIE DREXEL KNEW they were out there. She could *feel* them watching her house. She'd seen one of them fifteen minutes earlier, peeking around a tree. And where there was one, there had to be more.

She barely thought about the boy anymore. He'd been gone since the day before. To her, that was a lifetime ago. So much had happened since then. The world, as Owen had always told her it would, had gone to shit.

"You were right, big brother. You were right," she muttered.

Aren't I always?

For hours, she'd sat mesmerized in front of her computer, watching the news. Everywhere it was the same—death being delivered in dull metal boxes. That no one had died yet didn't mean anything. It was going to happen. She knew it would, like she knew why the men watching her house were there. Owen had told her.

Those boxes would be wasted out here, his voice had said. *Those are for the crowds. People like you and me, they'll come for us individually.*

He told her how they planned to do it—break in, hold her down, and swab the bug in her nose.

Too bad for them they've come to the wrong house, Owen said.

She smiled. "Yeah, too bad."

Lizzie wasn't about to die from the killer virus, but she *was* willing to die if it meant taking with her those who were trying to give it to her.

She went into the bedroom and opened the secret panel in the closet. Her sweet brother had prepared so much for a world he didn't live long enough to see.

Oh, I'll see it, he said.

She nodded. "Right. I just meant—"

I know what you meant. Now do what needs to be done.

Owen's big concern had been a civil war. He hadn't been clear what form it would take—race-based, religious, or class driven—but that wasn't important. He just knew it was coming. And while he wasn't interested in joining any of the sides, he wasn't about to let anyone take what was his.

He had two main means of preventing that from happening. The first was the four sniper nests he'd created under the eaves of his house. All he would have had to do was crawl from corner to corner to cover the whole house. He'd even lined the otherwise unfinished attic with steel plates for protection.

The problem with this option was that Lizzie was not the marksman her brother was, nor would her bad hip allow her to move around the attic in any kind of useful fashion. That left the second option—setting off the Semtex explosive that was built into the house right above the basement retaining wall, and in the garage along the base.

All she would have to do was wait until the killers approached the house, then *boom*.

She felt a bit sad that it had come to this. She'd come to love the house, but she was not about to die in it from some painful, draining infection.

Uh-uh. Not her.

She flipped the switches that turned the system on, removed the remote control from its clip, and carried it to the dining room window where she could watch and wait for the exact right moment.

THE HOUSE SAT near the edge of a clearing, a detached garage off to the side. They would have passed right by it if Miller hadn't noticed there were fewer trees in its direction, then found the broken twigs indicating a spot where someone had sat and watched the building like they were now doing.

Could it have been Brandon? Ash had wondered. Was his son right now inside the home, sleeping?

Both buildings were dark, and there was a faint whiff of smoke in the air, hinting at a dying fire in the fireplace. Someone was definitely home, but at this hour they were undoubtedly asleep.

Ash was tempted to walk up and knock on the door. It was only a warning relayed by Miller from Christina at the base that kept him from doing it.

"A survivalist," Miller said, summarizing what he had been told. "Or was. He died about a year ago and his sister moved in last August."

When Ash looked at him, surprised, Miller told him that the Resistance kept detailed notes about its nearest neighbors. The current occupant, Elizabeth Drexel, apparently led a very quiet life. She was an account who did all her work via the Internet, and since taking up residence, had only twice driven the thirty-five miles to town for supplies. Where she fell on the whole survivalist thing, they had not yet been able to determine, and that was the problem. Survivalists were a notoriously paranoid lot, and not fond of people knocking on their door. Especially at two in the morning.

"Did you see that?" Ash said.

"See what?" Miller asked.

"The window facing us, something moved along the edge."

Miller studied the window for several seconds. "There's nothing there now."

"There was."

Ash closed his eyes and played the movement back in his mind. It had been a curtain, but not flapping like what might happen if a burst of air rushed past. It had been more…subtle, controlled. Like someone pushing the curtain away from the frame so they could look outside.

One way to find out, he thought. He rose from his crouch. "I'm going in."

"Whoa. You're going to scare the crap out of her."

"I'm just going to ask her if she's seen Brandon."

"We should at least wait until the sun comes up."

Ash locked eyes with him. "My son is missing. I'm not going to waste time waiting for it to get lighter. I'll knock on the door and ask about Brandon. That's all."

Miller was clearly not comfortable with the decision, but he said nothing.

"You stay here," Ash said. "Less likely to scare the crap out of her if there's only one of us."

AS SOON AS Lizzie returned to the dining room window, she moved the curtain just enough so she could create a clear spot to peek through with her night vision goggles. She watched and waited.

It didn't take long for her intruders to make a move.

One moment the night was still, in the next the dark figure of a man stepped out from the trees and started walking toward her house.

You were right, little sister. They're really here, Owen said.

When the man passed the garage, she frowned. "Where are the others?"

Patience.

"Why aren't they all coming?"

Owen apparently didn't have an answer for this.

With each step the man took, she became more and more frustrated. She was supposed to take them all out, not just one guy.

Her thumb slipped down the side of the remote. "What am I going to do?" she asked.

Her brother still said nothing.

"What do I do?"

SO FAR, ASH had seen no repeat of the movement he'd detected earlier as he passed the garage and trudged across the cold, hard earth toward the house's small porch. He hesitated in front of the door for several seconds, then raised his hand and knocked.

LIZZIE WATCHED THE man until he disappeared from her view as he went around to the front of the house. She looked back at the woods, wondering once more where the others were, then stepped away from the window.

Was the man scanning her house for weak points? Or would he try to break in? She walked quietly toward the door, wanting to hear the moment he attempted to pick the locks. She was only a few feet away when—

Knock, knock, knock.

She jerked backward, nearly falling on the floor.

Knocking on her door was *not* something she expected.

Knock, knock, knock.

Pull yourself together, Owen ordered.

She took a couple of deep breaths to calm herself, and moved up to the door. The man was just a few feet away now, right on the other side. She looked down at the remote in her hand.

"Not yet," she whispered to herself. "Wait for the others."

Knock, knock, knock.

If she said nothing, he would get his colleagues, wouldn't he? And they would all come back?

"Hello?" the man called through the door. "Hello? Are you home? Ms. Drexel? Hello?"

She froze. He knew her name.

Of course, he knows your name, Owen said. *He and his friends are professional killers. They always prepare ahead of time. But there's no way they could have prepared for what you have waiting for them.*

That brought a smile to her face.

"Ms. Drexel, I just need to ask you a question."

"Go get your friends," she silently mouthed. "Go get your friends and I'll open the door."

"Ms. Drexel?"

Knock, knock, knock.

"I'm sorry if I've woken you. My son is missing. I need your help."

Son? What was the man talking about? His *son* was missing? It must be some kind of trick to get her to—

Then she remembered. The boy. And it all became clear.

The kid had been part of it. He hadn't just happened upon her garage to spend the night. He'd been sent to her place on purpose, to make sure she was the only one here, and to provide information to the men now out to kill her.

Oh, how tricky. Using a child to scout me out.

"Go away!" she yelled, then clapped her empty hand over her mouth.

Why had she done that? That was stupid. She should have just stayed silent.

"Ms. Drexel, my name's Daniel Ash. I'm looking for my son, Brandon. I think he may have come this way, and I was wondering if you might have seen him."

"No," she said. "No, I haven't seen anyone. Now leave me alone!"

"Are you sure? He probably would have come by here yesterday."

"I said no!"

The man fell silent.

She stood as still as possible until she could stand it no more. She moved over to the window next to the door to see if he had left.

She pulled the curtain back just an inch, but what she saw was not her empty porch.

The man was looking in at her, right on the other side of the window.

"NO, I HAVEN'T seen anyone," the woman yelled through the door. "Now leave me alone!"

Ash leaned forward a few inches. "Are you sure? He probably would have come by here yesterday."

"I said no!"

He stared at the door, unsure if she was telling him the truth. He turned his head and caught sight of the window just off to the side. Thinking that if he could get a glimpse of her, he might get a better sense if she was lying, he moved over to it and positioned his eyes as close to the glass as possible.

All he could see, though, was the back of a black curtain. There wasn't even a crack along the side to give him a peek into the house.

He was about to back away when the curtain moved. The woman, wearing a pair of night vision goggles, appeared directly in front of him.

They both jumped, then—

TWIN FIREBALLS ROSE into the sky as the double explosions of the house and garage shattered the night.

One moment Miller was standing behind a tree, watching Ash talk to the woman through the closed door, and the next he was sprawled on the ground, a dozen feet away. He rolled onto his hands and knees, and pushed himself up.

The two structures were gone, pulverized in the blast.

Miller ran out of the woods and weaved around flaming debris as he raced toward the house. All he could think of was Ash. He'd been right there, near the front door.

Miller stopped a dozen feet from where the porch had been. The only things left standing were bits and pieces of the retaining wall around the basement.

"Jesus," he said.

This clearly wasn't some accidental gas explosion. It was designed specifically to destroy everything.

He whirled around. The ground was covered with chunks of wood and bent pipes and things he couldn't even identify.

What he didn't see was Ash or the woman. She had been inside and Miller doubted there was much left of her. But Ash? Miller couldn't allow himself to think the same.

Starting from where he'd last seen Ash, he began searching. It wasn't long before he saw the rounded tip of something sticking out from under a ten-by-three-foot section of siding that had been blown from the house.

He grabbed the edge of the wood, and shoved it up. Ash was beneath it, his arms wrapped loosely around his chest.

Miller pushed the siding out of the way and knelt down.

Ash was breathing, and his pulse, though not strong, was steady enough.

"Ash?" Miller said, tapping the man's cheeks. "Ash, come on."

His efforts were greeted with a moan, but Ash's eyes remained closed.

Miller raised his hand to his ear to turn on his radio and call for help, but his earpiece was missing.

"Shit!" he said. It must have fallen out when he was knocked to the ground. "Hang in there, buddy. I'll be right back."

He sprinted over to where he'd been. There was enough light coming from the scattered fires that he didn't have to turn on his flashlight. His earpiece was on the ground, not far from where he'd been thrown.

"This is Miller. Do you copy?"

"This is Christina. Any progress th—"

"I need medical assistance right away," he said. "At the Drexel house. Ash is down."

247

31

AFTER LEAVING THE woman's house the day before, Brandon had continued east, knowing he would find a highway at some point. By early afternoon, he was exhausted, so he found a spot at the base of a large rock, and crawled into this sleeping bag. When he woke, the sun had already gone down, so as anxious as he was to keep moving, he'd thought it best to stay there for the night.

He had a cold dinner of baked beans and water. Afterward, he lay awake for hours, wondering if he would ever see his family again, before finally falling back to sleep.

It was the noise that woke him, a distant, rumbling roar that he wasn't sure was real or part of a dream. He opened his eyes, looked around, then sat up and listened.

If the noise had come from the real world, it was gone now.

Just a dream, then, he thought as he lay back down.

He was able to get a few more hours of sleep before he opened his eyes and knew he was done for the night. He retrieved a couple of granola bars and ate them as his breakfast. He put everything away when he was done, donned his pack, and started out again.

Clouds had begun to move in overhead, but in the east, where a half moon had risen not long before, the sky was still clear. Beyond the boulder where he'd been sleeping was a narrow, shallow valley. When he reached the top of the ridge on the other side, he stopped and stared.

"You're kidding me," he said.

Below him, less than half a mile away, was the thin ribbon of what could only be a highway. If he had kept going the day before, it was possible he would have slept someplace warm and welcoming.

Walking down the hill, he debated with himself what to do if he spotted a car. His experience with the woman at the house had instilled more than a little caution. Maybe he should just stay in the trees and follow alongside the road to a town. That might be the safest option.

As the sun took away the night and the morning made its slow journey toward noon, it looked like he wouldn't have to worry about what to do if he saw a car. So far, not a single one had driven by.

Around eleven he stopped for lunch. As he was eating another granola bar, he remembered what day it was. It was his mother's favorite day of the year, the first to occur since she died.

Christmas Eve.

The tears started before he even knew what was happening, then the sobs followed. It was over twenty minutes before either stopped.

32

WHEN SANJAY REGAINED consciousness, the sun was high in the sky. He started to roll onto his side, but made a poor choice of direction, and momentarily pressed his damaged shoulder against the ground.

He clenched his teeth as pain once more shot down his arm and across his chest. It wasn't as bad as it had been when the bone was dislocated, but it still hurt like hell. Cradling his arm so his shoulder would remain immobile, he sat up.

The wrecked motorcycle was exactly where he had last seen it, as was, thankfully, the bag with the remaining jars of vaccine. His relief at this knowledge was tempered by the fact he still didn't know where Kusum and her family were, and now he had no means of traveling around to find them.

He tried to remember where he was when the crash occurred. He was close to their meeting point, wasn't he?

With some effort, he rose to his feet and looked out at the road. Dirt, rough, narrow.

Yes, this was the road to the place he and Kusum had slept the night before. No, two nights before.

The good thing was, even at a slow pace, he should be able to walk there in no more than an hour. But the location of the crash also meant it was unlikely Kusum and her family were there already. Surely they would have seen the wreckage and found him lying by the road as they passed.

So what should he do? Go to the meeting spot? Or head the other way to the main road? They'd have to come from that direction anyway, so it really wasn't a choice.

He picked up the bag, slung it over his good shoulder, turned right, and headed toward the highway.

IT TOOK SANJAY forty minutes to walk back to where the road ended at the highway. Once there, he found a shady spot from where he could keep an eye out for Kusum, and sat down.

It was eerie how quiet it was. When he was driving around earlier, there'd still been a few cars on the road, but in the first hour he sat there, he didn't see one.

She's not coming. The voice was but a whisper in his head.

"She is," he said aloud. "She's coming."

She's not coming, the voice repeated.

"Stop it!"

He pushed himself to his feet and walked out into the middle of the road. He stared in the direction that led to Mumbai, willing Kusum to appear.

"She's coming," he said. "I know she is."

The highway, however, remained empty.

He staggered back to the side of the road, his body weak from the accident and the walk and the hours spent searching for Kusum. He needed something to eat, something to help him regain strength. He couldn't recall the last thing he ate, but he knew it hadn't been much.

Just down the highway was a roadside restaurant. Both the dining area and the kitchen were open air with a simple roof above, made from whatever materials the owners could get their hands on. Like everything else seemed to be, it was closed.

Instead of sitting back down, Sanjay headed toward it, hoping something edible had been left behind. Just as he reached the other side of the road, he heard the distant sound of a motor. He stopped, his head whipping around.

The sound had definitely come from the right direction, *and* it was getting louder.

He knew it was a mistake to think it was Kusum, but he couldn't help it. It had to be. It just *had* to be.

He placed his hand against his forehead to shade his eyes from the sun. The road went straight for as far as he could see. In the distance, something moved. Though it was no more than a small blob at the moment, there was no question it was a vehicle.

He took a few steps toward it, as if doing so would make it arrive sooner.

"It's got to be her," he whispered. "It's got to be her."

Another step, the blob growing and beginning to take shape.

"It's got to be her."

A square now. A white square. Only—

He stopped moving.

The square continued to grow.

He dropped his hand to his side. It felt as if his heart had fallen off a cliff.

Not a car. A large truck.

He could now see the canvas-covered back, and make out enough to know several people were in the cab.

He closed his eyes, willing himself to not lose control.

She's not coming, the voice from earlier said, stronger this time.

"She is," he fought back, not as convincing as before.

He started to turn away.

"Sanjay!" The voice was just barely audible over the sound of the truck's engine.

He paused, and looked back. Someone was waving from the open truck window.

Sanjay!" Louder now. A girl's voice. Sounding very much like—"Sanjay!"

There was a squeal as the driver of the truck stomped on the brakes, and Kusum leaned out the passenger window.

For a moment, Sanjay thought his mind was just showing him what he wanted to see.

The door flew open even before the truck came to a full stop. The girl jumped down and ran toward him.

"Kusum?" he whispered.

"Sanjay! You're here!"

Her arms flew open as she neared, and she wrapped them around him, squeezing him tightly. Though his shoulder screamed out in pain, he made no attempt to stop her. It *was* Kusum. And she was hugging him.

"You waited for us," she said, finally pulling back from him.

Of course, I waited. What else would I have done?

Her smile began to wane as she touched his face where the skin had been ripped away in the accident. "What happened?"

"I'm okay."

She took a good look at him, taking in his scratches and noticing his immobile arm. "You're hurt."

"I'll be fine." He paused. "I could use some water, though."

"Of course! Of course!"

She put an arm around him as if he needed propping up. When he took a step, he realized he did.

"Someone bring some water!" she yelled toward the truck.

"I thought you were…going to be in a car," he said.

"That didn't quite work out. Besides, it wouldn't have been big enough."

Big enough?

Before he could ask what she meant, Jabala ran up with a bottle of water.

"Here," the girl said, holding it out to him.

"Take the top off first!" Kusum scolded her.

"Oh, right. Sorry."

Jabala removed the top, and handed the bottle back to Sanjay.

As the water passed over his lips, he wasn't sure if he had ever tasted anything so good.

"Slowly," Kusum said.

He continued to drink, slower than at first, then poured what was left over his head. The cloud that had infiltrated his mind began to lift, and while he was a long way from being whole, he could feel some of his strength returning.

"Thank you," he said to Jabala.

"It is no problem," she replied, taking the empty bottle from him. "Would you like more?"

"Yes, please." He managed a smile. "And maybe something to eat?"

"I will be right back."

As soon as she was gone, Kusum said, "Tell me what happened to you."

He told her about the accident.

"It's lucky you are even alive," she said.

"But I am."

Kusum eyed the bag hanging over his shoulder. "Is that it?"

He waited, but she didn't say anything more. It took him a moment before he realized she was talking about the vaccine.

"Yes. I got it."

She looked relieved, though not quite as relieved as he expected. "I hope you have enough."

"Enough?"

"Come."

She guided him over to the truck. As they passed the cab, he heard a child cry out.

"Wait," Kusum said. She stepped up to the open door and leaned inside. When she pulled back out again, she was holding a baby. "This is Nipa. Nipa, this is Sanjay, the one I've been talking about."

Nipa looked at him for a moment, then hid her face against Kusum's chest.

"Where is she—" he began.

"Later," she said. "I have much to tell you. First, come."

She led him around to the open back of the truck. Sitting inside were Kusum's mother and her two cousins, but there were also nearly two dozen people Sanjay had never seen before, most of them kids.

He looked at Kusum, confused.

"We couldn't just leave them on their own," she said.

"Of course you couldn't," he told her. It had never been just Kusum's beauty that drew him to her. It had also been her compassion.

She smiled and squeezed his hand. "Everyone, this is Sanjay."

There was a chorus of greetings. He nodded and said hello several times, but the more he did, the more a question grew in his mind.

Did he have enough vaccine for everyone?

33

LI JIAO HAD a simple garden of potted plants on the small balcony of her second-floor apartment. Despite its lack of size, she took pride in what she'd been able to create. In spring she often had the most beautiful flowers on the whole block.

The news about what was happening in the rest of the world was frightening. She had watched for hours as reports came in from America and Europe and even elsewhere in Asia about the boxes and their deadly cargo. The endless reports were what finally drove her back outside, knowing she'd be able to forget everything else as she tended her plants.

So when she saw Madam Zhang step out of the apartment building across the street, she leaned over her balcony, yelled out a greeting, and waved as if it were just any other day. Madam Zhang, though, made no indication that she'd heard Jiao at all.

As Jiao started to call out again, the words died in her throat. Madam Zhang, who Jiao knew was only in her thirties, was moving like an ancient grandmother. She pressed a hand against the side of the building as if she would otherwise fall. Then Madam Zhang stopped and leaned wearily against the wall.

Jiao quickly set down her pruning scissors, and rushed

through her apartment out into the hallway. It took her less than a minute to reach the other side of the street.

Madam Zhang hadn't moved.

"Where are you headed?" Jiao said. "Perhaps I can go with you."

Madam Zhang took a labored breath. Jiao noticed sweat on the woman's brow. "I need…to get some medicine for my husband." She halfheartedly raised a hand holding a piece of paper with several items on it.

"I'm heading that way. Perhaps I can pick these up for you."

"I wouldn't want to…" She paused for several seconds. "To trouble you."

"It is no trouble at all. Here, I will walk you back to your apartment, then I'll pick up everything."

Jiao placed her hands on the other woman's arm and eased her away from the wall.

Without another word, they walked into the building, and slowly up the stairs to the third floor where Madam Zhang lived with her husband.

When they reached the door, Jiao carefully took the key from Madam Zhang and let them in. She led her friend over to a cushioned chair and helped her sit down.

"Where is Mr. Zhang?" Jiao asked. The place was quiet.

"Lying down."

It was clear he'd given whatever he had to his wife.

"Here. Give me your list," Jiao said. "I won't be long."

The woman handed the list over. "You'll need some money."

"You can pay me later."

"That is unnecessary," Madam Zhang said, but the look on her face was relieved. Jiao got the impression that the energy it'd take to look for her money was not something her friend had.

"You just rest," Jiao said.

She stopped back at her apartment to pick up one of her shopping bags, and headed out. As she walked, she decided she would cook something for Madam Zhang when she got back. The woman had always been kind to her in the past. It was the least she could do.

With a smile, she continued down the street, unaware that later that evening, she would be cooking her last meal.

BERLIN, GERMANY
12:23 PM CENTRAL EUROPE TIME

HAROLD WOLF DROVE past the Brandenburg Gate, an uneasy knot in his stomach. He had never seen Berlin so quiet. The only places with any action were the areas where the shipping containers had been found.

Thank God he hadn't drawn that duty. Instead he was ordered to enforce the twenty-four hour curfew, which had so far been extremely easy.

That was why he was nervous. Easy was always a warning signal to him. He knew it wouldn't last. And he was right.

The call came over his radio four minutes later. A problem at one of the hotels not far from the American Embassy.

Making a U-turn on the usually busy Ebertstrasse, he headed for the Dorint Hotel near the Gendarmenmarkt. The trouble was immediately apparent as he rounded the corner onto the block where the hotel was. There were at least half a dozen people standing outside the entrance, banging on the glass doors, and shouting angrily at hotel security staring back at them from inside.

Wolf pulled to the curb fifty feet away. Knowing it was more than he wanted to handle on his own, he radioed in for backup. Unfortunately, one of the people outside noticed him and headed over.

"You've got to tell them to let us in!" the man yelled.

"Please stand back, sir," Wolf said, climbing off his bike.

The man slowed his pace but didn't stop. "They won't open the door. We have rooms here. We're guests!"

"Please, sir. Just stand back."

He touched the gun at this waist, emphasizing the point. The man seemed to finally get the message, though his anger didn't subside.

"You need to talk to them! Where are we supposed to go? Those are our rooms!"

Wolf closed his eyes for a second as a wave of pain shot through his head. Great. Just what he needed. A migraine.

"Let me see what I can do," he said.

"We can't stand out here like this," the man said. "Who knows what's in the air?"

"Sir, just a minute. Please."

Wolf took a step toward the hotel, then stopped suddenly, a wave of dizziness rushing over him.

"Hey. Are you going to help us or what?" the man asked.

"Are you all right?" A woman's voice.

Wolf realized a few of the others had come over.

"I'm fine," he said. "It's just a long day."

Another step, and this time it was his stomach.

He was only able to turn partially away before his breakfast made a quick exit out his mouth.

"Jesus!" the first man said, jumping back. "You're sick! Dammit, you got some on me!" He started wiping viciously at his suit jacket. "Dammit!"

Wolf fell to his knees and retched again. When he finished, he looked up and saw the others staring at him as if he were death itself.

"Please, someone call for help," he managed before his stomach churned again.

MUMBAI, INDIA
4:12 PM INDIAN STANDARD TIME

TARU LEANED AGAINST the side of a car, exhausted. He'd been up walking the streets since six a.m. and it was now past four in the afternoon. That in itself would have been enough to tire most people, but he had to also carry the heavy container of anti-malaria spray on his back.

Up and down his assigned roads he'd gone, spraying the liquid along the edge of the streets. Whenever he started to run out, one of the suppliers would invariably show up and fill his tank again.

But it wasn't the walking or the burden that had caused him to stop. Though he didn't know it then, nor would it dawn on him later when he started to hallucinate, the cause was directly attributable to the fact he had stopped wearing his face mask not long after the morning had grown hot.

His exposure to the virus, in extreme amounts, was inevitable, but he also had a genetic makeup that accelerated the KV-27a virus's effects, making him one of the first to contract the disease.

He coughed, and was surprised that it hurt deep down in his chest.

He must be catching something, he thought. Ironic, given the mission of mercy he was on.

He coughed again then spit a wad of phlegm into the gutter.

"Just a few more hours," he told himself.

A full day would include an extra bonus, and that was money he sorely needed.

"Just a few more."

He pushed off the car and started walking again.

Forty minutes later, he was lying half in the road, the contents of the container on his back spilling across the ground.

34

MARTINA HEARD SOMEONE moving around, but she didn't want to open her eyes. Sleep was what she wanted, a place where she could pretend she was somewhere else. At school, perhaps, getting ready for the softball season. Or back home, helping her mother finish putting up the Christmas decorations. Or somewhere on the coast with Ben, finally spending enough time with him to solidify their relationship.

"Has anyone seen Laurie?" Mrs. Weber said.

Reluctantly, Martina opened her eyes and propped herself up on an elbow. Riley looked like she had just woken up, too, but both Pamela and Donny seemed to be still asleep. Laurie's sleeping bag was empty.

Mrs. Weber was standing near the front door, frowning and clearly worried.

"Did you check the bathroom?" Riley asked.

"First place I looked," her mother told her. "She's not there. Her coat's missing, too."

"Her coat?" Riley sat up. "What time is it?"

"A little after six."

The look on Riley's face began to match her mother's.

"Maybe she went for a walk," Martina suggested.

"Laurie?" Riley said. "Are you kidding me? She doesn't *walk*. And she would definitely not do it at six a.m."

"She's not in the house so she must be outside," Mrs.

Weber told them.

Donny rolled onto his stomach and covered his head with his pillow.

"Didn't either of you hear her leave?" Mrs. Weber asked.

"I didn't hear anything," Riley said.

"Neither did I," Martina added.

"I'm going to go check," Mrs. Weber said.

Riley pushed herself off the floor. "I'll do it, Mom." She started pulling on her clothes.

"I'll go, too," Martina offered, grabbing her jeans off a nearby chair.

Mrs. Weber looked unsure at first. She glanced down at her long nightgown, then nodded. "Okay. I'll go change and join you in a few minutes."

The two girls quickly finished dressing and pulled on their winter gear. Since the sun had yet to rise, they flipped on the outside lights before leaving.

At some point during the night, the storm had moved on. What it left behind was over a foot of snow that covered the ground as far as they could see.

Riley was about to step off the porch when Martina grabbed her arm. "Don't."

"What?"

"Look," Martina said, pointing at the ground in front of the porch. "No footprints."

The snow surrounding the entrance was a flat, white surface. It would have been impossible for Laurie to go this way without leaving a mark.

"See, she must be inside somewhere," Riley said.

"Or," Martina said, "she could have used the back door."

"Um, maybe," Riley grudgingly admitted.

Since they were outside already, they started to walk around the house, but as they neared the Webers' car, Martina noticed something. There were several small depressions in the snow close to the driver's door. Footprints from the night before, she thought, the snow having almost filled them in.

She angled over for a better look. Even though they had been partially filled, it was strange that the depressions were still smaller than her own prints. So it wasn't one of their dads she'd heard last night?

"What are you doing?" Riley said from the corner of the house. "Come on."

Martina looked up and nodded. Before she said what she was starting to think, it would be best to check the back of the house. If Laurie's prints were there, everything would be fine.

But everything wasn't fine.

"See, I told you," Riley said. "She's inside."

The snow outside the backdoor was as flat as it was out front.

"Come on," Riley said, reaching for the door.

"Did you hear someone go out last night after we went to bed?" Martina asked.

Riley paused, then shook her head. "No."

"I did. I thought it was either your dad or mine. Whoever it was went out to the car and turned on the radio, but I fell asleep so I didn't hear anyone come back."

Riley's eyes widened. "Do you think it was Laurie?"

"I don't know. That was around midnight."

They stared at each other for a moment. Riley then grabbed the knob and tried to open the door. It was locked, so she had to pound on it until her mother answered.

Mrs. Weber pulled the door open a few seconds later, her coat half on. "Did you find her?"

Riley rushed past her. "Dad!" she yelled. "Dad!"

Martina came in right behind her.

"What is it?" Mrs. Weber called after them.

But the girls ignored her as they headed for the bedrooms. When Martina opened the door to her parents' room, they looked up, obviously having been woken by Riley's yelling.

"Is something wrong?" her mom asked.

"Dad, did you go out to the Webers' car last night?" Martina asked.

"Why would I do that?"

"To listen to the radio."

"No," he said, shaking his head. "Your mother and I

went to bed the same time you did."

Martina whipped around and looked over at Riley, who was staring back at her from the doorway to her parents' room.

"He didn't go out," Martina said.

"Neither did my dad," Riley said.

THEY WALKED IN an ever-widening circle around the cabin, but there were no footprints or other signs of Laurie anywhere. It was like she had just vanished.

After a while, it was decided someone should take one of the cars and check along the road. Mr. Weber wanted to do that, but Martina's dad used the argument that his car was the only one with chains. Martina suspected it was more than that. Mr. Weber was starting to show signs of panic, and letting him operate a car would have been a mistake.

Martina sat up front with her father, while Donny had the backseat to himself.

Keeping their speed slow, her dad headed down the snow-covered road. Martina watched to the right, while her brother scanned the area to the left.

They were getting close to the main paved road when Donny said, "What's that?"

Their father took his foot off the gas and let the car roll to a stop.

There was a slight rise that started about twenty feet from the road on the driver's side. Donny was pointing at something toward the top—a flash of color peeking out from behind a tree. Lavender, like the color of Laurie's jacket.

Without waiting for the others, Martina threw open her door and ran around the car.

"Martina, hold on!" her father called out.

She ignored him and headed up the side of the ridge. When she reached the tree, she found Laurie there, sitting with her back to the trunk. The girl's face had lost most of its color, and her lips were ashen gray.

"Laurie?" Martina said, shaking the girl's shoulder.

For a second there was no response, then Laurie's chin moved up a fraction of an inch. Her eyelids parted just enough so she could peer at Martina.

"Dad!" Martina called down the hill. "Dad, she's here!" She looked back at Laurie. "It's okay. We've found you. We'll take you back and warm you up."

"Home," Laurie whispered. "I want to go home."

MARTINA'S DAD BLARED the horn as they approached the cabin and pulled to a stop. Her mom and Mrs. Weber rushed outside as Martina and her father jumped out of the car.

"We found her," Martina said, and helped her dad ease Laurie out of the backseat.

"Oh, my God," Mrs. Weber said "Oh, my God!"

While they carried the girl to the house, Mr. Weber, Riley, and Pamela ran out of the woods from where they'd been searching.

"Laurie?" Riley said.

"Someone open the door," Martina's father ordered.

Martina's mom ran around them and pushed the door out of the way. They took Laurie into the Webers' bedroom, where Mrs. Weber and Martina's mom stripped off her cold, wet clothes and covered her with blankets. Mrs. Weber asked everyone to leave the bedroom and let Laurie rest.

No one would admit it, but they had all thought they'd never see Laurie alive again. Instead, they just talked about how happy they were that they'd found her, and how they were sure she would be all right.

At one point, Martina heard a muffled cough from the Webers' bedroom. She assumed it was Laurie, her system reacting to her ordeal.

She was wrong on both counts.

35

THE CONFERENCE ROOM at NB219 had undergone a major overhaul in the last twelve hours. No longer was there a single monitor that needed to be split into sections when several people were on a video call. Now there were six monitors, all mounted to the wall, each capable of receiving a different feed.

The furniture had also been replaced with pieces Perez thought were more fitting for the new principal director's temporary headquarters—an impressive black metal table and a dozen padded leather chairs, the largest of which he was sitting in at that very moment.

Four of the screens were active, each displaying the image of a different person looking out at him. Of the former leadership committee, only Dr. Lassiter was present. On the other three screens were Renée Girard, Richard Chang, and Dr. Ronald Fisher.

"For all intents and purposes, Europe is completely shut down," Girard said. "Everyone has locked themselves inside. The only ones moving around are military and other government personnel."

"It's the same here in Hong Kong," Chang said. "And throughout the rest of Asia. Borders are closed, but it's an unnecessary step. No one wants to go anywhere."

"Any reports of illness?" Perez asked.

BRETT BATTLES

"Yes," Girard said. "It's scattered, but growing."

"Same thing here," Chang replied.

"Dr. Fisher, are we still working on the same timeline?" Perez asked.

With those who'd been at Bluebird either dead or at least temporarily out of communication, Fisher became the head Project scientist. He had been on the team who worked on perfecting KV-27a.

"Yes," the doctor said in his distinctive monotone. "Our latest tests of samples taken from dispersal points in various locations indicate the agent is working as planned. I would say reports of illness will no longer be 'scattered' by midnight."

It was exactly as Perez hoped.

"Kind of ironic," Dr. Lassiter said. "That it'll basically hit tomorrow."

"Not ironic at all," Dr. Fisher told him. "I believe that was the plan."

No one said anything for a few seconds, then Perez leaned forward. "All right. We'll reconvene at midnight my time."

As Perez reached for the keyboard to turn off the system, Dr. Lassiter said, "Merry Christmas, world."

Perez paused for a moment before disconnecting the call.

36

IT HADN'T BEEN a simple matter to get Ash back to the Bunker. The only vehicles that hadn't been wrecked in the attack on the Ranch were three motorcycles kept in the Bunker, and with Ash unconscious, there was no way he could be transported on one.

Lizzie Drexel's vehicle was also not an option. It had been blown apart with everything else when the garage exploded.

The best they could do right away was get one of the motorcycles down the tunnel, muscle it up through the hatch, and send their only medic, Lily Franklin, out to do what she could. Ten minutes later they sent a second bike with two men, the one in back carrying a stretcher.

Once Lily had Ash as stabilized as she could get him, they loaded him onto the stretcher, and alternated between carrying him and pushing the motorbikes back to the Bunker.

Matt was at the end of the tunnel when they arrived.

"How is he?" he asked Lily as soon as she climbed down through the hatch.

"A broken arm. Ribs cracked. Undoubtedly a concussion. There might be some internal damage, too, but there's not much I can do about that." She took a breath. "We need to get somebody here who can handle that kind of thing."

"Is he conscious yet?"

"No."

Once they had maneuvered Ash through the hatch and into the Bunker, they took him straight to the medical area and transferred him to the bed next to Gagnon.

A moment or two later, footsteps pounded down the hall, skidding to a stop outside the door. A half second later, Josie rushed in.

Matt grabbed her around the shoulders. "Josie, you need to stand back."

"Let me go!" She squirmed in his arms, trying to break free. "He's my *dad*! Let me go!"

She twisted again, dropped down out of his grasp, and ran to the bed.

"Dad? Dad, can you hear me?"

Tentatively she touched her father's shoulder and shook it.

"Dad, wake up."

"He can't," Lily said. "I gave him something to keep him under."

"Why?"

"If he wakes, he'd be in a lot of pain. It's better if he rests now."

"Is he going to be okay?"

Lily shot a worried glance at Matt before looking back at Josie. "We're doing all we can."

"That's not an answer."

Matt stepped in next to them. "It's the best answer she can give. You don't want her to lie, do you?"

Looking dejected, Josie shook her head.

"You want to stay here with him?" Matt asked.

"Yes," she said quickly.

He nodded toward a chair sitting against the wall, and one of the men brought it over. Josie sat down and slipped her hand into her father's.

Matt waited a moment, then quietly left the room. With the exception of Lily, the others did the same. Once they were far enough away from Josie, Matt said, "I need a man on each bike to head out and find a doctor, preferably a surgeon, just in case."

"I'll go," one man said.

"Me, too," another offered.

The man beside him raised his hand. "And me."

"No," a new voice called out from down the hall. "I'll be the third."

Chloe was walking quickly toward them, the look on her face daring anyone to challenge her.

After the two bikes that had been used were refueled, and the third was lifted out of the Bunker, Chloe and the other two raced off.

Matt watched them until they disappeared. Then, instead of going back down into the tunnel, he walked over to the edge of the woods, and looked for the first time at the still smoldering hulk that had once been their headquarters.

A snowflake fell on the back of his hand, and another flew by his face, but he barely noticed. He stared at the remains of the Lodge, remembering all that had happened there, the good and the bad. It had been more than just a place to meet and make plans.

It had been his home.

But, as devastating as it was to see it this way, he knew the horrors that were about to come would be much worse.

37

THE MOOD AT the cabin is somber. Though they've been able to warm up Laurie, her pulse is still weak, and when she speaks it's like she doesn't know where she is. She needs a doctor.

While there may be one somewhere in the area, the only doctors they know about for sure are the ones down the mountain, back in Ridgecrest. But because of the snow, the drive would be dangerous at best, and quite possibly deadly.

Mr. Weber sees no choice, though. He can't just sit and watch his daughter fade away.

Because the Gables' car is the only one with chains, Martina's father agrees to let him take it. At least this means those at the cabin will still have a radio.

Mrs. Weber wants to go, too, but her husband insists on her staying. Her sniffles are disguised by her tears. As much as she wants to believe she got out of Los Angeles without being exposed, it is just wishful thinking. Soon she will be too sick to get out of bed, and by then she won't be the only one not feeling well.

But that is hours away. Now they all stand near the front door, watching Mr. Weber drive Laurie away.

No one says what they're all thinking, that they wonder if the two will ever come back.

They won't.

But Martina is the only one who will know that for sure.

PALE HORSE

JOSIE REALIZES THE drug in her father's system is supposed to keep him asleep. But his eyes have started to move under their lids, and every once in a while his body jerks one way or the other.

"Wake up," she says, keeping her voice low so the woman who's been taking care of him doesn't hear her. "Come on, Dad. Wake up."

But he remains unconscious, living through whatever dream is playing in his mind.

"Wake up, Dad," she said one more time, knowing he won't.

CHLOE DRIVES FASTER than she should in the falling snow, but she has finally reached the main highway, and can't help but go as quickly as possible. Ash's life is on the line, and she must do everything she can to save him.

It's dark now, the gloomy day turning into an even gloomier night, making her task all the more difficult. But she keeps going.

At one point there is movement off to the side of the road, but she's already past it by the time it registers and she can't take a chance looking back. One wrong move and the bike could slip out from under her, which could mean a death sentence not only for her, but for Ash, too.

For half a second, she thinks she hears something, but it, too, is gone, and soon she forgets about both the noise and the movement as she continues racing down the highway.

KUSUM IS THE one who ends up having to give everyone the shots. Because of his injuries, Sanjay is in no condition to do it himself. Besides, his only experience stems from the one shot he gave Kusum.

Still, he is part of the process. Each time a bottle of the vaccine runs dry, he removes a new one from his bag. This way, he is the only one who knows how few containers are left. Right from the start, he has Kusum give each person an amount that's less than what he'd given her, hoping that will be enough to make the vaccine last.

Even then, the supply is dwindling faster than he would like. He knows if his mind were clearer, he would be able to figure out if there is going to be enough for everyone. But math is beyond him at the moment.

Kusum's father is the last in line. When his turn finally comes, Sanjay breathes a sigh of relief. There are still two precious bottles left.

These, he shows Kusum. Her eyes widen at how close they have come to running out, but then she smiles and says, "Good. Then we still have some if others need it."

Her words make him feel better until one of the children she has collected asks, "So now what do we do?"

Everyone looks at Sanjay. Even Kusum's father seems anxious to hear his response.

He stares back at them, then says the only thing that comes to his mind. "We stay together, and we survive."

It's not a plan, or a course of action. It is merely words, no different than an advertising slogan meant to evoke an emotion in consumers.

But it seems to work. There are several scattered smiles, and a few nodding heads. And, at least for the moment, no one asks, "How do we do that?"

THE DAY IS growing short. Brandon can't see the sun because of the clouds, but dimming light is enough to tell him that the sun is low on the horizon.

About two hours earlier, it had started to snow. He had walked in it for a while, but was getting too wet, so he moved into the trees just off the side of the road, and gathered enough branches to build a lean-to against a large trunk. It's not perfect, but it is keeping most of the snow out.

Should he have stayed at the woman's house? At least he had shelter there.

No. I did the right thing.

To warm up, he unravels his sleeping bag and crawls

inside, but he remains sitting, his back against the tree.

Tomorrow he needs to find a house, or some kind of building, hopefully someplace with a phone that he can try to call the only number he knows—his father's cell phone. He's not sure if his father even has a signal where he is, but Brandon doesn't know what else to do.

He doesn't even realize he nodded off until the noise wakes him. It's the sound of a high-pitched engine. Given the weather—it's still snowing—he wonders if it might be a snowmobile, not knowing that the thin cover that has fallen so far is not enough for one of the machines to operate on.

It seems to be coming from somewhere down the road. After another few seconds, he realizes it's heading in his direction. He unzips his bag and tries to pull himself out, but his foot gets tangled in the bottom. He twists it around until it finally comes free, then shoves his feet into his shoes and stumbles through the darkness toward the highway.

After a whole day of not seeing anyone, he is no longer worried about who he might run into. He needs help. He needs to find someone, anyone.

The delay at the sleeping bag causes him to arrive at the road just seconds before the snowmobile passes. He sees the single headlight and starts waving. As it goes by, he realizes it's not a snowmobile at all, but a motorcycle.

"Hey!" he yells, already knowing his voice will be drowned out. "Hey!"

But the red taillight recedes at the same speed the headlight came toward him.

Brandon rushes to the center of the road and jumps up and down. "Hey! Hey! Come back!"

The motorcycle continues on, and soon the light and the sound of the engine fade to nothing.

IN HIS DREAM Ash is playing catch again. The air is springtime warm, and on its breeze the smell of barbecue.

Brandon arcs the ball into the air, and Ash takes a few steps back so that it'll land right in his mitt, but he stumbles as he catches it, and falls onto the grass.

His son breaks out into hysterics, doubling over in laughter.

On the porch in front of the house—a house that kind of looks like the one they had in Barstow—Josie, book in hand, is also laughing.

He always loves it when she laughs. It reminds him of Ellen, his wife.

Just as he thinks this, Ellen walks outside carrying a plate of brownies. Never mind that she's been dead nearly nine months. She's here now.

"They're still hot. Who wants one?" she calls out.

"I do!" Brandon said.

Josie looks up. "Me, too."

"How about you, sweetheart?" Ellen says, looking directly at Ash. "I know they're your favorite."

They are indeed. No one can make a brownie like Ellen can.

"Get up," Josie says to him. "Come on, Dad. Wake up."

THE ROOM IS many rooms. The locations, too numerous to count.

Lit or dark, it doesn't matter.

The only thing important is the sound of the cough.

The Project Eden saga returns in Fall 2012, with

Volume Four

ASHES

CPSIA information can be obtained
at www.ICGtesting.com
Printed in the USA
LVHW042216120420
653202LV00016B/2584

A simple push of a button
and the world will never be the same.

Martina Gable returns home to spend
Christmas break with her family, but
the relaxing vacation she expects is not
even close to what she'll get.

Sanjay knows more than he should
about Project Eden's plan, and will do
whatever he can to keep the girl he loves
alive and safe.

A boy named Brandon Ash runs for his
life in the hills of Montana, wanting only
to see his family again.

But first there is Daniel, the boy's
father, who watches Olivia Silva's finger
hover over the enter key that will decide
the fate of humanity.

Do you think you're safe?

Praise for
the Project Eden Thrillers:

"...not only grabs you by the
throat, but by the heart and gut
as well. Buy these books now.
You won't regret it."
– Robert Browne –
best selling author of
TRIAL JUNKIES

"You think Battles was
badass before? He just cranked
it up to 500 joules. CLEAR!"
PopCultureNerd.com

Brett Battles is the Barry Aw
winning author of over a doze
novels and several short storie
He is a member of Internatior
Thriller Writers and Mystery
Writers of America.

He lives and writes in
Los Angeles. More is availabl
at his website:
www.brettbattles.com

ISBN 9781477608838

90000

9 781477 608838